CALLIOPE

The Slave of Athens

CALLIOPE
The Slave of Athens

A novel by

Cindy Stockler

Translated by
Michael Nicolau

Adelaide Books
New York / Lisbon
2021

CALLIOPE
The Slave of Athens
A novel by
Cindy Stockler

Title of the original:
Calliope: A Escrava de Atenas
Translated from Portuguese by Michael Nicolau

Published by Adelaide Books, New York / Lisbon
adelaidebooks.org

Editor-in-Chief
Stevan V. Nikolic

For any information, please address Adelaide Books at
info@adelaidebooks.org
or write to:
Adelaide Books
244 Fifth Ave. Suite D27
New York, NY, 10001

ISBN: 978-1-956635-09-6

Printed in the United States of America

"History does not only study material facts and institutions; its true object of study is the human soul; history must propose itself to the knowledge of what this soul believed, thought and felt in the different ages of life of the human race"

Denis FUSTEL DE COULANGES (The Ancient City)

"Well, you noticed that the face of the one who looks into the eyes of another appears in the part of the eye that is in front of him, as in a mirror. (...) Therefore, if one eye looks at another eye and fixes what is best in them, what allows them to see, they can see them-selves...Well, the soul, too, if it wants to know itself, will have to fix a soul, and especially the part where the soul's virtue, wisdom, or any other object that resembles it is found."

SOCRATES (The Republic, by Plato)

TWELVE GODS OF OLYMPUS

ZEUS – king of gods and men

HERA - protector goddess of women and marriage

POSSEIDON - god of the sea

HEPHESTUS – god of fire, artisans and blacksmiths

APOLO - god of poetry, music, sports, hunting and the art of healing

ATHENA - goddess of wisdom and peace

APHRODITE – goddess of beauty and love

HERMES - god of commerce and messenger of the gods

ARES - god of war

ARTEMIS – goddess of the forest and hunting, protector of girls

HESTIA – goddess of the sacred home and family, protector of the house

DEMETER - goddess of sowing and harvesting

Author's Note

Here is the story of a family of ordinary people in Athens in the 5th century BC – the so-called "Golden Century", the century of Pericles, of democracy, of the Peloponnesian War, of the great arts, of the great names. I admit that it was a bold gesture to have given the inspiration freedom to write it. But meticulous research supporting the account, combined with observation and reflection on the intricacies of the human soul, excited and encouraged me, becoming so valuable that it ended up being part of the book, in the form of a numbered Appendix.

It is possible to think, at first, that this novel should have been written obeying the rules, form and language used in the tragedies and epics written at the time it describes, such as Euripides, Homer, and so many others. However, there is no intention here of equating this novel with the great classics of ancient literature, whether in its form, language, approach or content. It is, in the novel, a story of fiction, a fantasy, a wonderful trip to ancient Greece, seeking to captivate, enchant and entertain the reader, referring him to this time in history that, I well know, can do without such pretenses to be appreciated, admired and studied. The issue of language, however, has not been forgotten.

Should a language and mode of speech similar to those of the aforementioned classics have been employed, aiming in this respect for strict fidelity to the time? Could current language be used without jeopardizing the credibility of the story or robbing the value of deep research about the time, its values, institutions and facts, research that led the entire production of the work with the aim of giving it substance and consistency? Such was my question in front of the blank screen and the brain full of scenes, episodes and events wanting to be transcribed, put on paper and, finally, read.

I acquiesced to the urgency of the story to be told, and chose to write it in the common language, the one with which the non-academic reader is more accustomed, so as not to discourage its reading, taking it comfortably into the home of this Hellenic family , which, the reader will see, was not so far from our own homes and hearts. Interestingly, it was reading Aristophanes – a comic playwright from the 5th century BC – that showed me that I had chosen the right path.

Divided into 12 chapters, each bearing the name of one of the twelve gods of Olympus, as they are mentioned by the characters, the text also has a numbering in parentheses, which refers to the Appendix - this one in didactic form and language, bringing all the research notes, so that the novel is aligned with the historical facts and characters, customs, laws and passages of the period described.

I hope that, as it happened to me, the reader finds in this trip to the past a link between the ancient world and the 21st century.

Cindy Stockler

Introduction

In an age where image prevails, I remain an old-fashioned reader; in the world of high-tech and cable TV, I still prefer a book.

I love to sink comfortably into my favorite chair, hold the book in my hands, smell the fresh ink, and feel the texture of the paper on my fingertips. There is nothing to compare!

And then I abandon myself to the writer. I let myself be taken to a whole new world for me: the author's fantasy world.

And if the author is talented, he will take me with him on his wings, lead me into the realms of his imagination, and present his wonders to my expectant eyes, thus binding me to his story.

This is exactly what happened when I read Cintia Marques' novel *Callíope, the Woman of Athens*.

Although I have devoted my entire life to the study of ancient Greece and its institutions, and although I have read many historical novels whose plot unfolded in Greek antiquity, this book really moved me. Couldn't stop turning its pages; it was as if a time machine had taken me back 2,500 years ago, through the streets of 5th century BC Athens. I could see the monuments and statues that adorned the city, could hear the hubbub of the crowd heading to the Pnyx to take part in the ultimate function of Democracy, I could smell the food slowly cooking in the small houses.

Because Cintia Marques is not simply telling a story, her vision of the time and people is not cold and indifferent, and her heroes are not mere caricatures, on the contrary, they are alive and real, and the reader quickly sympathizes with them, and can feel and understand their passions, needs, and disappointments.

However, the book is not limited to mere entertainment, it is also educational, as the author describes not only the politics, laws, philosophy and customs of those times, but also talks about commonplace things like slavery, the inheritance and property rights, access to citizenship, marriage, and much more.

11

Her clearly in-depth research and her academic background in Law (being a lawyer herself) helped her achieve the difficult task of presenting us with a carefully documented story and, above all, a pleasurable read.

Welcome to a new ancient world!

Prof. Nikolaos A. Vrissimtzis
Athens – Greece

MAIN CHARACTERS

Calliope, *daughter of the citizen Ganymede*

Ganymede, *landowner outside Athens*

Theodoros, *slave of the family of Ganymede*

Iphigenia, *mother of Calliope*

Cassandro, *husband of Calliope*

Calypso, *slave of the Ganymede family*

Athenian, *fictional citizen*

DISTINGUISHED CHARACTERS

Alcibiades, *Athenian General*

Aristophanes, *comic playwright*

Hippocrates, *physician, creator of the medical school on the island of Cos*

SPECIAL PARTICIPATION

the Spartan

Chapter I
Hermes – God of Commerce, Messenger of the Gods

Ganymede gets up and, asking for passage among the other citizens, begins to walk towards the door, shaking his head in an sign of dissatisfaction. The Ecclesia – People's General Assembly– which he had been waiting for so long, ended up coming to nothing. He had come to Athens also to make various purchases of provisions for his house, but his main objective was this General Assembly. He thought that several issues of interest to landowners like him, grain producers, as well as customs and merchant issues in the port of Piraeus, and other important items of the program - the agenda - would be debated in order to finally change the laws that only harmed citizens and prosperity of Athens. But that had not happened: Council members always found some "more important and urgent" matter to put on the agenda at the last minute. In addition, the huge number of troublemakers in the assembly - citizens who understood nothing about a text of law, not least the finances of the state, but who had their way of life in the assembly, given that they received an obol to participate in each session - the discussions were so disruptive that it seemed that none of the items on the agenda would be pursued. They made that afternoon useless to all those present, except for themselves, who, in addition to having fun, were also paid for it. They immediately forgot the words they had just heard from the priest:

"Keep silence, religious silence; pray to the gods and goddesses – and to Glorious Athena, protector of this city – so that everything goes as smoothly as possible in this assembly, for the greater honor of Athens and the happiness of its citizens".

Since the preliminary votes to decide on the viability of the proposed laws, the turmoil began, and not even a law had been put up for discussion, let alone put to a vote. The speakers had not yet begun to speak – only when they did would there be silence.

"Where are you going? You cannot leave before the end of the session!" - said the guard to Ganymede, barring his exit.

"Can't I ? And these gentlemen you see making such a fuss, making it impossible even to hear the herald calling out names? They can do it?"

"Everyone is paid to be here and participate in the vote!"

"Well, don't worry about that," said Ganymede, taking from the folds of his chiton – the long tunic – the drachma coins he had received on entering, and handing them to the guard.

"But, sir... this is irregular..."

"My friend, in a matter of irregularities, we both would have a lot to debate here this afternoon..." Ganymede replied, leaving at last, while, on the speaker's podium, another citizen, with a crown on his head, was waiting for the noise to finish before starting his speech.

Leaving the building, Ganymede finds Pan, on the ground, who extends his arm to ask for a coin.

"Have you finished the session, Mr. Ganymede?"

"For me it is over now!"

Pan was a beggar who lived from begging throughout the city, posting himself at the doors of temples and palaces whenever there was a large meeting, when he would collect many drachmas. He was known to the entire population, and many joked about him calling him "the true fulcrum of Athens," as he was always seated at the foot of a column. No one knew his real name: he had become known as "Pan" for his unbroken fallacy, his lack of manners in vocabulary, and his constant glee, though he was crippled in his left leg and arm. The obscenities he said to the women who passed alone drew laughter from the men around him, making the passerby enraged. He knew everything that was going on in the city: if anyone wanted to have any news, just walk around the area and would soon find him, always seated by the same column, and he felt honored to pass the news on to everyone who wanted to know – in exchange for some gratuity, of course.

"Have you seen my daughter Calliope and her slave?" Ganymede asks, handing him a coin.

"Yes, I saw that piece of juicy hip!" he says, working out the syllables.

"Watch your mouth, Pan! Or I'll call guards to teach you a lesson!"

"Here is the slave, Ganymede!

His daughter and her slave were still walking through the market, mixed in with the colorful bustle of people, stopping at every stall, wanting to see everything, know everything – and buy everything. They had agreed with their father that they would come to meet him at the end of the assembly, and that in the meantime they would go for a walk and do some shopping.

For Calliope, those were being the most happiest days of her life – her long life of 14 years. She had come with her father and two slaves to Athens and Piraeus, which was great experience for her, who rarely left the countryside. The last time she went somewhere had been a year earlier, when Ganymede, somewhat unwillingly, had been forced to take refuge with his family within the walls of Athens on account of the threat of Spartan attacks. He had rented a house in Melite, a district west of the Acropolis, and he did not allow the women and children to even think about stepping outside. Those had been tense weeks, when the Athenians didn't know what to expect. The older ones fearfully recalled the times when they had seen the city razed to the ground by the Persians fifty years before. Times when the Spartans, before being rivals, had been allies, with Leonidas at their head, perishing with their soldiers in the pass of Thermopylae, trying to stop the advance of the invaders.

However, none of this had been engraved in the memory of Calliope. Only now was she really getting to know Athens. She swallowed with her eyes and ears everything that passed by her, enchanted with so many people together, taken by the joy that filled the air of the city, whose more than four hundred thousand inhabitants swarmed on all sides, going to and from, restless, loud, each with their activities, as varied as possible.

Born in the year in which General Pericles had been elected a leader of Athens for the first time, she was smiling and admiring, on that sunny afternoon, the streets, squares, temples and monuments of the city that the statesman Pericles had beautified during all those years he had been in power. That great politician who now, at almost seventy, was too depressed to walk his city…

Tired of the excesses of politics; attacked by opponents – especially for his connection with Aspasia, a woman of dubious reputation, but with a high degree of culture and education, of foreign origin, who wrote speeches and conversed with philosophers, and whose influence over the great general was the preferred target of antagonists ; misunderstood by his people; exhausted by the war against Sparta, which he had at first calculated would be swift, but which now seemed to unfold in unforeseen paths, Pericles was still facing his own family drama. He had lost several friends in the plague first, then his sister, then his eldest son Xantippus, who had always been hostile to his father, and finally Paralos, his youngest son. He had endured each of those losses with the strength for which he was known, escaping discouragement, not even having gone to visit the graves of loved ones, standing firm and unshakeable. But when Paralos was taken to him, no longer able to bear it, he succumbed to grief, like any citizen in a similar situation, and the people then saw that great general, for the first time in his life, bent over the body of his dead son. At the moment of placing the crown of olive branches on his head, weeping aloud, shaken by sobs, giving in to the despair that comes from impotence in the face of death. Adding to his bitterness, he was still facing the magistrates in an attempt to legitimize two other children – Pericles and Athena – that he had with Aspasia. The Athenian people, somewhat regretting not having reelected him the last time, and feeling sorry for so many misfortunes, were already considering returning him to the post, from which, they now saw, he should never have been removed.

But of these things, Calliope knew little. For her, Athens was a party.

Her dark, wavy hair, almond-shaped eyes in the same color, like those of her mother, Iphigenia, could occasionally be seen in Calliope's eyes as a ray of annoyance, as she was full of ideas and her own thoughts – a very rare thing, because the girls were not given to moments of reflection: either because they weren't fond of it, or because they didn't have much time for that, since they already helped with household chores from an early age, in simple families as well as in the more affluent. But Calliope, who did not shy away from her domestic duties, always found time for her daydreams and musings, and now she would have ample material to do so: on her walks through the city, she had seen many novelties in terms of women's fashion: hair ornaments, tunics in bright colors, the earrings, necklaces and bracelets, the ankle rings – the city magistrates went crazy, creating laws that demanded moderation in women's clothing and behavior, different objects, people, gestures, words, manners , behaviors, riches. His teenage eyes didn't see the poverty, the malnutrition, the pain. Athens was a big party. But the most interesting thing was in Piraeus...

She had met a young man in that port city and the two had fallen in love in a moment. There were vows of undying love and promises of a future together, filled with lyres, dances, veils, fountains in a central courtyard and chubby babies. All this in the few minutes the slave had left her alone to go to a fish stall. Alexis, the boy, the son of a customs inspector, intended to become a sailor. Calliope already imagined tearful farewells every time he left for the sea – which would be frequent, she soon realized.

"Oh, what a pity! It's the father, with the carriage, waving at us downstairs!!"

"Is it the time to go? – asked the slave, carrying several things in her tunic.

Arriving in the carriage, taken by the slave down the street, Ganimedes called his daughter and maid.

"Come on, girls, it's time to get on our way home! The day is short, and the sun will set fast! So, Calliope, do you have any money left, or did the city's handymen take everything you had in your pockets?

"Papa! When will we return to Athens?"

"But we're not even out yet! - He said, laughing. – Come on, kids! Are all the bags there? The vegetables and fish that Iphigenia ordered, is everything there? Look, you know what that woman looks like when she's short on onions and celery!

"Yes sir!" the two girls answered together.

A farmer on the outskirts of Athens, Ganymede always had in his service few slaves that he occasionally bought, and to whom he would soon give freedom, keeping in his house only those who did not want to risk the uncertain lives of freed slaves. He paid them as he could. Given that he did not always obtain high incomes from the sale of grain, wages did not provide the ex-slaves with a means to support themselves. But Ganymede was good, and country life pleased those who were with him. He called everyone "children", whatever their age. He often came to the city to sell his produce, close deals, buy tools, seeds, grains, fabrics, medicines, supplies, and also for the public assemblies, as he was very interested in business and laws, especially those concerning the price of goods and, in general, to the farming business. He would always bring a slave with him, for the heavy work of unloading sacks, pulling the mules and arranging the carriage. This time he decided to bring Calliope, despite his wife and Calypso having been against:

"A decent young girl walking alone through the city! What will people say?" Iphigenia had said.

But Ganymede knew what he was doing. Calliope was already fourteen, and it was time to be seen. Furthermore, he would stay with his daughter practically all the time, and he had even brought the slave as a companion, who did not let go of the girl when he went to the assembly. The fact is that he had not been able to resist the pleas of his dear daughter who had slyly convinced him to take her to the city this time.

"Calliope, don't talk to anyone, don't look at anyone, don't look sideways!" Iphigenia had said.

"Mom!"

"Be very careful, my love, do not eat or drink anything you are offered, and do not touch anyone!" Calypso tells her, handing her a package with some breads, cakes and fruits, and checking if the water amphorae were already in the carriage, when the small group was leaving.

Still frightened by the plague, the women considered it irresponsible for Ganymede to take the girl.

"With the five hundred of the delegates!! – exhales Ganymede, after a few minutes on the road. – We failed again!!

Coming down from the carriage, snorting, he goes to see what happened to the back wheel of the carriage, followed by the slave.

"If we had a paved road like the one that goes to Piraeus!

Ganymede made the journey between his lands and Athens at least every six or seven days. It was painful because of the bad road, but he was used to the bumps and bumps, not without the usual curses, of course. He criticized the Council of Five Hundred – for its delay in taking action, even though he himself had been a member of that body, years before, when he had been drawn to take the place of prytanes for a year. So it was every day that he faced the potholes, to go to work like an ox in the affairs of the city. More than ever, he suffered on his skin – and on his hips – the bad state of the roads, but even so, he still managed to pass the projects that interested him personally.

Furthermore, this public service had taken up his time almost entirely, and he had been forced to neglect his lands and his business. So it was with relief that, every year, he saw his name not being drawn or nominated for any other office of state.

Although used to the bustle of the city, he preferred the country life, which he did not want to abandon. Even last year, when the simplest peasants soon took refuge in the closed city, fearing Spartan attacks, Ganymede and some other landowners refused to do so until the last minute, considering this measure too drastic: to take all the family to Athens and being ill accommodated, waiting for who knows what, and even when, the abandoned lands, seemed an exaggeration to him. He stayed only a few weeks and then returned to the countryside: he preferred to risk it because, more than the Spartans, Ganymede feared, yes, it was the plague that was ruining the city. Definitely, the rural values, which he inherited from his parents, grandparents and more distant ancestors, prevailed in his way of life, even though the younger ones, like his son Helios, wanted to convince him of their urban superiority.

"We'll have to go down, kids. And push the wheel out of the hole, or we'll spend the night here!"

"I'll help, dad!"

"No, daughter, we men ..... take it... uuuuifff.... don't worry..." he says, pushing the carriage with great effort, "hmmm... now! Ready!"

21

The wheel comes out and immediately rolls back into the hole.

"I think the mules didn't understand that it was to take a step, sir!" the slave jokes.

They finally managed, and everyone goes up again.

"It would be nice if we had some horses, sir!"

"Horses? What good would horses do, with the road like this? They would fall into the holes too! It's no use, my dear, it's no use. For years I have been trying to get into the minds of those unfortunates in the assembly that all trade in Athens would gain if the roads connecting them to the countryside were improved; but what do you get with the five hundred of the delegates? Five hundred mules, that's what they are! Discard all our projects! And they say it's a strategy to leave the path bumpy like this: in this way, the enemy can't get through!"

"If Theo had come, I would have helped you two and it would have been easier!" - Calliope says.

"I could not leave your mother alone in the field, daughter. And he had a lot to do there."

Theodoros was a young slave that Ganymede had purchased as a boy of six or seven. Not that it needed the work of a child, but it caught his attention when, at the Market, as he passed the moment when the slave trader was finishing the day's sales, that sad-looking boy was left, and would have to return with the merchant to be dropped somewhere until the next sale. His origins were not exactly known, and he had no recollection of his parents. He was the same age as Calliope, and Ganymede felt his heart soften when, when asking his price, he saw her little eyes light up with hope and, as he paid the merchant, a smile broke out on the little one's face. With a quiet temperament, but gentle, affable and obedient, Theo grew up to be strong, intelligent and hardworking, even learning some things from the slave teacher. He had loved Calliope from the moment he saw her for the first time, when he arrived at the house and was led into the kitchen by Ganymede's hand. They grew up together and became true and inseparable friends. Theo was very fond of the family - the only family he had ever known - and he considered it his home.

"I can't wait to tell Mom and Lypso everything!" Calliope says, looking at the trinkets she had bought at the Market.

Iphigenia and Calypso, the slave who helped her in the house, did not want to go into town. Not counting the previous year, which was so unusual, it had been a good five years since Iphigenia had not been to Athens. The last time had been at the opening festival of the Parthenon, when she'd been so afraid of losing Calliope in the crowd that she'd squeezed the girl's hand until she had calluses. For the rest, Calliope and Theo, who had also gone, remembered nothing about this festival, as the crowd was so large that they, squeezed in between so many people, saw only legs, tunics, sandals and the remains of fruit on the floor, which was all that reached their field of vision. When, following along with the procession, they were almost reaching the Propylaeum, at the top of the Acropolis, who ended up getting lost was Calypso, and then Iphigenia saw nothing more of the party, as she had to go all the way down and ask a guard for help, with whom she left Calliope and Theo, insisting not to let go of them so she could go look for her friend. The two children then spent what seemed like hours standing there, holding hands with the guard in his dress uniform, plume helmet and all, while Iphigenia, desperate, bulged her eyes in all directions to find her dear friend, who finally appeared. And of course it took them a few minutes later to find the guard again, which made them even more nervous. They guided themselves by the tufts of their uniforms, going to them, but there were so many guards that they were wrong several times: one was slapping a young man who had tried to steal a woman's money; another was talking to a girl and didn't even seem to know he was there on business; another still had another lost child with him. The two women ran together, muttering together "Oh Divine Athena, in the bosom of your city, bring back my children" and "Oh goddess Artemis, protect my little daughter with your heart". Finally they found the guard and the children, in the same place they had always been. The whole thing cost Iphigenia an extra good lock of gray hair. She was so traumatized that she preferred not to return to town. And of the Parthenon he saw only the facade, from afar.

Arriving back home was always a joy – for those who arrived as well as for those who had stayed.

The grandparents of Ganymede's grandparents had acquired the first pieces of land, and with time and a lot of work, the new generations increased the property, when they then found that small sheltered hill, away from the road that reached the land, only being known to others local peasants and family friends. Then Ganymede's grandparents decided to build a new house and moved there.

It was a bigger house, already following the molds of the well-built houses in the city, and Ganymede often adapted it to the new construction and needs of the family. Spacious, with only one floor, it had in the center an inner courtyard, surrounded by a colonnade – the peristylium . Facing the front, next to the entrance door, were the kitchen and the living and dining room. On one side and at the back were the three bedrooms: Ganymedes and Iphigenia's, Helios's, Calliope and Calypso's, and a small room to store chests with fabrics, tunics, blankets, etc. On the opposite side was the reception room for the men – the andrónion – and two small isolated rooms used to cram all sorts of things, especially furniture, the large clay pots, the braziers for the winter, and household utensils in general. In one corner was the bathroom – with a wooden bath tub, and a latrine with a rudimentary sewage system, a novelty recently introduced by Ganymede. Beside and behind the house, Iphigenia and Calypso had a garden where they cultivated, on the floor and in the beautiful pots brought from Athens, beautiful plants and flowers – especially primroses, tulips and anemones, and in a corner, a small vegetable garden.

"My herbs! Be careful, don't step on them!" Calliope said, when she caught someone walking carelessly through the vegetable garden, where there was a corner of her own.

The servants' quarters were in the barn, in a building some distance away, along with the well, the stable, the pen, the straw store, and the mill.

White, covered by several coats of lime paint, with some stones adorning the facade where ivy climbed - and which in spring/summer was almost completely flowered, sheltering the door there was a small roof, supported by two slender columns in Ionic style, near which were some vases with the women's flowers. The mere sight, in the distance, enchanted those who approached.

It was as if hidden by tall trees, to the west, and facing east, on top of the small hill - safe from the waters of rare rains and enemy attacks, in a wise position that gave no one from the countryside any vision of its existence. To get to it, you had to go around the road, when it was seen from below, an olive tree welcoming you. From the front window, too, you could see whoever arrived at the foot of the road. Thus, every time a cart or horse was sighted, everyone in the house was already stationed to receive it, accompanying them up the path. Calliope liked to get out of the carriage and walk the path when she returned from an exit.

Beside the barn, somewhat camouflaged, Ganymede had built a small covered tower, from which one could have an overview of practically the entire property, so as to see possible unwanted invaders, and be able to take action in time.

The trip had been tiring for Ganymede, who had to go down several times to curse the holes and take the wheels out of them. It was with relief that he stopped the buggy at the door of the house, where his wife was waiting for him.

"Woman, bring me a cycéon cup, my throat is on fire!" he said as he was getting off the carriage.

"And Helios?" Iphigenia asked, as she hadn't seen her eldest son for several days.

"With friends, as always!"

"Before leaving the assembly, Ganymede had looked for his son Helios with his eyes, among the men present there, and had seen him with his friends, oblivious to everything around him, in a very lively conversation, certainly on some subject far removed from those on the day's agenda. He wanted to know if Helios was going home that night, but he had given up: Helios certainly wouldn't. Since turning 20 and reaching adulthood, it had been almost a year and, together with a good number of other young Athenian citizens, he had taken the oath of allegiance to the Hellenic homeland (6): "...wherever the wheat grows , the vine, and the olive tree", Helios hardly slept at his parents' house: he had many things to do in Athens.

Helios was the pride of the family. First child, he had been brought up like so many other Athenian boys: with a view to the honorable mission of becoming a soldier and defending his homeland – Athens! To do this, he went to school in the city from the age of seven, taken every day by Castor, a highly educated slave, who had completed his studies, and had also taught Calliope and Theo to read, to do math, to play the lyre, to sing and recite Homer's poems.

The strong and robust type, Helios soon showed that he would be a good athlete and soldier. He spent afternoons in the gym exercising and training. Since then he made a large group of friends, who went with him into the army. At the age of eighteen, while his friends went to discover the mysteries of love with the prostitutes, entering the houses of tolerance in the most remote and poorer neighborhoods of the city - and some other young people knew such mysteries in the gym, among their colleagues and certain rich young men in the city, Helios fell in love with Musságora, widow of a meteco, twenty-eight years old, inhabitant of the Cerâmico neighborhood.

The young widow – Sássa, as he called her – was a constant target of gossip from the neighborhood, who saw the coming and going of government agents knocking on her door and maliciously attributed to her beauty the fact that she continued to live there, in the house to which she had no right. They speculated maliciously where she got her money to survive.

In fact, she barely survived. Alone, she had lost her husband and her two small children to the plague. As a widow, she managed to sell almost all the objects made in ceramics by the deceased, who was a potter, and somehow managed to get money for permission to stay in the house, but not without difficulties. She began to weave sheets and tunics for men, which she sold as a street vendor in the Market, always afraid of being caught by the sellers, who sometimes repressed her, sometimes bought some tunic. But there was little she earned, having to see her pantry empty and the house crumbling, with cracked stucco, broken doors, and leaks everywhere. Often, without money to buy food or oil for the lamps, she would stay at home for hours, plucking up the courage to go to the market to steal a fruit or vegetable, but she would never carry out this plan, and would turn to the side in bed , the stomach growling. This the neighbors did not see. Helios suffered to see her in difficulties, but there was little money he could bring her to help. Meanwhile, the two let themselves be carried in each other's arms, in long hours of love, which made Helios even more in love.

"Sassa! My Sassa…"

It was a delight to spend the night with her, and it was a double delight when she, having managed to sell something or when he gave her a few drachmas, prepared that dish he loved so much: she had invented a dish where she mixed onions, cheese, a little of meat in small pieces, when she could get some, and eggplants – a vegetable not very widespread in Athens; for some because it is very expensive, since it is imported, for others because it is not very appreciated, since it is unknown. With the addition of the spices she cultivated in her little garden – especially basil, the smell of the delicacy made the neighbors even more sullen: after they were snooping around, they didn't have the courage to knock on her door to ask for a piece, or for a recipe. Helios feared he would not have his father's permission to marry her; he would have to accept a marriage to his father's taste, and be content to keep Mussagora as his mistress. Now, at the age of twenty-one, Helios already participates in the People's Assemblies, but actually only does so when on the agenda there is some debate about laws that are linked to the situation of his beloved. When not, it is in her house that he would take refuge.

Theo at first listens, delighted, drinking the words of Calliope, who tells him about the trip. Without letting go of her eyes, he barely pays attention to the words, just hears the sound of her voice. Suddenly, he frowns and leaves, saying that he has a lot to do, vines to clean, remove the caterpillars and weeds, seeds to spread in the field, sheep to search the pasture, wheat to thresh, in short, all luck of services more important than Athens and – above all – much, much more important than Piraeus and its sailors.

"Wheat to work out?! But we are in Elaphebolión[4] !!" Calliope says, not understanding anything and returning to the kitchen, lifting the hem of her chiton with her fingertips, so as not to trip, as she had seen elegant ladies doing in the city.

The family thought it was very funny how she walked around the countryside and around the house with this Athenian affectation, and the habit of playing had even been incorporated, every time someone quoted Homer and the Achilles' heel, the other added: "and the ankles of Callíope".

But she didn't care, and continued to impose on her family everything she had seen that was different and "better" in the city, such as women's hairstyles.

"Honey, you know I don't care about these fads! All my life I wore my hair in this bun, with a bow at the back, and nothing else!" , said Iphigenia, sitting in front of Calliope who was standing behind her, trying to fix her mother's hair as she had seen in Athens.

"Calm down, mother, you'll see, you'll be as beautiful as those women I saw walking in the Market!"

She had come back from Athens full of ideas and with her head full of all the news she had seen, everything so different from the countryside, so colorful, so vibrant, women so elegant, with their tunics in different colors, the neat hems! The father definitely didn't know how to shop for women; she would have to go to town more often, to bring all those things, so important! And with this excitement, she had convinced his mother to try a new hairstyle: her hair arranged in an intricate way, intertwined, with strips of fabric holding the strands together and giving it a very interesting finish. The problem is that Calliope wasn't exactly a female beauty artist, and the locks refused to stay where she wanted them, insisting on falling over her forehead, by the sides, and falling down on the back of her mother's head, who patiently and amused at the way of his daughter, she was letting herself beautified by the girl.

"Lypso, come learn how to do this hairstyle, I want to be so beautiful when Alexis comes to see me!"

"Still thinking about your "Hermes from Piraeus", my love?" the slave asked. The two women joked with Calliope about the port inspector's son, in a reference to Hermes, the god of merchants and travelers.

"You'd better forget about this boy, my dear," says the mother, brushing a large strand of ribbon from her face. "It is not good to be in the hope of seeing him again ... much less dream of marrying him."

"But why not, mother?"

"Your father already said he has plans for you…"

"What plans? Mom, you won't tell me he's thinking of getting me some old man, whose face I've never seen, some fat guy…"

"Calypso, help me…" the mother pleads. "It's time to have that conversation…"

The slave approaches, with her calm and slow gestures.

"Calliope…" she says, carrying in her arms the pot where she mixed grains with oil for a dinner plate. "When you were with this little boy… did he touch you?"

"What do you mean, did you touch me?"

"Did he try to put his hand on you, touch any part of your body?"

"Oh, there was a time when he… took my hand…"

Calypso stops stirring the cereals.

"Honey, is that all he did?"

"Yes, yes! He took my hand, that's all! Why this concern?"

"There is little care with the hands of men, they are capable of anything to advance those hands, as for that they are true animals!"

"And even when the problem is the opposite, the complication is for the woman anyway!" mother said.

"What do you mean, the problem is reversed?" Calliope wants to know.

"Like the case of your aunt Leda, when grandfather gave her in marriage to a young man from a prosperous family, and who on her wedding night did not "untie his belt", and after more than a year of marriage, he didn't even touch her…"

"But is it to play or not to play?"

"Her grandfather wanted to know why she wasn't pregnant yet, and she told him how things went between her and her husband… or how they didn't…"

"And what happened?" Calliope asked, getting interested. "What was going on?"

"Her husband was the type who… only touched other men's bodies…"

"What??" Calliope asked, not understanding.

"Your grandfather was furious and ended the marriage, taking your aunt back home; it was a scandal, there was all sorts of slander, because people, as usual, sometimes cursed the boy, sometimes cursed Leda, saying that she was guilty of not having 'stoked' him."

29

"Like this?"

"It was a riot in the family, this whole story; his grandfather wanted to settle as soon as possible and immediately married his aunt to another man, sending her to Thrace."

"To Thrace? Why to Thrace? Is it the punishment for women whose husbands are not teased?" Calliope asked, at this point lost in the conversation.

"Since then we haven't heard from her anymore..." the mother said, with a thoughtful air.

"What if the new husband was also like the other? What good was the grandfather getting rid of his aunt?"

"Your father often tries to find out news when he goes to Athens."

"In Athens? But he has to go to Thrace! And they didn't even see if this other one was a fat one!"

"What's wrong with him being fat? Everyone ends up getting fat, not able to control their desires, of any kind!"

And Iphigenia, along with Calypso, starts to laugh, while Calliope, giving up her hairdo, leaves sullen, because she couldn't understand the women's ironies.

"Go after her, Lypso! Finally, try to explain how things happen, it's time for her to know."

Calypso was already a slave in Ganymede's house when Ganymede and Iphigenia got married. It was an immediate affection between them as soon as Iphigenia had come to live there, and the two began to treat each other like two true loving sisters. They raised the two children together; they went through all the troubles and pains together for all those years. Shortly after his father died and he assumed the position of head of the family, Ganymede brought Calypso to the dinner table, so that she effectively became part of the family, although she did not accept Ganymede's release. She was afraid of freedom. She said poetically that her heart was the eternal slave of that family. Iphigenia always turned to Calypso in the most delicate situations where tact was needed, such as saying difficult things to her husband or children. Now that Calliope was close to marriageable age, they had decided it was time to prepare her for the meeting between husband and wife. And it's obvious that it would have to be Calypso who would recount this matter in detail.

"Daughter..." she says, approaching the girl and putting her arm around her shoulders. "Don't take this wrong way; we're just embarrassed to talk to you about certain things..."

Calliope loved Calypso perhaps more than her own mother. Her name had been chosen by the slave. There was no problem, no cloud hanging over her heart, that she didn't trust the woman, and she soothed her soul with her words and sometimes even her sympathetic, welcoming silence.

"You say things I can't understand, and laugh at me..."

"We don't laugh at you, we laugh at ourselves! Because we are two old fools who can't talk about such a natural subject..."

"Babies....?" Calliope asks, guessing.

"Yes."

"But what do Alexis' hands have with it?"

"Many problems in life can come around, my dear. Mainly for us women. An unwanted pregnancy can determine the end of a woman's life, her misery. It is not easy to have a child, much less alone and helpless. The woman ends up going to the street..."

"But why is it such a big problem? If she doesn't want the baby, just put it in the basket as soon as it's born, and leave it by the river. Isn't that the way they do with babies you don't want?"

The slave's eyes fill with shadows and pain. It wasn't that simple.

Here and there people could still hear about the archaic practice that, when girls or children are born with malformations, or in an already large family, people choose not to let them live, exposing the newborn to its own fate, and alleviating the awareness in the belief that when the baby was left out in the open, it would die not because of their hands and guilt, but because chance did not want him to live. But in Ganymede's family there was no news that this had ever happened. However, with Iphigenia a second pregnancy in a year of drought and poor farming, Ganymede felt threatened by hunger and misery. As if helpless, as Iphigenia's womb grew, he ceaselessly made sacrifices in honor of his father, who had recently died, trying to get from him an answer to his doubts and fears. He had grown up hearing from his father, and before him from his grandfather, whose ancestors had been repeating from generation to generation for centuries, the teachings of Hesiod:

"If you want to thrive, work even in winter. Don't marry early. Have only one child because more than one is difficult to support. Offer sacrifices to the gods regularly. Remember the happy days that work gives you and avoid the unhappy ones. Otherwise the animals will get sick and the wheat will rot. Be friends with your neighbors, because they will be around if you need them. Besides, with a bad neighbor, you never know what might happen to your cattle. Never borrow, don't lend anything and don't trust anyone."

Their forefathers had seen very difficult days, and Hesiod's words had guided them. The rigidity of these words led the family to prosper in fact, even making them differentiated, as they were peasants accustomed to the culture, went frequently to the city, and educated their children in the schools of Athens. But that was a year of scarcity and bad weather and Ganymede, afraid of the future, seeing a girl born, stunned by the threat of hunger, decided to expose the baby, placing her in a ceramic vase on the road, far from home, to entrance to Athens.

Repentance came almost immediately. Ganymede went the next day to the spot on the road, but the vase had already been collected. Probably, once the girl's body had been found, an end had been given to her, the details of which Ganymede feared to discover. Iphigenia spent years without sleeping or eating properly. Calypso spent a long time without finding within or without the words that could cleanse her heart. In the end, it would not have been necessary to expose the girl: the year had ended well and in the end there was no hunger, much less misery. Ganymede felt unworthy and saw life very differently, and that was the first time he gave freedom to slaves. Iphigenia became pregnant twice more, the babies were born weak and, despite the family's struggle for their health, they died. One before he was a year old, and the other just three months old. All attributed this to the abandonment of the baby. Then, on a fifth pregnancy, when Calliope was born, strong and smiling, it was with immense joy that the whole house watched her go through the critical months, get even stronger, start talking and walking. The family saw in the girl the redemption of that nebulous fact in their memories. Wanting to spare Iphigenia, Ganymede took her to Athens to visit a doctor, who gave her a controversial but effective contraceptive, and she never became pregnant again. At great cost the whole episode of the abandoned baby was being, if not overcome, at least softened in their consciences. But life would still charge them for that ignoble stumble.

"It's not that simple..." said Calypso. "A baby... is a joy in people's lives... Do you remember when we talked the day you... when you..."

"On the day I got 'what you have when you don't have a baby' for the first time?"

"Yes... Calliope, my dear, soon you will get married, and then there will be the baby... And your husband will play a big part in this..."

"Like what?"

"Well, on your wedding night, when you go to live at your husband's house, you will be alone in his rooms, and then he will untie your belt..."

"Calypso finally finds courage and tells the girl step by step, who listens attentively to her like a good student, her eyes fixed on the floor.

"... And this is how a girl becomes a woman," finishes the slave, triumphant for having successfully completed this delicate task and with such painful memories.

Under the summer sun, taking with her a cloth to pick some loquats that were already ripening on their feet, Calliope slowly walks across the land, through the plantation, until she reaches the small plain, the inviting fresh green grass, where she and Theo so often they used to lie down, after a tiring day of work, to talk, looking at the blue sky, watching the clouds pass by in the most varied forms. Taking a moment to look at the landscape, she sees Theo a few meters away, also standing, looking at the horizon.

"Hey!! Theo!!" Calliope screams.

Seeing her, he approaches.

"Calliope! Are you going to get the fruit? I heard when your mother asked you…" he says, in his soft and low voice.

"I will take a look. What a beautiful day! It was so sunny in Athens, too. Ah, Theo! You had to be gone! I've never seen so many people together! But the most impressive thing… was seeing the sea… You need to go one day, Theo, to see the sea up close…"

"Hmmm…" Theo doesn't really want to hear her talk about the sea or Piraeus.

He had never stepped on the edge of the sea – or, at least, he did not remember having done so. Until now, at the age of fifteen, he had not had the opportunity to go with his boss to shop or do some work in the city and in Piraeus. An older slave was always taken for this service. And Calliope, no matter how much she described it with her countless words full of admiration and superlatives, she could not convey to him the damp image of the sea.

"I already know!! Let's play our 'thought-seeing' game?" she says, stretching out on the grass. "Go, lie down behind me, let's try!"

Since they were small, the two used to play together, playing five pebbles, playing with the small animals, running around the house, playing ball, and when tired of the handrail, they would lay on the grass looking at the sky, talking, singing, identifying the shapes of the clouds. Sometimes a silence hung in the air.

"What are you thinking about?"

"I won't say!"

"So I'll guess!"

And that's how they invented their favorite game: "passing the thought" to the other. Stretched out on the grass, with the tops of their heads touching each other, one concentrated and imagined a scene, or an object, or even a sentence, and the other tried to "visualize", as if the thought of one "passed" to the other's head. They spent hours entertaining themselves in this way, to the anger of their father, who needed Theo in the house or in the fields, and their mother, who needed Calliope in the kitchen.

"Concentrate, huh!" says Calliope, with Theo stretched out on the floor behind her, their heads touching. "I'll tell you, to help, okay? Then, before your eyes, you see a huge blue blur... a blue that takes over your entire vision there is nothing but this blue... no trees, no house, no people, not just animals... . blue... Gradually... you will see that they are two different blues: it is as if it were divided in half, lengthways; the top half is light blue... the bottom half is a darker blue... And it's like there's a line dividing the two blues... The top blue is the sky; the blue below is the sea. Then, you notice some small white spots, very small, here and there, in the lower blue, the dark... and you see that the dark blue moves...”

"Does the blue moves??” Theo asks, wanting to laugh.

"Don't get distracted!! The blue moves, yes... and when the blue moves, it makes the white spot... Then you realize that the dark blue is water and the white spot is a wave, raised by the wind, by the movement of the sea.”

"Hmmm...”

"So, what are you seeing?”

"A ram, followed by a battalion of armor!”

"What???” she says, seeing that he was joking.

"Yeah, look at the sky, the clouds,” says Theo, pointing to the sky.

"You weren't paying attention!! And what's more, you have to close your eyes, it doesn't work with your eyes open! Where are you seeing a sheep??” She says, looking at the clouds. "It's a carriage! Pulling a car with hay!!”

"Sheep, yes! Look at the paws!! And the armored battalion follows. It's a sheep rebellion!!” He says, laughing.

"Is it possible, it's so clear, it's a carriage, and now it's no longer hay, it's... it's... onions!!”

"What? Onions? Where did you see onions?” he says, standing up and turning his head to see from her point of view. The figure of clouds begins to unravel.

"Oh, now there's not even a carriage or a mutton or anything else,” she says.

"Yes, I can still see it, Calliope, look over there... one of the wheels of your cart...”

"You didn't take me seriously, I wanted you to see the sea! It worked that once, remember... I so wanted you to see the things I saw…" she said, sitting down and hugging her knees, a little sad, a little angry, while Theo sat down too, your side.

"But I don't need… I just have to look into your eyes," he said, in his soft voice, looking at her closely. "I see everything in your eyes… everything that is most important in life to me… Why do I need to see the sea, if I see your eyes?"

They fall silent, a silence filled with words, looking at each other closely, and Calliope finds herself reflected in Theo's eyes. A blush coming from her insides rises to her cheeks, making her jump with a start:

"Mom's loquats!!"

Calypso was wrong. This was not the way she had told her that a girl became a woman. She felt she had become a woman under that gaze from Theo.

"Woman, send Calypso with me to town with the list of necessary purchases, and get ready for the girl and the party: in a month Calliope is getting married!"

The news was totally unexpected for Iphigenia. She knew her husband was making arrangements to find a husband for his daughter, but she didn't think it was that way. Calypso didn't even have time to think: a month was too little time, and she needed to finish preparing the girl's trousseau, which had already been made for some years. Theo felt an arrow cross his chest. And Calliope knew that this day would come, anyway, but she didn't know exactly what to expect. She had already forgotten the "Hermes from Piraeus", so she didn't mind the idea of marrying someone else.

The visit to Athens, almost a year earlier, had had the effect Ganymede had hoped for. Several citizens had seen the girl with him. And it was a matter of Ganymede to talk here and there, and see which suitor seemed more suitable to him. Found the ideal guy, just set the date and some details, and everything was arranged. Although he had in his son Helios his legitimate and universal heir, Ganymede counted on Calliope and his future son-in-law as an additional guarantee of his line of succession.

Chapter II

Artemis – goddess of the forest and hunting, protector of girls

The wedding night did not leave a good impression on Calliope. She thought that was very weird. Calypso had told her everything in detail, including the sordid details, the day they had "the conversation." It is true that, like all girls, she had already been groomed from childhood to become a housewife: she had learned to pick and wash seeds and fruits, to select vegetables and clean meat, to cook food, weave tunics and sheets and tidying the house, making prayers and devotions to the family god, leading the servants. But nothing had prepared her for this. Nor the details and allusions of Calypso.

At least, she thought, he was the 'hot-up' type, and she wasn't in danger of being sent to Thrace like her aunt, whose husband didn't touch her. The husband her father had chosen was just the fat one she feared so much, and he was already bearded and balding. Cassandro was a thirty-seven-year-old childless widower, also a landowner in Attica but northeast of Athens, whom Ganymede had met in the Market and turned out to be the only good catch he could find: he wanted Calliope to marry a country man, where his daughter had grown up and was used to it.

After the first few nights she got used to it, and even got used to her husband's presence in her bed all night long – a habit she hadn't expected: Calypso had been so distressed to tell her about their love affairs that she'd forgotten to tell her about it. To say that she would sleep with her husband by her side forever! Cassandro, moreover, quickly liked that young woman who had been given to him as a wife. For the first few days, he stayed with her in bed in the morning, taking a long time to decide whether to get up and go to breakfast, much to the horror of his mother, who thought it was shameless.

"What world are we in?" Calliope would hear her mutter in a moralistic tone to a slave.

This was one more thing she hadn't been prepared for: her mother-in-law. She had seen her for the first time, as well as her husband, on the very day of their wedding. Her family from then on!

The wedding feast had been prepared with all the rigors prevailing in Athens, although in the countryside things usually went more simply. Ganymede invited many friends and their wives, making the house, normally so quiet, an unusual fuss. Helios also took some friends, soldiers like him, and Cassandro only took his mother – who was the only family he had. Three rams and two pigs were sacrificed in honor of Zeus, Hera, Artemis, Aphrodite and Demeter, the goddess of the house, and all the gods. Ganymede had ordered several amphoras of sock- like wine from Chios. There was also brawl,[5] more to the taste of peasant guests. After all, it was his dear daughter, joy at home, who was getting married, and Ganymede wanted the party to be memorable. He had thought of killing an ox, but Iphigenia and Calypso dissuaded him, fearing the neighbors' gossip, as the guests would not be that large in number, and at that moment they did not have an old ox to sacrifice: they were all young animals, and were being used in farming.

The house, normally blooming and full of plants, was even more tidy: Ganymede ordered flowers for the vases and garlands to come from Athens. Tables were placed outside, and Ganymede ordered extra couches and chairs from the city as well. Zeus contributed by not threatening the party with dark clouds: the sun was shining and the sky was blue. Nobody felt bad, not even a sneeze had been heard. Good omens for the ceremony! Sign of a happy union that pleased the gods!

Calliope was a little nervous, a mixture of feelings since the day before, when she went to bed for the last time at her parents' house. She had woken up early, distressed but happy, and the women soon took her to the cleansing bath: rituals were one of the most important parts of the day. After oiling her body, they removed the excess with new cloths, thus cleaning her skin, and then she entered the tub of slightly heated water, where Calypso poured some of the essential oils she had brought from Athens, especially for the occasion. This was already one of the most solemn moments of that special day.

"Oh, mom! It's hurting me!"

"Calm down, Calliope. We have to scrub you with the loofah! - Calypso tries to calm her down."

"Honey, did you do what I told you last night?"

"What, Mom?"

"Your toys…"

"Ah… yes… I put everything together, as you said…"

This had been a difficult moment for Calliope: she was leaving her life so far behind, she was becoming a woman, she had to abandon her children's toys, consecrating them to Artemis. But she didn't want to get rid of his treasures! How was she going to live without them? It was with immense pain in her heart that she placed all the wooden dolls and the little animals – her little woolen sheep! – in a chest brought by the mother days before. She should have done it since then, but she didn't think Iphigenia wouldn't notice and she could take everything that belonged to her with her to the new house. Iphigenia, however, every night, when she came to kiss her before going to sleep, she charged her daughter:

"Haven't you packed them yet, my dear?"

And finally, the day before, she had to.

After scrubbing the loofah with the oils, the slaves emptied the tub, washed it, and then new water was added – this time, purified water, through prayers and libations. As Calliope went back into the tub, her mother and Calypso recited the hymn – a special song for the occasion of weddings. The women's voices, in the sacred chant, showed how emotional they were. Prayers were always the most important moments in a family.

"Lypso, the tunic!"

Iphigenia was a little nervous. For someone who didn't like riots and parties, that day was exceptional. I had to take care of so many things! And her daughter's wedding garment had taken up most of her time. She wanted her to look very beautiful, for the husband who would see her for the first time that day.

"Is he going to be beautiful?" Calliope asked, coming out of the tub, wrapped in the cloths, beginning to realize what awaited her in a few hours, at her husband's house.

Her tunic was new, made of fabric from Egypt – fine, in pure white, with a heavy, elegant drape. Calliope had always been thin, and the fabrics thus emphasized the harmony of her few curves. Edged in bright blue threads, forming delicate designs, they adorned the hem and neckline. And the belt – a nice twisted belt, in a blue a shade a little stronger than the welts, gently marked her waist. The women then fixed her hair, and on her head they placed a wreath of flowers, which held the veil, in a very fine, transparent fabric, which did not show her face, only the outline.

And then she was taken by the women to the room where her father and Cassandro were waiting for her, and where Ganymede prayed at the hearth – the family altar, where the sacred fire was, and where Iphigenia poured every morning a handful of grains as an offering to the gods. Ganymede waits for everyone to post next to him and, taking a deeper tone in his voice, with the traditional phrases of the ceremonies, he declares that at that moment he was delivering his daughter to her husband:

"...To, with him, in his house, to adore the husband's gods, keep burning and offer libations and pray at the husband's home, bear his children, honor and respect him, submitting to he, and disentangling himself from this house where he was born. May Zeus, Hera, Artemis and Aphrodite protect her, and may her husband's gods receive her."

Ganymede had been thrilled. Remembering that he would no longer see Calliope every day by his side, he was beginning to regret not having postponed his plans for his youngest daughter a little.

"Well... he's really chubby... half bald... half big...." It was all Calliope thought about during her father's prayer.

Cassandro couldn't see her face because it was still covered. But she could see him very well through the veil: face, belly, bald head, beard and everything else.

"Does this girl have a good memory? Is she intelligent? Will she quickly learn prayers in her new home?" the mother-in-law asked, in a harsh tone, on the way to the tables for the banquet.

Iphigenia and Calypso look at each other out of the corners of their eyes for a few seconds without saying anything, sensing that little Calliope was going to have a lot to face. The feast of the feast followed, with some musicians Ganymede had hired to cheer the guests, playing, dancing and making riddles and riddles, many of them with allusions to Athenian politicians of the day – although Ganymede had warned them that this was a family feast without political motivations – and which men laughed and women could not understand. After all the dishes were served - lettuce, watercress and broad beans salad starters, vegetables, fish, partridges, meat, and finally the fruits and honey sweets, then the most significant moment occurred. of the ceremony, when Calypso took off Calliope's veil, who only then showed her face to her husband, all eyes on the couple waiting for his reaction.

Cassandro was surprised to see her. How young she was! She looked like a child! His first wife was also about that age when he married her, but she wasn't all that...youthful... The new wife was very pretty, that was true. And all dressed up, he was delighted. Calliope, moreover, blushed at that moment, with all those looks on her, and her blush and shyness made her even more charming in her husband's eyes.

And with the cheers of the guests – mainly Helios and his friends – the men retired to the andrónion – the men's room, where they would drink the wine taken from the craters by the employees. Ganymede had ordered the wine to be mixed with the water in a proportion of 1 to 3, because although it was a feast day, he was not given to the excesses of the symposiums of the city, as he had already seen sometimes at banquets in Athens. At his house, this moment of gathering the citizens was intended only for a small extension of the salutes and greetings for such a solemn occasion.

As the afternoon was falling, it was time for the couple to leave for their husband's house, where more ceremonies awaited them. Two carriages were being prepared for this. In the first, the couple would go, alone. In the other, the mother-in-law with the two slaves who had accompanied them, and also those present, part of the trousseau, and some of the bride's objects. Several men took turns trying to load so many chests and packages into the carriage, and they couldn't seem to agree on how to do it, starting to get exasperated that they couldn't get anything away:

"Put the biggest one first."

"That; now, that one over there!"

"Help here!"

"This one, on top."

"Not!"

"It will fall! It will fall!"

"Take that one away!"

"Not like this! Besides!"

"Let's take everything out and start again!"

"There!"

"Ready!"

And, wiping their hands, proud in front of the crowded cart and with no free space, they look to the side, on the floor: two more big chests were missing...

"But who forgot those?"

"Are you sure this has to go?"

"I said it was better from the side!"

When the heat of the discussion between them made them simply move away from the carriage so that they could better gesticulate in exasperation, Iphigenia, Calypso and two slaves took the task for themselves and, with a few moves, quickly arranged everything, in order, safely, and still leaving good space for the three passengers. Calliope was approaching her carriage, carrying a dog held by a rope by the hand.

'Where are you going with that animal? The dog is not going to my house at all!" said the mother-in-law, peremptorily.

"But...", Calliope looked at her mother.

"Come on, honey... Leave him here with us."

Calliope pouts like someone about to cry. Until then, everything was going well. Leaving the parents and the dolls away was going to be difficult, but she would get over the pain. But Sour didn't! The Sour she had to take! She was beginning to think that this marriage story was turning out to be too complicated for her. It was the puppy, she and Theo had been born and raised together! They even wanted, when he was ten days old, to perform an acceptance ceremony, walking with him around the sacred fire, as was done with newborn babies. But Iphigenia had thought that would be mocking the gods, giving the animal a treatment equivalent to that of men, and she hadn't allowed it—although Ganymede said the puppy certainly had more intelligence than several members of the Assembly Council. Callíope and Theo, disobedient, lit a small fire away from home and performed their small ceremony anyway, but were caught by a slave, who told Iphigenia everything. They were grounded for an entire afternoon, only being saved by Ganymede at dinnertime. He and Ifigênia, moreover, when alone in their room that night, they laughed a lot at the children's mischief.

"Calliope, darling... he'll be fine here," says Calypso.

She looks for Theo with her eyes, and goes to him with the dog.

"You take good care of him, huh, Theo... Our Sour..."

"I'll take care..." Theo says, picking up the rope from the dog without looking up at her departing friend. He didn't really feel like talking.

Finally the couple climbed into the carriage, with the other following behind bringing her mother-in-law and the servants, carrying torches to light the way in the soon to fall night. Helios and his friends, along with some of the younger men, wanted to organize the procession to accompany the couple, but given that Cassandro was getting married for the second time, he no longer wanted the tumult that boys usually make on such occasions. And it was a good thing that it happened, because they would have seen when, arriving at the house, Cassandro, not without much effort, took Calliope from the carriage, taking her in his arms and, staggering, carried her into the house, without her touching her feet. on the threshold – which was the most anticipated moment in every wedding, when the boys wanted to see the strength of the groom and play games. The memory of him breathless after that effort was for a long time a reason for laughter between the two of them, and also among the slaves who had watched the scene. At her husband's house, in front of the fireplace – the home – they ate together sweets and dried figs, symbolizing their union and integration. And then they went to Cassandro's rooms. Already in the stable were the six pure horses of Thessaly that Ganymede had given as a dowry.

In the house of the bride's parents, after the betrothed people left in their carriages and disappeared on the road, with the sky already beginning to darken, stars appearing here and there, when some guests began to prepare to leave, and Helios and his friends already somewhat inebriated they were having fun with the grotesque game of kottabos – throwing the remainder of the wine from the bottom of the glass against a suitable target, a man on horseback is seen below, on the road, climbing, out of breath, towards the house, where he arrives almost without strength, under the gaze of curious men and women, stunned by that surprise. He dismounts and barely greets everyone, turning to Ganymede, his breath missing, a deep silence waiting and following at the end of his words:

"Sir…"

"Easy boy! Breathe a little!" says Ganymede.

"Sir… I come from the city… by order… of Mr. Helios' superior to inform the family… and call you together with your colleagues… back to Athens with urgency… Pericles died."

That night, oblivious to the stupor caused in the house and throughout the city by the news of the death of the great general, his head full of brawl and wine, which he was not used to, and the image of Calliope in the new white chiton without leaving her in front of his eyes Theo no longer had any connected thoughts, had no desire to speak or move. He felt as if the next day wasn't going to dawn, as if the sun wouldn't rise again, as if his life had been stolen from him.

Theo had always had an older brother in Helios, whom he admired and sought to emulate. When, on coming to live in that house, he was introduced to the family cult – in a purifying ceremony, in which Ganymede made him circle the home – the fireplace, where the sacred fire was constantly lit – and, along with it, he made the prayers and libations , asking the gods to receive that new member in that house, Helios had made a terracotta doll especially for him, giving the boy a gift and welcoming him. Theo had never owned a toy, and that gesture had enormous meaning for him. Helios, in turn, also had great affection for the boy, and taught him everything he could, as when he taught him to swim, imitating the tone of voice of his gym teachers:

"An Athenian can read and swim!"

Theo felt embarrassed, knowing his inferior status as a slave, and that he wasn't actually "an Athenian." He tried to learn everything Helios taught, but he was of a totally different temperament from the boy. Helios was a talkative, athletic type, working out at home as soon as he got back from the gym every afternoon. He ran, took long jumps, kept throwing a stone away, and wanted one of the employees to come and train with him in the fight. Ganymede didn't like this part: there was always someone hurt, and that wasn't good for the farm, which needed all possible arms. But the great joy was when he and Theo went down to the stream that sometimes formed below and began swimming. Theo was a good swimmer. Helios, by the way, thought he would also be a good athlete, as he was growing up and getting stronger. In vain he tried to convince Ganymede to send him to school.

"Son, slaves don't go to school."

"But what if you release him? He could be a soldier too…"

"… Nor do they become soldiers…"

As a teenager, Helios knew nothing about the city and citizenship.

"Why, Dad?"

"Serving the army and fighting for the motherland are an honor reserved for citizens only."

So, although he barely left the field, never going to the city, Theo closely followed Helios' evolution in sports. He knew his brother was fond of that. But when Helios became a soldier, becoming a more serious man, he turned away from Theo, revealing little to him about the things he learned in the army. And even less about Mussagora. Helios' life was taking new directions.

When, however, the Olympics came and he was called to take part in the pentathlon, Helios saw this as perhaps his last chance to take part in the games, and he did not hesitate to take Theo with him as a helper.

For the little boy it was a rare occasion to leave the field, and attend such a huge party. The walk would do him a lot of good, taking him out of the doldrums and sadness he'd been in since Calliope got married.

All cities made a truce from hostilities during games, and athletes gathered in Olympia for games and celebrations. (11) The city was packed with people. The men competed for places in the stands. Some athletes went to the city months before the event, to exercise, in Élis gym. All Hellenic, of course, and free by birth.

Theo and Ganimedes arrived in Olympia in the late afternoon, just in time to see the torch lit in the prytaneum, starting the games that year. Helios was already in town with his group of friends – some athletes like him, others just spectators.

"We're here, my son!"

"Dad! How long it took! Were there any problems on the trip?" Helios asked, approaching them in the area where he was practicing the jump.

"Hmm! Every Hellenic city has a Assembly and its five hundred, from what I've seen. The road looked like the end of war, carriage bogged down on all sides. Not even the destruction of Eretria left so much devastation!

Ganymede often referred to things from the past. He spoke of the Persian attacks as if he had personally witnessed them, although he was not born until nearly ten years later.

"What an exaggeration!" Helios laughed. "Did you find the inn that my master indicated?"

"Yes, we already took our things there. Well, I'm going to find a place to sit, these old bones are now broken! All! Pheidippides himself, arriving in Athens putting his blows out, did not feel as much pain as I am feeling at the moment."

"Was the trip so bad?" Helios asked Theo, laughing at his father's antics, when the two return, alone, to the training site.

"Not so much... On the way out of the house, it took us a while to find the way. Other than that, until we came well... Helios... who is Pheidippides?"

"It was a guy who fought in Marathon, when the Persians invaded us. He was champion of races, and was charged with bringing the news of the victory to Athens, because the people were eagerly waiting to hear how things had turned out. He ran the entire course, over two hundred stadiums[6] , without rest, and when he arrived, out of breath, he spoke to the first person who came across: 'Victory! The victory is ours!'. And dropped dead."

The sanctuary of Olympia was indeed worthy of being seen, it was no wonder that all Hellenic peoples respected the truce and gathered there to see the competitions, visit the Áltis forest – a sacred place that contained many temples – and participate in all the side events that occurred during the games.

Although he had to accompany Helios during training, carrying the equipment, the oil jug and the estrigil - metal hooks specially designed for scraping the skin, after being greased with oil, to clean it from dust and sand, which they always stuck to the sweaty bodies of the athletes - as well as towels and bandages, Theo was able, in his free time, to listen to lectures and speeches made by professors and speakers from various cities, as well as appreciate the works of art that were exhibited especially on the occasion - when such events were open-air and open to all, of course.

On the afternoon of the second day, he attended the games reserved for teenagers – boys between twelve and eighteen years old – who just didn't play wrestling and boxing. Of course, among these young people there were almost only children of aristocrats, and equestrian competitions, the most expensive sport to maintain, were where they stood out the most. In the games themselves, where the men competed, Theo found that the competitors belonged to all social classes.

But without a doubt, of all the things he saw – he, who had hardly ever left the field, what impressed him the most was the temple of Zeus. Following Ganymede, full of fear and respect, he entered the place with the clear feeling that the god was there indeed, looking at everyone, ready to unleash his lightning on all the missing. After passing through the galleries that surrounded the temple, they approached the back of the enclosure, where they finally glimpsed the immense statue of the god, seated on an ebony throne and inlaid with precious stones, as well as sculptures and paintings representing the other gods. Zeus held an eagle scepter in his left hand, and Nike – the goddess of victory – in his right. The body in ivory, the tunic in gold, the head almost touching the ceiling, some forty feet tall. Zeus, lord of men and gods, who had shared the government of the world with his brothers: Poseidon, lord of the seas, and Hades, who reigned in the underworld. Zeus, who had the power over atmospheric phenomena, shooting lightning and shaking the whole earth with just a frown. The most enlightened men recognized in him, if not the only god, at least the supreme god, sovereign, omnipotent, but just and good, ruling all things and sustaining order, both in the physical world and in the realm of morals. Simple people saw in him a god closer to human beings, given to adventures and intrigues. At first dazzled by the size and beauty of the temple and statue, Theo was immediately intimidated by its magnitude. That statue frightened him, at the same time that he felt that there was a mutual indifference between them. Zeus did not know of the existence of slaves like him.

As the competitions were held and the winners were announced by the herald, a crown of olive branches was placed on their heads, hymns and songs were heard, and the athlete's joy was immense and contagious, as well as that of the spectators who they had supported him during the competition. The great orators, full of pomp, extol the victors, reminding listeners that victory reflects the athlete's innate excellence, discipline, skill, willingness to risk, and moderation in the joy of success. There were also those expressions of repudiation of the results and the referees. Theo learned a number of new words on this occasion among the disgruntled spectators. But the bad losers were soon calmed by their coaches, who took them to a corner, exalting them to "virtue". It was still on everyone's minds the terrible episode that occurred in the Olympics years before, when an athlete named Cleomenes, deprived of prizes for causing the death of his opponent, furiously hit the pillar that supported the roof of a school, where there were 50 children, causing the death of all.

Helios was doing well in the competition. From high school his teachers knew he could be a great athlete, but in the army, although he continued to train, specializing in pentathlon, he thought he would no longer have the opportunity to participate in the games. His coaches, however, seeing his chances of victory, intensified his training in those months before the start of the games, and encouraged him to go to Olympia.

Helios was not as robust as several of the athletes gathered there – many of whom were even truculent, especially those who played the pankrácio: the very tough fighting modality where it was only not allowed to bite or attack the eyes, nose or mouth of the opponent, everything else being absolutely legal, including punches and kicks in the belly, and the players didn't use the himantes, gloves to protect their hands. Nor was Helios as tough as the athletes who ran the special race, running two to four stadiums (384 to 768 meters) wearing the armor and carrying the equipment of the thirty-pound hoplite soldier. But he was excellent in disc and javelin throws.

The pace and precision needed in throwing were considered as important as the athlete's strength. Made of stone, bronze or iron, in the shape of a plate, the disc had sizes that could vary according to the age of the pitcher.

The javelin, made of wood, at the height of a man, with a metal tip, had a leather handle placed in the center of gravity, for the thrower to place his fingers, thus increasing the accuracy and distance achieved by the flight. And it was in the javelin throw that Helios stood out the most.

The entire stadium paid attention to him only when he was starting to prepare for a pitch. Tall, focused, muscled well, legs strong and slender, he took the first steps and moved his body deftly and with full force, throwing the dart into the air, like an extension of his arm, his slender body stopping with the movement. , straight and elegant, while he, as well as the entire audience, his breath caught, followed with his eyes the dart that took flight, gaining height as if to stop, then stopping in the air, in a fraction of a second, starting the fall , and finally digging into the ground, to the frantic applause of the spectators. His brands were always the best, and his attitude had won most sympathy. Certain men there would like to watch Helios throwing the javelin forever.

But not everything was that simple.

Although, in the family, "Calliope's ankles" were the most famous, it was his, his left ankle, which was the most work. He had fallen once as a child, twisting it, and since then he had told himself and everyone that he was already healed, but every now and then he felt his footing fail. He forced him when it hurt, and often hid from the coach the excruciating pains that nearly kept him from standing. And yet, he got the best results in the tests.

In the race test, everything went well.

In the jumping test, he didn't do as well as he expected. Although he felt nothing in his foot as he jumped, throwing back the stone that served as a counterweight to increase the distance of the jump, he realized, still in the air, that he would not hit a good mark.

But already in the throwing of the disc, he felt a small failure, when he turned and supported himself on his left foot. And now, as soon as he released the javelin on the last throw, he scrunched up his face, holding back the pain, trying not to let anyone notice.

After cleaning the naked body, scraping it with the strigil, he commented to Theo:

"It would be good if we had Calliope here, with her little tables!" he said, as Theo lets go and re-bandages his ankle.

Calliope had inherited from her maternal grandmother the knack and instinct to heal. At least, she was the one who took care of the vegetable garden where she planted those herbs and leaves whose medicinal benefits she learned here and there, always attentive to everything related to the subject. Her parents said it was a gift, and they didn't discourage her, as they soon noticed her abilities. It was always called when someone was sick, sick, had discomfort, etc.

"Go to sleep and dream of Asclepius[7] for him to tell you in a dream how to cure these pains!" One would say a patient.

"To dream of Asclepius! Call Calliope, and she resolves you of all pains!" was Ganymede's answer.

"If only women could come and watch the games![8]" ,Theo answered, doing what he could with Helios' ankle strap, who finally gets up for the fight.

"Married women should be able to come – after all, what they would see would be nothing new! And Calliope has now seen Cassandro!" said Helios, laughing, or trying to laugh, because the pain was unbearable.

'Cassander. Why had Helios come to remember him? It was so good, distracted by the competition, with all the people, with the coming and going.' He hadn't thought about Calliope for nearly half a day.

The first two opponents were relatively easy to eliminate. But the pain persisted, and increased. When he saw the third competitor – very strong and very hostile looking – Helios felt he was going to have to try harder. He tried to make the moves that would save his left foot, but it was very difficult, as he got distracted from the fight every time he worried about leaning on the other. And the first fall was inevitable[9] . No longer able to support his ankle, he lost the fight in a third fall in which he was already agonizing with pain, and he didn't even see his opponent receiving the applause, as he was immediately taken to a special place for the wounded and injured, where several awaited doctors specializing in athletes' injuries.

Helios didn't even try to hide it. His disappointment was pitiful. For years he had dreamed of participating in the Olympics, and it would be foolish to say that he was not interested in winning. Silent in the carriage, he barely heard what his father and Theo were saying on their way home. Ganymede mixed sadness for what had happened with apprehension for his son's health – that foot would stay with him for the rest of his life. And Theo came all the way comforting his older "brother", saying that the winner had been very lucky, that the rules were wrong, that the judges were blind, that in four years everything would be different. But Helios was too overwhelmed and frustrated, and no words could soothe his thoughts. Only Mussagora's arms could really comfort him, and he could hardly wait to be with her again.

"Sassa!"

"Come, my dear..."

Pelopia, Cassandro's mother, was a mystery to Calliope.

She was a woman much older than Iphigenia. In fact, he was about the same age as his father. It was a totally different style of woman from what Calliope was used to. It had grown up around ancient people, with constant references to the hard facts that marked those lives, who saw and felt the most difficult years, the misery and disease, the excesses of tyrants and the attacks of the Persians.

Even more than Ganymede, Pelopia was immensely anxious to see Cassandro and Calliope beget children. In fact, this anguish was the whole reason for her life. However, while for Ganymede it was a matter of the succession of land and property, a matter only of heritage – the future of his daughter, in short – for Pelopia the concern had deeper roots, living remnants of his immeasurably archaic upbringing, where marriage was nothing more it aimed at the perpetuation of the family, since the lands "did not belong to the one who was in it, but to all the ancestors", and to lose them would be "to rob the dead of eternal rest, condemning them to wander forever in limbo" . And simply having children was not enough: it was necessary to generate a male child, one who would continue the tradition and the family name, always keeping the house's sacred home (12) lit – the "savior of the paternal home", as the ancients said . Where had she gotten so much atavism? The fact is that Pelopia contained within itself all the traditions long extinct, or at least greatly diminished in strength and habit, and dumped all that weight on Calliope's shoulders.

Such a rigid view of things had made her an inflexible and very difficult woman.

And adding to Calliope's annoyances, there was the fact that Cassandro was her mother's "favorite"... Having given birth to a boy early in their marriage, Pelopia had felt proud of having fulfilled her only obligation as a woman: she was the succession and peace of her husband's ancestors guaranteed! When she then gave birth to another boy – Cassandro – then she felt the true love of a mother. He justified his stated preference by repeating even older words that said: "The firstborn was bred for the fulfillment of duty to the ancestors, others are born of love."

Thus, it was not without antagonisms that Cassandro and his brother grew up together, without any other brother or sister. But fate wanted the eldest to fall ill when he was still young, dying after much suffering for him and for everyone. And Cassandro became the savior of the paternal home.

At first Calliope found it strange that her mother-in-law checked the intimacy of her garments, looking for traces. Pelopia became angry and even more grumpy every month when she found out that Calliope had not become pregnant. Afterwards, Calliope tried to complain to Cassandro, who, by the way, had never faced her mother in any domestic matter.

"Until you give my son an heir, you will not be the mother of this house, and I will still be the one to consecrate the grains to the sacred fire," Pelopia said solemnly in the morning, when she made offerings and prayers to the gods of the house – Hestia, above all – with Calliope a few steps away, looking still.

At the beginning of married life, however, she was still too young to be aware of all this, as well as the various weaknesses and nitpicking that characterize the human being.

Despite all the differences felt by Calliope, she was adapting well to her new home and her new activities – in and out of her bedroom. It certainly wasn't because of Cassandro's lack of effort that the babies didn't come.

The only thing that altered the girl's mood a little was her mother-in-law.

"Cassandro..." she begins one night, when alone with him in the room "... what was it like with your first wife...? Did Pelopia like her?

"Hmm... I don't know... Why do you ask?"

"It's just... I think she doesn't like me... I don't know why... What have I done that bothers her so much?"

"But of course you didn't do anything, what would you have done?"

"It's just that she talks to me in a way... worse than my mother, when I did something wrong..."

"Impression of you, Calliope..."

Calliope, however, felt that hostility was spreading to slaves and servants.

"I don't know why, but Syra also looks at me in a strange way, I never did anything to her! I even want to talk, but she responds rudely, as if I were an enemy!"

"I think you're exaggerating... They have their things to do, that's all!"

"Then! I wanted to do it too, help in the kitchen and everything, but they always put me out, they don't let me prepare the dishes I know how to cook... Why don't they like me?"

"Don't worry, honey... Soon this will change."

Cassandro was referring to the fact that his mother would treat Calliope better when she became pregnant and had a baby, but he himself was not mistaken: he had the impression, with his first wife, that she was perfectly healthy, and that their children had not had them. coming on his own.

"Let's see if you can find a less useless one!" Pelopia had said about her deceased daughter-in-law, while she was still alive.

Now, after nearly three years with Calliope, Cassandro was pretty sure the problem was with him. Pelopia, by the way, was smart enough to realize that it was his son who was barren, but he would never recognize this. It was easier to continue attacking the "intruder".

"Cassandro is not lucky even with women! Another infertile in this house!" Calliope had heard her saying to the slaves, one morning she had passed through the kitchen door, without permission to enter.

However, her mother-in-law's campaign against her had contradictory effects because, without friends, Calliope had ended up clinging to Cassandro, the only person she could talk to - because Pelopia, although she wanted to, had no way of interfering in the couple's intimacy. . And Calliope soon realized that. Instead of being annoyed with the fact that her husband did not stand up to her mother on her behalf, she began to feed the union and complicity they both shared in bed, talking and laughing a lot, and exchanging tender looks and small sentences full of malice in the morning, at breakfast, a habit that exasperated Pelopia, in her impotence to poison her son against her daughter-in-law as well.

"With the five hundred of the Assembly!" screams Helios.

Since the first time he had gone by horse-drawn carriage to visit his parents, he had joined the ranks of citizens who, in assemblies, pleaded for improvements to the roads around the city.

He's heading back to town. He had come to say goodbye to Ganymede, Iphigenia, Calypso and Theo, because he was being sent with his troops out of Athens. He had been promoted to lieutenant, and had a very large number of soldiers under his command; he had become a man whom the generals were beginning to pay attention to, as he was extremely thoughtful and intelligent, despite being only twenty-six. However, during conversations with his father, he had not been able to talk about what mattered most to him: Musságora. I would have to talk anyway the next time I came to see the family! He was determined to go his own way. General Pericles himself had fought for his love for the foreign Aspasia! I needed to talk to an orator who knew the laws well to know exactly what he could and couldn't do.

The fact is, he couldn't be content with having to hide his love for the widow. They had been together for years, and their bond had only grown stronger. He was already able to bring her some money, lightening her wife's burden, finally supporting what he already considered his home, even having already gone through the papers to buy it. The problem during those years was that, being an only child, his father would certainly want to marry him to some girl of interest, with a view to the succession of lands and businesses. And Helios knew that Mussagora would not be the woman chosen by his father. How many nights had he spent awake, with her asleep in his arms, or with his colleagues snoring in the nearest litters, in the barracks, thinking of a way out of the black future that awaited him. But it seemed that things would finally have a happy ending for him: Calliope's marriage had brought new hope to his plans. He didn't need to succeed his father after all; everyone knew he was not made for country life, he had adapted so well to the city! He didn't care if the children he had were not citizens; he wanted to be able to live freely with the woman he had chosen! Cassandro to become his father's heir through Calliope! And their children, to the lands of both farmers!

But the children of Calliope and Cassandro did not come.

There passed nearly four years, and nothing.

Chapter III

Ares – god of war. Son of Zeus and Hera, he was hated by the gods

Cassandro returns from Athens one late afternoon that spring, annoyance stamped on his normally placid and cheerful face. The women – including Calliope – are in the kitchen, where he enters quickly, dropping some things on the table, and heading straight for his wife.

"My name was on the list," he says, anxious to get out this news that since early afternoon has been hammering his thoughts.

"What list, Sandro?" Callíope asks.

Pelopia stops what he was doing and approaches the couple.

"Are you sure?"

"I have. I'll have to go, Mom."

"Go where? What list is this?"

"The annual list of those drafted, Calliope... This year I'll have to serve in the army..."

"But... how are you going to do it? Are you going to be gone all this time?"

"I still don't know how it's going to be... I just know that I have to present myself at the end of Skirophorión. I may not return home that day.

Pelopia leaves without saying a word.

Cassandro at war. It was like a death sentence for her.

"Sandro... why do they want you?" Callíope asks, still not understanding. "I wonder if they don't have enough soldiers, trained? There are so many who also end up going to war, why are they looking for those who have so much work to do here in the countryside?"

"Callíope... if I said I don't want to go, they would say I'm a coward, wouldn't they?"

"But the city is full of men who want to show their bravery, people who do nothing, who just want to earn some change, fighting... I don't think it's cowardly of you not wanting to go... Besides... and the lands? What about us here alone?"

Cassandro was a great farmer. His lands were even wider than those of Ganymede – it had almost thirty hectares – and, like his father-in-law, he was part of that group of farmers who did not want to meddle in the things of war, were too attached to their properties, to the his crops, his grain business, his country life, to give himself to the heroic reveries of battle. Like his father-in-law, when the threat of Spartan attacks a few years before, he had been reluctant to take refuge in the city, and had quickly returned to the countryside, after the first fears had passed. It differed from Ganymede in some points, however. Perhaps influenced by his mother, he was more rigorous both in the administration of the property and in the treatment of slaves, with whom he was not benevolent, giving them little benefit, and never freeing them, despite treating them well. He hired extra workers throughout the year and had a foreman who advised him in the different stages of planting: pruning the vines; the foot care that was beginning to bear fruit; harvesting and knitting the grains and preparing that field for fallow; the repairs to the barns and the house; the harvest of the grapes after being laid out in the sun for ten days; the harvest of olive trees; the preparation of the land and sowing of the wheat; the shearing of sheep and the weaving of wool for the winter; supplying the house for cold days; animal care. There was also the whole part of the commercialization of the production, the trips to the city to take the grains and trade them, the payment of taxes, the collection of debts.

Cassandro didn't like the idea of leaving it all for a year. And even less to leave Calliope and her caresses for even a day.

"Your mother will have to give me a truce for a year!" says the girl, trying to find something good in her husband's summons to war.

But not even that truce had succeeded. Imbued with the desire to pursue her, as soon as Cassandro had enlisted, Pelopia started harassing her with a supposed fear of seeing her get an adulterous pregnancy, trying anyway to find a way to denigrate Calliope.

Now, unlike the times when Cassandro was at home, every month he searched his daughter-in-law's clothes to make sure she wasn't pregnant!! Calliope, in turn, had already acquired more self-confidence then and, surprisingly, the absence of Cassandro made her stronger in relation to her mother-in-law. And with her kind and playful way, she discovered that the slaves had a completely false impression of her, and little by little she was showing them who she really was.

"But I thought you hated this dish, that you had "nausea" when you saw this food, that you think it's a poor man's dish."

"Hate? Me?? But I love maza with cooked vegetables! It's what I ate every day at my house!"

The maids, moreover, were nothing like what her mother-in-law made her look like, when she told – or made up – things they would have said or done.

"Look, Syra, there's no need to clean the sheets like this, I know it's tiring and unnecessary, since they'll be inside the chest. I know I came from another house, and you don't like my way of tidying up, so you don't have to do it like that.

"But no problem, no! Who says we don't want to clean up? We always thought that your way was better, because when it's time to use, the sheets are clean and ready, without needing to be fixed again, as in the boss's way…"

Calliope had made friends and, grudgingly, her mother-in-law had to admit that she knew how to run a house.

Since Calliope's marriage, Theo has taken on greater responsibilities in the lands. Helios having established himself in a military career, Ganymede already knew that he could not count on his son for any matter connected with agriculture. Theo, in turn, showed himself to be suited to the farming business – both in administration and in the work itself, in the care of the land, grains and animals. He also went to town more often, accompanying Ganymede and the other servant, and he was used to taking some tools with him. For many years he had seen his boss complaining and tiring on those trips, and he had long wanted to be able to do something. Every time the buggy got stuck, he gradually straightened out the road, covering the potholes, widening trails, clearing and leveling. Ganymede, who had even given names to the holes, began to see that in this and that they no longer fell, as they had disappeared.

"Theo is worth five hundred!" he told his wife, in the eternal allusion to the Assembly advisers , when he arrived back at the house, on trips that were starting to get shorter.

Theo smiled, following Ganymede with a glass of cycéon.

He was now a stocky young man with a thick beard – a beard he shaved every other day, just because Calliope had said years before that the fashion in town was for men to shave, and that she thought they looked much better. In the same way, he kept his hair the way she'd once cut it for him, saying it suited him just fine. Calliope once insisted on cutting her straight black hair, thick and long. She made him sit in front of her, and with not very skillful hands, tried to make the cut that she had seen the Athenians using and, not getting the expected result, ended up leaving Theo's hair in a straight cut, which fell to the sides. , over the ears. And she thought it looked great, she kept looking at it. Since she got married, he'd cut his hair himself, pulling it all the way up and running the scissors in one go. The hair then formed a streak down the middle of the top, falling to the sides, coming to rest almost at her ears, as she had said she liked. When they grew up, he tied them with a leather strap across his forehead, tying it back so it wouldn't cover his eyes, as he had to keep running his hand over his bangs all the time, pulling it back. Little did Theo know that his effort to keep up with Calliope's tastes was unnecessary, for it was his light brown eyes, almost honey-colored, with the very black lashes, that she liked best.

So much preoccupation with appearance did not interfere with his country routine. He had grown up in the country, and that work was his life. He woke up very early, like all peasants, when it was still dark and there were many stars in the sky, and he worked hard all day. Most of the time, he only returned home after night had fallen, having spent the whole day working the land, farming, inspecting the work, watching over the property, taking care of the animals. In place of sports, it was the plow and the hoe that formed his strong, rigid musculature. At night, after washing himself, he would wait in the kitchen for Ganymede to tell him the things he had seen and done during the day.

He never got sick. At least, if he was sick, he didn't even notice, he went out to work, no matter what. No discomfort prevented him from putting on his peasant's chiton, in summer, and over it the sheepskin, in winter, to go and cultivate the land, in cold or heat, in rain or even under snow, which in some winters he was coming to descend on those lands. What would make an Athenian limp and bedridden made no difference to him. He got to his feet and went about his business. Calypso and Iphigenia occasionally watched his haggard countenance, a little fever in his eyes. In his face, with very thick eyebrows, black and well defined, almost joining in the center, contrasting with his skin, which, in winter, was incredibly white, and even the hooked nose, this dejection made him more serious than usual.

"Theo, my son, wouldn't it be good for you to go to bed?" Asks one of the women, seeing him cough heavily.

"Me? Why? I am not sleepy!"

"What would Calliope say, if she saw him wanting to go out like that, and with this weather, what is he doing?" Says the other.

"She would order him to go to bed right away, and bring him a plate of mazza."

"But to us, no one respects."

If she were there, he would let himself be pampered a little. But she wasn't, and he couldn't stay away from work. It was his life and his healing.

His only distraction was to stay in the tower at the end of the day, watching the landscape, watching the colors change in the sky, dreaming of Calliope, waiting for her to come visit, imagining she was preparing him a dish of mazza.

It was a very sunny morning in Athens. It had rained a little during the night, the air was clean and fresh, a scent of summer plants and flowers scenting the air. The floor of the Market still had some puddles of water here and there, and the people were happy and talkative, especially the women: that dawn a large number of carts had arrived from Piraeus bringing an immense quantity of vegetables, fruits, fish, spices and all. Good luck. It was a day of plentiful and assorted tables in every house in the city, as there was food at all prices. The women were delighted with the fruit: they had never seen it so fresh, fragrant and ripe! One of them, already in her tunic loaded with figs, was fiercely struggling with others in choosing the famous fruits, while bargaining with the seller, since she had already spent almost all the few coins she had taken that morning. Having finally made her purchase, as she turned to leave, not seeing where she was stepping, she stepped right into a puddle of water, and then there was a spectacle that for a long time would gladden the memory of those who watched her. : she flew upwards, as if propelled by a spring, with her legs spread in a grotesque "V", showing her pudenda shamelessly, all her vegetables scattered on the ground, rolling to all sides, and still, in the fall, she hit the edge of the fruit stand, which came to the ground with her in one piece. The accident lasted only a few seconds, but for those who saw it, seemed like minutes, all those pairs of eyes together following the rise, the "V", the contents of the vertex of the "V", the descent, the arm in the tent, the jaw dropping from the greengrocer, the delicate fruit dropping to the ground, and the final thud. There were people who got sick from laughing so much. A man had to sit on the floor to laugh better. The children immediately picked up the fallen fruit and fled.

"Poor woman!" said a rich lady, hiding her laughter with her hand, as she passed by her maid, who was laughing with all her teeth.

"It's worn out soles, it needs new sandals!" Said another, looking at the ground, worried about not falling too.

But there was still more to come: a burly man who laughed so hard he had to bend down and rest his hands on his knees, stepped on one of the berries, and made the second flight of the morning, crashing to the ground and breaking one of the stones with his weight. It was the account. The young poet Aristophanes himself, with his most recent comedy "Arcanenses", presented at the Odeon, at the time of the last Dionysian festivals, had not managed to obtain so much joy from the public.

"Warn the people at the Pendelikon that we've discovered a new technique to break the stones!

The only one who was in a very bad mood when they told him the story was Pan:

"Filth! Why didn't it happen in front of me?"

And while the people in the Market, oblivious to the affairs of state, laughed to tears at the ordinary events of the morning, in the boulevard, the five hundred assemblymen, extraordinarily assembled, approved of Cleon's proposal to order the attack on Esfactéria, the small island to the south. of the Peloponnese, deciding the fate of Athens and its citizens, and continuing the war against Sparta.

Sparta and Athens. The two greatest powers in the Hellenic world. The opposition of races – those Dorians, these Ionians. Those aristocrats, these democrats. The former is a continental empire, this is a maritime empire, aimed at supremacy in commerce – this is indeed the greatest fear of the Spartans.

Poor soldiers who were not born with bearing and athletic strength: they suffer a little more in battle. The hoplite equipment they have to carry, alone, already requires training, as it is quite heavy – both in kilograms and in money, as everyone has to buy it at their own expense, paying the equivalent of the quarterly salary of an average worker .

In the phalanx - the method of making war, placed side by side in rows - they had to continue without undoing the formation, carrying the almost thirty kilos of metal: the armor, which was a linen coat reinforced with metal plates; the helmet; metal leggings; and also the hoplon, the emblematic weapon of the hoplites: a circular shield 90 cm in diameter, in bronze or in amalgam of wood, wicker and skins, carried on the left arm, held by a central brace and a bronze handle. The sword was slung across the shoulder and, in the right hand, the wooden spear about 2.5 m long, with a metallic tip, in iron or bronze, and finally a short sword for melee, attached to the leg. But, in fact, having all grown up being prepared and even waiting for the war, which was part of their lives, no one was surprised or regretted. It took years, since childhood, to exercise the body and mind for the moment of battle, which consisted of advancing in formation, carrying weapons, with the bravest on the front line, in a real challenge of strength.

Arranged in several rows, the phalanx is a compact group, with the space between the combatants being more or less one meter. The wings are populated by some contingents of light troops and knights, with the function of opposing the attempts of encirclement and creating confusion among the enemy lines. Once a meeting place for battle has been decided, a divine favor has been invoked, and a sacrifice offered, the ordered march towards the enemy begins. The Spartans, dressed in their red tunics, follow in profound silence, only the sound of a flute guiding their spirit. The frontal impact only gives rise to lateral maneuvers, the phalanges shifting naturally to the right, given the propensity of soldiers to move to the opposite side of the shield. Relatives, friends and neighbors, purposely placed side by side by the Athenian generals, thus remain firm in their posts, solidarity, more than military discipline, ensuring that no one abandons their comrades.

The cold, gray afternoon at the end of the year did not invite her to put even her face out of the house. Calliope is in the kitchen, laying the vegetable slices on a platter, while two slaves knead the barley for soup and bread, when the foreman rushes in:

"Lady Calliope! Lady Calliope! Come quickly!"

"What is it? What happened?

"An employee of your father arrived, he wants to talk to you, he says it's urgent! He's almost out of breath, he looks like the living dead! His carriage mule even lays down!"

Calliope leaves her plate and wipes her hands, stepping out into the courtyard, where she actually sees one of her father's servants. She immediately feels it is something bad. Too bad.

"Mistress Calliope," he says, finishing a glass of water that had been offered to him. " Mistress Calliope, Master Ganimedes told me to come and get you running, you need to go, everyone is waiting for you!

"What happened?" she asked, not wanting to hear the answer.

"Helios…"

Calliope's vision blurs, and she feels the ground softening under her feet. The employee's voice seems to fade and come back, so she hears only snippets of his sentences. An urge in the pit of her stomach makes her put her hand to her mouth and turn to sit on one of the benches in the courtyard.

Helios had been killed in action, and the family was expected in Athens for the year-end funerals, when all dead soldiers were buried in a solemn ceremony, which was supposed to take place in a day or two.

She quickly gets a change of clothes and climbs into the carriage with her father's servant, saying goodbye almost wordlessly to everyone, and asking her mother-in-law to pray for all of them, and especially for her dead brother. Pelopia felt for the first time for her daughter-in-law, seeing in the girl's eyes how important her family was to her.

The carriage arrived at the foot of the small hill, and her father's house had never looked so gloomy. How many times had she looked at the house like that, from a distance, and felt an immense joy that always made her jump from the carriage and run to the door, calling everyone by name, asking for water, bread, a fruit! This time she had neither the strength nor the will to go down, but she did when he saw Theo approaching.

"Theo… Theo." her legs wobbly, she went to meet him.

Theo had his gaze as if covered in mist; the lump in his throat made him even more tense. Helios had been his older brother, the boy he looked up to, his hero. He can't say anything to Calliope, just look at her to see in her eyes the same pain he felt.

"How was it? Where was? Where is he?" Calliope's words come out broken; her voice choked.

"The father ordered the cart to be prepared; let's go to Athens, that's where he is…"

"Do you know something? Was it a single scam? Did he… suffer…?"

"I do not know."

"Was there... cruelty? Will it be?" now there was a mixture of sadness and anger.

"I don't know, I don't know anything, no one knows..." His eyes turn away from hers.

"Oh, Theo... he died..." Calliope covered her eyes with her hand, and holds back her tears.

Theo wants to put his arm around her shoulders, but restrains the gesture, and they walk in silence.

"How is the mother?" she asks finally, as they approach the door.

"Not well... She closed herself in her room... Only Calypso can come in and see her. It seems she hasn't said a word since they came to bring the news... She squealed, and went to her room..."

"And the father?"

"He..." Theo controls his voice. He loved Ganymede like a true father. "It's wrong... Can't speak the sentences properly... I had to help him with everything..."

"Is that you? - Calliope asked when they reached the door of the house, which remained closed, a deep silence coming from inside.

"And you?" he asks.

The family can barely look at each other. They all climb desolate and amazed in the carriage, taking the path to the city in silence. And for the first time in so many years, Ganymede makes the journey between his lands and Athens without even noticing the potholes in the road.

Funerals were full of pomp, as was the case for heroes killed in war. There weren't that many this time. Athens had emerged victorious, taking the island of Sphateria, off the southwest coast of the Peloponnese, and bringing three hundred Spartans prisoner.

The family enters town wearing brown tunics, the color of mourning, including Theo. Ganymede had allowed him, though a slave, to wear a small brown cloak over his raw tunic. Besides, he was also the only employee, save Calypso, to accompany them to the city. Each one brought Helios an offering, an object of the boy's predilection, to be placed next to the coffin. Ganymede, the first sword his son had learned to fight. Iphigenia, figs and honey, their favorite foods as children. Calypso, her winter cloak, which she had made when he was at the age at which boys became adults. Calliope, two terracotta figurines representing a boy and a girl, which Helios had carved for her when she was little. And Theo, a wreath of olive leaves, the crown of an Olympic champion, which he had made, his eyes filled with tears, as soon as he learned of his brother's death.

As the carriage passed, the people in the streets were silent in the face of mourning, and all of them focused their gazes on the mother, wanting, as in a tragic spectacle, to see her expression of anguish and grief. Iphigenia, who had not been to Athens for years, did not even notice the countless changes in the city, the new monuments, the new squares, the new temples. In fact, it was kind of absent from everything and everyone. Her eyes saw nothing, her ears heard nothing. The soul had fled her. Other families were also in mourning, and in groups of bowed people, united in pain and color, they looked at each other in sympathetic and resigned silence. The air was filled with that dreary and sinister aspect that surrounds people when a loved one leaves.

A tent had been pitched and, under it, long tables had the bodies side by side for the visitation of relatives. The next day, the day of the procession and ceremony, they would be placed in cypress coffins, one for each tribe. An empty coffin was always taken to be buried, representing those dead soldiers whose bodies could not be recovered.

In one corner of the tent, four soldiers in special uniform stood guard around an individual coffin propped up on a table. In it was the body of Helios.

The family was surprised, as they knew that the bodies of soldiers were all exposed together before being placed in the urn common to their tribe. But Ganymede and Iphigenia were too shaken for any reasoning.

A short distance away, the superior general of Helios, who would deliver the speech at the ceremony, as was customary since the most remote times, with a very serious countenance, was waiting for the family of his lieutenant to come to say goodbye to his son. Calliope learned from him, while waiting for her parents to say the last goodbye, that Helios had died a heroic death, saving the lives of some companions, and this was the reason for being in the spotlight. He wanted to know more details about the blows and injuries, but the general was reticent and said no more.

"But why closed coffin?" she asked herself.

First, Ganymede and Iphigenia approached him. Holding on-to each other, they rested their hands on the coffin in silence, look-ing at the wood as if not understanding what it contained. Then, alone, Calypso, acting as a second mother, approached the coffin. And she seemed to be talking to the boy, as if he were sleeping in-side. Then it was Calliope's turn. Afraid, she takes Theo's arm.

"Come with me, Theo... Please..."

And then came the most difficult moment. The two ap-proached the coffin and Calliope, whose heart until then had seemed almost stopped, suddenly feels it beating unevenly and as if jumping out. Also look at that wooden box that was said to contain your deceased brother. She was obsessed with the idea of knowing if there had been excessive cruelty in the fight that had killed him, she wanted to know details of her brother's death. And, taken by a pain-filled disbelief, a desperate hysteria, she begins to try to open the coffin, her little hands prying on the lid, her face contorted with anguish, wanting to see the body and to believe in that death. Theo held her, but he also ached with the same morbid curiosity.

"Lady Callíope..." said the general, quickly approaching and holding her carefully, while the soldiers, who were about to inter-fere, returned to their position. "You can't do that... Take it easy..."

"I need to see! I need to know! — she said, struggling with Theo and the general, the words coming out of her guts. "It's my brother! Who will stop me? I'm going to die... if I don't know how he died."

Her voice completely altered, her breath missing, her hands continuing to force the coffin open, and with a force that amazes the men around her, Calliope ends up releasing the lid, just as the general, after an impasse, looks to two of the soldiers standing guard, nodding, assuming a totally irregular procedure. The soldiers approach, carefully lifting the lid of the coffin, into which Calliope and Theo bend their heads, immediately seeing the skull pierced by a huge hole, loose from the neck, the rest of the bone apparently intact.

Calliope turns her face into Theo's chest, and Theo drapes an arm over her shoulder, horror in her eyes, unable to pull them away from her brother's remains.

Like all soldiers killed in war, Helios had been buried in the Ceramics necropolis, in a tomb erected during the three days before the ceremony.

The spectacular funeral procession was conducted soberly and without noisy demonstrations. Women from bereaved families and others, hired to make the lamentations, went ahead. A large group of soldiers lined up, in parade uniforms, in honor of the dead. Other soldiers had been bringing the tusks of war - armor and equipment of the vanquished, and the three hundred Spartans themselves, humiliated and offended, their hands tied, tied together by ropes at their feet that barely allowed them to walk. Members of the families of the deceased soldiers, as well as strangers and the curious, increased the procession, crowding into the necropolis, always fascinated by mass emotions. But the really great moment, the most awaited one, was the funeral speech, the panegyrics, which every year was delivered by a citizen chosen among the wisest. From the first year of the war, when Pericles had made his famous speech, tearing tears of emotion from all Athenians, everyone else chosen for that role had tried unsuccessfully to match him. That had been an especially cold winter, both in temperature and in the hearts of the Athenians. They were guided by that great general, from whom, at that time, they hoped to hear some word of comfort. When the time came, Pericles climbed onto a small platform, to be heard by as many people as possible:

"Many of those who preceded me in the task I now have praised the one who made this speech a legal obligation – he had begun –, considering his pronunciation at the funerals of those who fall in battle to be correct. As for me, I believe that the value shown through great acts would be sufficiently rewarded by manifesting only in acts the honors we pay them, such as those now seen in these funerals prepared at the expense of the people. I wish that the reputation of so many brave men were not put at risk, exalted or belittled according to the greater or lesser oratory talent of a single individual. For it is difficult to speak properly at a time when it is not possible to assess the credibility of the speaker's words. The well-informed and favorably disposed listener will perhaps think that due justice has not been done in the face of his own desires and his knowledge of the facts. On the other hand, one who is oblivious to the subject, hearing about a feat beyond his own capacity, will be led, by envy, to suspect some exaggeration. For men bear the praise of other men only as far as they can persuade themselves capable of equaling themselves in the reported feats; past that point, envy overtakes them, and with it unbelief. However, since our forefathers gave their approval to this practice, it is my obligation to obey the law and try as best as possible to correspond to the wishes and aspirations of each one of you".

Among the listeners, the one who was most attentive was Thucydides, a noble and wealthy citizen, who absorbed Pericles' words and transcribed them, as he understood that it was important to leave the precise and accurate account of historical facts to future generations, to that the truth be known.

Pericles then spoke of the glory of the ancestors and their achievements; he praised the Athenians present there for maintaining and further adding to the city's grandeur, its self-sufficiency, and the independence of its resources in war and peace.

"Our Constitution does not conform to those of our neighbors. She is, rather, an example to be followed. The state here is administered in the interest of all, not just that of a minority. This is why our regime is called democracy. As far as differences between individuals are concerned, equality is guaranteed to all by law; but as far as participation in public life is concerned, each is considered according to merit, with less importance for the class to which he belongs and more for his personal value. Poverty is not a reason for anyone, being able to provide services to the City, to be prevented from doing so because of the obscurity of their condition".

Each person listening to that speaker went along with him deepening the meaning of his words.

"As a city, we are the Hellenic school, and my doubt is not small as to whether the world is capable of producing a man who, having only himself to look for strength, will face emergencies and be master of versatility just like the Athenian."

He drew attention to the art and beauty spread throughout the city, and also to the shows, games and religious rites that met the needs of leisure and obligation to the gods.

"When put to the test, Athens, and none other among her contemporaries, proves to be greater than her own reputation, never giving rise to her opponents to be angry at the antagonist who defeats them, nor to her citizens to question her merit as an authority."

In the military aspect, it showed the differences between Athens and its antagonists:

"Our confidence is based little on military preparations and cunning, and much on the firmness of mind that we are going to look for in ourselves when we act."

An absolute silence had taken over the city; not even the birds dared interrupt the general.

"If I expand on the character of this country, it is to show that the risk we take in fighting for it is not the same as those who do not have such blessings and attributes to lose."

So the great strategist had spoken to his attentive listeners at the Ceramics, in front of the buried coffins and the teary eyes of the mothers and fathers of those heroes.

"This is the Athens for which these men, bent in their determination not to lose her, nobly fought and died, and so be their successors equally ready to atone for their cause."

Tears flooded the faces of bereaved families.

"Choosing to die resisting, never subduing themselves, they not only saved themselves from dishonor but, facing danger, face to face, in a brief moment marked by fate, they surrendered their lives not to fear but to a moment of glory. So these Athenians died".

There was not a noise in the air interrupting the speech, not a faint rustle of trees, not an uncontrolled sigh. Even the breaths were held.

"This panegyric here comes to an end, for the Athens I celebrate is nothing more than what made it the heroism of these men and their equals."

With such an emphasis on the honor of soldiers, he had finally managed to bring some comfort to those hearts so eager for comfort.

"And now that you have finished mourning for your loved ones, you may go away."

Six years after that emotional speech, at the funerals of Helios and his companions, fallen in the victorious battle of Esfactéria, although the eulogy had not been so emotional, the tears of the families were the same, and the same was pain in the mourning hearts.

When, at slow, sad and resigned steps, everyone had left the necropolis and night was falling over the city, a woman wearing a hooded cloak, carrying a package, sneaks to the soldiers' tomb, approaching the one of Helios and of the offerings left by the boy's family. He had a little girl by the hand who could barely walk, whom he left a little away from the grave while he unwrapped her package: a plate of food that she had prepared especially that afternoon. After placing it with the other offerings, she looked around to make sure no one was watching her, and then she cut off a lock of her hair as well as the girl's hair and, tying it to a strip of cloth, put it on. them also at the foot of the tomb, with their eyes closed saying a few words, in an almost imperceptible voice. And then, taking the child by the hand again, she left in silence.

It was Mussagora.

Calliope stayed with her parents for three days, for the funeral feast, which is attended by the neighbors and some friends of Ganymede from Athens. She needed to help with the cleaning and support her mother, who was slow to recover. Iphigenia still hadn't let go of the pain she was feeling. Didn't cry, or couldn't cry. Shocked, her eyes seemed to have no expression, her face showed no reaction. He neither understood nor accepted that Athenians and Spartans were in that senseless struggle. They were all Hellenic. They had fought together on more drastic occasions, where the danger was real. Every now and then she was surprised to stare, her hands together, her thoughts far away, until, finally, a sigh leaving her lips, she said aloud to herself:

"They are brothers..."

Calliope helped the women make ribbons and wreaths, and prepare food. But her father thought she shouldn't be long, freeing her from the feasts of the ninth and thirtieth day, ordering Theo to take her back to her husband's house.

It was a slightly longer journey than that to Athens, and the two, side by side in the carriage, made the entire journey practically silent. Calliope recalling the image of the pierced skull. Theo, eyes on the road, dreaming of her resting her head on his shoulder and sleeping peacefully.

It was night when they arrived, and both were exhausted both from the silent and bitter journey and from the cold and serene that left them stiff and eager for shelter. From the road Calliope sees a light inside the house: some slave must have noticed them arriving, and got up to light a lamp. But it is with sudden joy that she climbs out of the carriage and sees Cassandro waiting for her at the door, holding out one hand to embrace her, while with the other he leans on a wooden stick.

"Cassandro!" she exclaims as Theo drives the carriage to the barn, where he's going to spend the night, to go back the next morning.

As if finally able to let go of the anguish that she had been carrying in her chest for so many days, Calliope hugs her husband and bursts into tears, crying convulsively for everything she hadn't cried before.

Sadness and tiredness, added to the joy and relief of seeing him at home, make Calliope feel an unexpected wave of affection for her husband.

"Let's go; Syra is just finishing warming up the food for you guys" he says, sitting down to keep her company while the slave, who had risen to welcome them, brought them a very hot dish of rophema of peas with barley and wheat bread.

"Come eat, Theo!"

"I'll eat in the barn…"

"Come sit down, I'm inviting you, how stubborn you are!" she insists, and Theo looks at Cassandro, who nods.

This had been one of the few habits in the paternal house that Calliope had managed to introduce into her new home, much to her mother-in-law's disapproval. She would sit with her husband for meals, which her mother-in-law considered a breach of tradition and decorum. A man and a woman eating at the table together!

"Decent couples eat their meals apart, with the man being served on the divan and the woman seated in some out-of-the-way chair at a decorous distance!" she would say.

But this was an innovation that Calliope did not admit to giving up, as she particularly enjoyed talking to her husband like this, peacefully, at the kitchen table, having learned from her parents about the peace and harmony that this moment invokes. Cassandro, in turn, approved and enjoyed all the things his wife did, especially those that contradicted his mother's rigidity. For the rest, the healthy habit of eating at the table, sitting in a chair, which Ganymede had brought home so long ago, at the time he was drawn to make up the Assembly for a year, and he learned that this was how prytanes ate, and had suited him very well. Tall and very overweight, the back pains that had bothered Cassandro so much since he was young, made the reclined position on the couch at mealtimes an especially painful ordeal. A slave at the table, however, was only possible because Pelopia was fast asleep at that late hour of the night, and did not even know of her daughter-in-law's return.

"He had a huge hole in his skull, Sandro… like that…" She makes the shape of the hole with her hand. "How did they do this to him? Don't you think they attacked him while lying down?"

"I don't know, honey … Why keep thinking about it? He's gone now…" Cassandro takes the bangs that fall over his wife's eyes with his fingers.

Quiet, yet full of his own opinions and impressions, Theo eats from his plate without looking up from his plate. Passing the bread in the thick, salty broth, he gives a word here and there, when asked, uncomfortable with the couple, tormented by this moment of tenderness between Calliope and her husband. He wanted to go to the barn and get the image of the two of them together like this out of his eyes.

Cassandro, in turn, also had a lot to tell, and Calliope, traumatized, wanted first of all to check that he had no injuries. In her room, as he spoke, she reviewed his arms, his legs, his back, and finally came to his right foot, bandaged and a little swollen. He had fallen from a structure his infantry group was erecting – an ingenuity of his own making, so that he could more quickly transport sacks of food to the soldiers entrenched there. His general, although aware that he was not cut out for combat, very upset had sent him home to recover, regretting losing a man with above average intelligence, able to trace some lines on paper and draw solutions to practical problems of the life in battle.

Cassandro was given to imagining and executing innovative ideas both in construction and in tools for treating the countryside. When he went to Athens, it was always with the architects that he wanted to talk. He learned new techniques and shared his ideas, his sketches, and everyone pored over these features to visualize a new way of putting up a wall, or some jumble of wood and pulleys that turned and made something go from place to place. He was even part of a group that was studying a revolutionary way of collecting sewage.

He had never been fond of war, especially that one, which in his view, as well as that of so many, only sucked Athens' coffers and blood. He had always endowed the crop with the inventions that his skill created, facilitating production and everyone's life, saving effort and, above all, gaining time. He wanted to continue his country life and take care of the property, which was his passion, as well as the other: his wife, about whom he had not stopped thinking for a moment, and whom he had left in the clutches of his petty mother.

"Thanks, Syra, go lie down," he tells the slave who has come to stoke the brazier in the master bedroom.

"Do you want anything else, Lady Calliope?

"No thanks, Syra. Go to sleep, it's so late! Warm up, it's very cold tonight!"

Cuddled up, little by little, they fall asleep, trying to find in their sleep some of the peace that the last events had robbed them of.

"Anyway, I've already decided that I'm not going back to war: I'll hire a foreigner who will go in my place and I'll stay here, which is where my life is" said Cassandro, kissing Calliope on the forehead, before she fell asleep.

In the barn, with the image of Calliope beside Cassandro clouding his mind and bittering his soul, in a mixture of anger, jealousy and revenge, Theo ends up possessing Syra, who had sneaked up to him, curling up to his body after he had gone to bed, leaving him no other way out. The next morning, he left without saying goodbye to anyone, when everyone was still asleep, even before sunrise.

Chapter IV
Hestia – goddess of the sacred home and family, protector of the house

"Here in this house, no one is in mourning!!"

Pelopia had come to the kitchen after walking a little with her son in the garden beside the house, and was talking about the door, even before entering, seeing her daughter-in-law eating breakfast, wearing the brown tunic, the first one at her side. hand that morning after he came home from the funerals.

"Mom!" Said Cassandro, who came after her, without her noticing, and surprised her in his unfortunate phrase.

The slaves alternately looked at Pelopia and Calliope, sympathetic to their young mistress's pain, exulting in Cassandro's testimony to such hostility that, for them, was so commonplace.

"My wife's brother died. Her pain is my pain too."

"Cassandro" Calliope gets up, delicately. Lady Pelopia is right. In this house there is no mourning, I will change the tunic. It's just an outfit after all. What goes on in my heart, however, about that neither I nor anyone else has any power."

Cassandro was very upset with his mother's attitude. Those few months in the army, away from home, made him think of a series of things he had been seeing in his life. He could no longer accept his mother's subjugation of Calliope in that way, although her wife had already gained her space in the house by her own strength. Pelopia had to accept and strive for a good relationship with her daughter-in-law.

A new episode, however, immediately changed the routine.

Pelopia falls ill the day after her son returns from the army.

He had spent the night feeling ill, and the morning had been unable to get up. To her dismay, the only person indicated to take care of her was precisely Calliope who, seeing her lying in bed, her face downcast and her eyes dry, had felt a compassion that had driven away any and all resentment. She had taken under his care her mother-in-law, the house, and everything that Cassandro did not take care of himself.

Not knowing exactly how Pelopia felt, he began by administering those simple herbs that took care of intestinal ailments, such as the infusion of purslane stalk, which had brought some relief to the patient's pain.

Taking care that she didn't have a fever, Calliope did not leave her bed, constantly checking how she felt, how her breathing was, if she felt comfortable, if she wanted to go to the bathroom. It aired the room and kept it clean and tidy. Her gift of caring for the sick was accompanied by this devotion, this feeling of affectionate responsibility, which at first upset her mother-in-law, but soon made her realize her daughter-in-law's sincerity.

"Sandro, I haven't seen any improvement in Lady Pelopia..." she said at dinner one night.

"But she hasn't been complaining about pain, has she?"

"No, but that's not enough... She's still indisposed, she can't get up, she's having trouble... It would be nice if we took her to town, to see someone with better medicine."

"Do you think she can handle going to Athens?"

"If we accommodate it well, I think so."

"My mother doesn't like the city, Calliope... I don't know if she'll want to go."

"We'll have to find a way to force it, Sandro. If she stays like that in bed, it can perpetuate this ailment that afflicts her, when a visit to a doctor could cure her at once."

Cassandro knew his mother well. Pelopia did not even want to hear about Athens, or shrines, or doctors and their theories. She refused to go, and would not allow them to force her. She was used to Calliope's company; he no longer felt pain, with the medicines his daughter-in-law gave him; and he'd even gotten into the habit of telling his son's wife about his life, a sinister longing creeping into his voice.

"My father was very strict," she said one day. "Once he hit me and my sister hard because we didn't want to eat the meat of a sacrifice he had made. We were so little! We were afraid of the days of sacrifice, and we felt pity for the little sheep, we knew them all and even gave them names!

Calliope knew that feeling: she felt sorry for the animals too, even when they were shorn, when they were naked to give their wool, and she and Theo were amused at how skinny they were.

"This sister was the person I loved the most in my life, after my son Cassandro. She was married before me, but her husband died early. And then, having met a young man in town, she wanted to marry him, but my father wouldn't let her, as it was a meteco, and she spent time trapped in the house, until my father married her to a Spartan. Permission had to be obtained from both States for the marriage! She didn't want to go, but she was forced, and right then this war began, I never heard about her again... What harm must they have done to her? The hostilities must have been brutal." Pelopia says, getting distressed by the memory.

"I don't think so, mother..." Calliope said, trying to calm her down. "Being married, she should be loved by her husband. She married him in times of peace, and she certainly built a family like everyone else."

Pelopia had teary eyes fixed on Calliope.

"Are you feeling all right? Let me see if it's fever..."

"Good... to hear you say that..."

"But I really think so... Women form homes, with their husbands, whoever they are..."

"No... Calling me... mother... A daughter... I've always missed you so much..."

Calliope takes her hand, and feels her mother-in-law's weakness.

Despite all her daughter-in-law's care, Pelopia's condition was more serious than imagined, and after a few days in bed, with an amulet hanging around her neck, she died, calmly, without pain, with her son and daughter by her side, guaranteeing her prayers and peace.

Calliope removed her brown tunic from the chest where a week before she had placed it, and the house was in mourning.

Cassandro felt his mother's death, of course. It had been her only family for so many years. And like every funeral, this one had been very sad, with the lamentations, the brown clothes, the people speechless and not knowing what to say and what to do with their hands. And the flowers, which at funerals took on such an ominous look and smell. For all Pelopia's sullenness, he was going to miss her terribly. He felt his mother's death more than he had felt his father's death.

It is true that his father's death had been very painful, as it had left him and his mother alone, and he was then no more than a boy. He already knew how to take care of the land, but he was suddenly responsible for all the property, for all the decisions, and for so many people under his orders. He had never gotten along very well with his father. Respected him, that's for sure. But they had never been close, they had no affinity. The father was more concerned with his brother, to whom he tried to teach everything he knew. He could never imagine that the eldest son would leave so soon. When the latter was gone, he turned to Cassandro, discovering that he had another son perhaps much more like him, whom he had neglected for so many years. They didn't create affection, especially because at that point, in addition to lack of identity with his father, Cassandro already had his own ideas about how to manage the property, innovations that would be of great value, another way to treat employees, etc. When his father died, he felt the loss, of course, but he hadn't suffered from affectionate bonds that never had been.

And now, with his mother gone, he suddenly found himself remembering that father whom he had never tried to understand. Phrases of the old man came to his mind, and only now did he see meaning in them. Attitudes of the father that, at the time, he had criticized so much, now seemed to him coherent and full of wisdom. His father's own face, which he had not thought of for years, appeared in his memory with an inexplicable clarity, and he saw in that face traits and expressions to which, in life, he had not paid attention. He saw him as a man who, like himself, had to face the hardships imposed on him against his will, and without questioning. And who also, like him, had no one to talk to, no one to turn to, nowhere to seek advice. He had to go through situations that he might have preferred to avoid, and that he carried on through uncertainty and fear. A man with feelings, desires and disappointments, who had loved and perhaps hadn't been loved very much.

That father whose actions he had interpreted so heavily, and whom he had hastened to criticize, judge, and condemn, for differences between the two that had nothing personal, only now did he understand. He continued to have opinions and views that were even opposite to those of his father, but he realized that they were just different ways of looking at life, nothing more. His father had been, like him, a man who lived and tried to do what he thought was best, under the circumstances in which life had placed him. Cassandro felt a mute understanding for him rise in his soul. As well as an immense desire to see him again in front of him and tell him how much he understood him now, how much he loved him, and how much he wished to be able to talk to him, it hurting his heart to be unable to do so anymore. Why did he think so much about his father, when his mother was leaving? A tear welled up in his eyes, and he knew it wasn't for Pelopia.

"Sandro…" Callíope approached her husband at night, when he was outside the house, looking into the darkness. "Aren't you coming to sleep?"

"I'm going…"

"Are you feeling all right? Haven't eaten anything so far, since yesterday."

"I'm not hungry, Calliope…"

Calliope did not know what to say to her husband to comfort him. She herself still carried in her soul the shock of her brother's death so few days before. She could only imagine what he felt, and she wanted to show her support, but she didn't know how.

"You're going to miss her a lot, aren't you…" she said, putting her hand on his shoulder. "It's been so many years that you two stayed together taking this house… You know, she and I were even friends, now in the last few days…"

Cassandro took a deep breath to speak, as if until then he's barely been sending air into his lungs.

"She found out too late that there were so many good things around her, and that it was better to have had goodwill rather than looking for mistakes in everything."

Callíope wondered at the tone of voice, even a little austere, with which he refered to his mother. In fact, he was not referring to his mother, but to himself. Or maybe both.

"Each one lives according to what life imposes on him."

Cassandro looks at his wife surprised at the wisdom of what she has just said.

"You know, Calliope... my mother died... but I miss my father more than her... Am I a bad son? I should be suffering more for my mother... Dad has been gone for so long... Why is it I think about him nonstop?"

Calliope looked at this man over forty who asked her these questions, to her, a girl who was beginning to blossom, to stop being a child. Who would have the answers he was looking for? Who would know the human heart so deeply, to say that word no one could find? She wanted to say something that would soothe her soul, but she herself was looking for so many answers.

In the times that followed, Cassandro became more circumspect, and spent many hours alone, reflecting, looking far away, thinking about the past. When he went to the city, he began to frequent sects and alternative religious groups, in search of answers to the questions that rose to his mind from the depths of his soul. Questions of the spirit dominated him, and he began by trying to better understand the Eleusinian Mysteries, worship of the goddess Demeter in her sanctuary in Attica where only "initiates" were admitted, who were committed to keeping the ceremonies completely secret, concerned with purification of the soul, retreat and fasting.

But throughout the city, a reaction to the religion of the polis fostered the emergence of new spiritual outlets, in a deeper domain of the soul, addressing man as such, distancing himself from the limits of citizenship. Then Cassandro began to delve into the issue of purification of the body and soul, which would be "desecrated from birth".

Still unsatisfied, Cassandro then went to the Orphics, a group that proposed a way of life that was totally opposite to that of the citizen, since the latter got rid of his stains through a simple ritual. Open to all people, men and women, free or slaves, as well as foreigners and peripheral communities, marginalized intellectuals, poor and rich, the Orphs imposed a radical change in the way of life, with obligations and prohibitions, in search of a pure soul , addressing the most intimate and deepest issues of the human soul. It was a totally opposite view to the religion of the polis, for which the core of religion and of the citizen was to be together, to belong to the group, and to comply with the rituals. For the Orphs, who rejected the city's violent way of life with its bloody sacrifices, the polis was a segregator of the weak, and the salvation of the soul lay in purification through renunciation of eating meat and committing impure acts. All this was very different for Cassandro, who had never given any more refined importance to spiritual matters.

And in the wake of the uprising of thought, there were still incipient movements, less religious and more political, like the intellectual philosophers, putting everything in the city in check and overturning the rules of the old politics; the sophists, fighting against traditional institutions and against the prejudices of the prevailing religion, preaching a fairer, more humane, more rational order; the cynics, denying the concept of homeland, saying that man is a citizen of the universe; the Stoics, returning to politics, but extending the concept of citizenship, extending it beyond the walls of cities, emancipating man, declaring that all men are fellow citizens, as if they all belonged to the same city, rejecting the servitude of man à polis, warning him that his main work must be individual improvement, with a free and independent conscience.(18)

Cassandro spoke of these things to Calliope, who always listened attentively, and thought that his wife was just fulfilling her role as a listener. He was wrong. Calliope assimilated those words, and then kept mulling over so many thoughts, so many ideas, so much innovation in the way of thinking. The husband, however, continued to search for the paths of the soul.

"Tomorrow some people will come here to talk to us, Calliope. – he said one day, coming back from town.

"Yes? About what, Sandro? Anything serious?" Calliope asked, noticing a different tone in her husband's voice.

"No, nothing serious. They just want to talk."

"Will it be a symposium? Shall I make the wine?"

"No, no... I don't think they drink wine... It's good to leave some amphorae of ciceyon, and maybe some refreshment."

"You're so mysterious…"

"I met this group at the Market, and it doesn't have a fixed place to meet either, it usually visits the people who call them, just like the Orphs."

"Another group of religious people", thinks Calliope, who respected her husband's feelings, and somehow supported him in his search for answers, although she didn't see how those people committed to denying the city's religion could get anywhere.

"And what does this group say?"

"More or less the same as the others, except that they have some ideas about life after death… That people die, and then come back to live in another body several times."

"I think I heard Syra talking about it, in the kitchen."

"Syra?"

"Once, some friends of hers came here, from Chalcis, and they were talking about these things…"

"They follow what Pythagoras said… about the soul being immortal, and separating from the body, when dead, returning to live in different bodies, including those of other animals, completing a cycle. Always looking for the purification of the soul, freeing it from the impurities of the body."

Now Calliope understood her husband's interest in this particular group. Cassandro was a great admirer of master Pythagoras, that man of triangles, who had been born on the island of Samos and later moved to Magna Graecia, almost a hundred years earlier, and who had left behind so many mathematical, astronomical, philosophical, musical and, now she had learned, religious teachings as well.

Cassandro called all the slaves and employees who were interested in listening to his Pythagorean guests, and was surprised to see how large the number of those who came to hear the speaker, who explained everything very clearly:

"After going through several lifetimes in various mortal bodies, of higher or lower condition depending on the level of purification reached in the previous life, the soul can finally end this cycle of births in order to finally return to the divine, where it originally came from, and from where he had turned away, by contaminating himself in the corporeal world with the vile acts committed by men.

Calliope wondered what so tormented her husband that made him worry that way about the salvation of her soul. The fact is that Cassandro was convinced that the pain he felt was an expiation he was going through, and with which he accepted, perhaps finding the explanation for it in those religions.

Although deeply affected by these philosophical-religious thoughts, which were so far removed from everything he had learned and which was current in the polis - in the spiritual issue as well as in daily life - this distancing which, moreover, affected most of the population, who no longer understood the meaning of the rites, although he dared not stop practicing them – Cassandro had to end up giving up his moments of reflection, as life continued, and he had to return to pay attention to the land and his crucial problem: generating an heir.

At twenty, Calliope had finally taken responsibility for the house where she had lived for almost five years. Cassandro had already got used to the things she had quietly managed to introduce into her daily life, and in the end the changes came for the better. However, despite the impression that Pelopia's absence would be a relief to all women, this had not happened. If in domestic driving she was not needed, her absence was felt at almost all times. Calliope had decided that she would not allow the habit of saying bad things about her deceased mother-in-law, and she gently taught the maids to keep to themselves any comments or thoughts that were not meant to remind Pelopia in a pleasant way. For everyone's sake, and especially for her husband, who was unable to soothe his conscience in relation to his dead.

If there was no longer any claim to Pelopia for the heir, it was now Ganymede who had taken on a personal and urgent interest in this matter.

"Daughter..." he began one day, visiting Callíope, a few months after his mother-in-law's death, "How are you and your husband?"

"What do you mean, papa?"

They strolled through the garden that Calliope had just finished, with pots and plants brought by Cassandro from the city.

"You know, my dear, that... now that your brother is gone... you will be the one who will give me an heir..."

"Ah, the heir", thinks Callíope, "here we go with it".

"I believe that under the circumstances, Cassandro has already realized that he is the one who cannot have children..." Ganymede continues.

Calliope knew where he was going. The talk of Ganymede's succession had already reached her ears. The fact was, she must have had a son to guarantee both Cassandro's succession and her own father's, now that Helios was gone. An only child, she had no right to her father's inheritance. Her husband would receive her share as administrator. And then, her son would finally inherit the properties of his maternal grandfather. This was a topic that was occasionally discussed fruitlessly in assemblies, when bills were presented that gave greater rights to daughters to inherit and manage the property left by their father. And Ganymede had never really given them their due. Now this problem lived in his own skin. Here he was in the unusual situation of seeing his lands threatened to end up in the hands of the State, due to the lack of successors. Everything would be fine if Calliope had a child. But this one didn't come. And their situation was peculiar, as both Ganymede and Cassander had no a male successor, were the last in line in their families. Ganymede could test in favor of Cassandro, but what good would it do if the two had no children?

"You know I can... I'm thinking..."

Ganymede couldn't even finish his sentence. He wanted to tell his daughter that he, the father, had the right to annul that marriage for Cassandro's sterility, but he didn't want to have to. He liked his son-in-law. She couldn't have found a better husband for her daughter.

"Dad... Why don't you talk to Cassandro about it? He has as much interest or more in having a child."

"But it is such a delicate subject, my dear."

"Precisely, father... What would you like to happen? You show up here one day, put me in the carriage, and tell Cassandro the marriage is over?"

"No, I would never do such a thing!"

"Cassandro and I have been talking about it, too... he has some ideas... Maybe you should talk to him."

They were actually thinking of putting some of the old ways into practice. Couldn't they have children? Well, but so many people had children, and they didn't want them... They could adopt a child... Or even... take as their own a child who had been abandoned.

Pelopia would probably turn in the grave. But Ganymede, more practical and less attached to the old traditions, immediately incorporated the idea. It would be a way out, anyway! He knew that blood ties were irreplaceable, but on the other hand, he also knew how much affection could exist between people without any blood ties. Why couldn't they do it? There was the solution. He had come so glum to his son-in-law's land and left full of renewed hope. He just didn't laugh because, since his son's death, his countenance had acquired an apathy that no longer seemed to want to leave him.

"Selene has a lover. And the husband is very suspicious!" Calliope said.

"How do you know this?" - Cassandro asked, interested, like an old pimp.

"He sent an employee to follow her into town."

"And the lover? Is it serious, or something fleeting?"

Callíope and Cassandro passed from that upright and sober couple to two of the most gossipy human beings who had ever set foot in Attica. They talked about all the neighbors. They speculated on the intimate lives of people in the city they had never seen. Above all, they were looking for the spicy details of the stories, which were already so spicy without this effort. Dinner became a moment of fertile debate about the comings and goings of others. They vibrated mostly with the changes in women's bodies.

"She got fat."

"Let's see if she get more fat."

But the gossip was not based on the simple petty squalor of women who have nothing more to do than lead a simulacrum of life, sipping the facts of the lives of others. They wanted to know about those cases that had a chance of a tragic outcome, with some child being abandoned. Then they would take action. But not everything was going as they expected.

"A child was born. But they put an olive branch at the door."

"That cuckold!"

The olive branch meant that he was a boy, and that the husband accepted him into the family as his rightful one.

Cassandro kept an eye open for any baskets on the side of the road.

The poorest families were the most likely to give up on babies. But it seemed that a wave of optimism was sweeping the region. Everyone believed in a rich future. Is it possible that those people didn't realize they were in times of war?!

"The settlers came to invite to the celebration of the new boy who was born."

"Shit!"

Slaves likewise did not escape his lynx gazes. But they all seemed to be taken by a sudden shame. Even Syra, whose taste for adventures with the servants had already become legendary. None spent the night out, none had bad moods or hysterical outbursts, much less fainting, dizziness, or anxiety.

"Damned virginal nymphs!"

Ganymede also participated in the undertaking. He worked as a delegate for the couple on the other side. More bashful, he was a little embarrassed to find out about things, but he managed it, and brought a fortnightly report on the neighbors' waistlines.

"Look at that belly, father-in-law!" ecommended Cassandro, when saying goodbye to his wife's father when he was leaving for home. A proximity of accomplices linked them all.

But time passed, and it didn't seem like a baby, whatever, would come to belong to that house. Cassandro was discouraged. He thought about the old laws, and what would happen if he had a brother or a cousin, for example, on his father's side. And he even had absurd ideas.

"Who knows if you're going to spend a few days in town. Alone, with one or two slaves... If you're discreet... You can find some... boy, and..."

"Cassandro!!"

"Why not?"

"But how can such a thing go through your head?!"

"It would be a way, wouldn't it?"

"I can not believe!"

"I would accept... I would end it all. And it would be yours."

"Stop, because I don't like the joke. And what's more, suppose I accepted such an aberration, who can guarantee that when it was born you wouldn't repudiate it?"

"... I was going to have to drink pure wine all day, all the time you were there, with "him.""

"Enough of this conversation, which is making me sick."

"That's enough for me too!"

"Sandro... calm down... You'll see, sooner or later, there will be a baby around... After all, the world has to go on, doesn't it? If babies stop being born, the world ends! So, why would we want to bequeath the lands?"

Only the babies were running out. Whether it was because the families kept them at home, or because the war took the men away and the women didn't get pregnant, the fact is that none was left for them. Cassandro was considering the idea of the will. But they still had the alternative of adoption. Cassandro started looking for orphaned children, or children of poor citizens. He was in no hurry, in that case. It was a child who searched those little faces.

Chapter V
Demeter – goddess of sowing and harvesting.

From the top of his tower, at the end of the afternoon, Theo watches the horizon, that view he knew so much in every one of its details. Every tree, every rock, every pasture, every crop, every bit of dirt path. His vision reaches far, almost the entire property, and his ears can catch even a small animal screaming at the edge of the land. He knows where each of the sheep is, and he can even see the flight of a bird among the seedlings at the end of the field. Nothing escapes your listening ears and your trained eyesight. In this warm and quiet late afternoon, it is with this keen vision that he sees something strange moving where the wheat ends, where the closed trees begin, on the property's limits. The unexpected movement makes him uneasy, and immediately he has a bad feeling. He runs down from the tower and, taking his machete out of his boot, runs as far as he can, and as silently as he can. He doesn't have time to call other slaves, and he doesn't want to alert Ganymede. He had a bad feeling.

As he approached the place where he noticed the unfamiliar movement, he sneaks away, hiding among the trees, among the branches, inert, as in hunting, in which he hid from his prey before attacking her. He knew those woods with his soul, could recognize where he was even with his eyes closed. Very slowly, without even touching a branch, the movements imperceptible, he hears a noise, a rustle of leaves on the ground, like indecisive steps. That much closer, the movement and the sound showed that it was not a small animal, a bird, but something bigger, much bigger. Fear creeping into his soul, Theo wonders if he would be able to face something far beyond his strength. Moving his face behind the trunk that blocked his vision, breath held, heart pounding, sweat already pouring from his forehead, Theo feels his heart skip a beat as he finally sees in front of him, stepping out from among the other trees , a soldier, mounted on his immense horse, in breastplate and plumed helmet, with the shield in his left hand, lowered, and the sword in the other. His red tunic and beard, without a mustache, left no doubt: he was a Spartan knight. He had certainly gone out on a reconnaissance quest in the region where his troops were, to inform his superiors for a later attack and, distancing himself far from his camp, he ended up going through the dense woods, getting lost in the trees, and finally being sighted by Theo. Both feel a shiver down their spine when their eyes meet.

Time seems to stand still, for both of them. They stand for a few seconds to stare at each other, the soldier mounted and dressed, their gaze haughty and menacing. Theo on the ground, in chiton and rough boots, wielding a farmer's machete.

He knew that the soldier would finish him in a few strokes, and worse, he knew that where there was a Spartan there were many more, who would come and ravage everything they saw, killing off all the harvest, tearing down the house and other buildings, and who knows the doing with family and employees. Theo sees these horrific images, and still his whole life, flash through his mind in a split second, like a spark, as he looks each other in the eye. In the seconds the two held each other's gaze, time and space were still.

When the Spartan straightens his horse and swings his sword to attack, Theo realizes that at the time there was no point in thinking, he would have to fight him, seeking within himself all the strength he could find. It was kill or die. He had to protect that house, those lands, those lives. In a flash of reasoning and instinctive reaction, at the animal's first step, Theo brings his thumb and forefinger to his mouth and gives a long, high-pitched whistle, startling the horse, which rears up once, standing with its front legs in the air. , falling back to the ground. The Spartan staggers a little, but manages to hold on, when Theo then repeats the whistle, startling the animal even more, which rears up twice more, the soldier struggling to keep from falling. On the fourth prancing, the soldier breaks free and finally falls, and Theo, slapping the horse on the rear, lets him run away. The soldier, fallen but still a combatant, was already getting up, throwing himself at Theo, who had kicked his sword away and, by instinct for survival, engaged him in a physical fight for which he was not prepared, but he felt his strength rising. through the bowels. With the shield torn from his other hand, the soldier was trying to pull his machete out of his hand, while reaching for his own knife that was attached to his boot. Theo, with a force he didn't know he possessed, hit him as best he could, with blows that he delivered to the soldier without dropping the machete, hitting him on the head several consecutive blows with his forearm, accompanied by kicks to impede the movement of the man, who falls back to the ground, when Theo kicks him off his helmet. He had hit the soldier so hard that he, even though he was wearing the armor, had wounds he could not bear. Dropping to one knee on the ground beside him and raising the knife-wielding hand to slit his throat, the eyes of the two men cross, the soldier, frightened, seeing death in the sun's reflection on the blade, waiting for the blow. fatal. It was then that Theo was reluctant, in that crossing of eyes; a sea of images coming to mind. He didn't know anything about the army, he hadn't been prepared for battle, let alone hate the Spartans. He understood nothing about the war and the reasons that caused it. All he had in life was work on the land, and his family to protect. But there was the memory of Helios. He looked at the Spartan surrendered under his feet, with life in his hands, and he was reluctant to do what he wanted to do. He had a vision of Iphigenia saying "They are brothers". And he felt that a powerful force, much greater than he, held his hand suspended in the air, preventing him from delivering the blow. He then kicks the soldier, turning him face down, pinning his hands behind his back, never letting go of his machete, checking to see if the man would still react. But the soldier was almost unconscious.

Within minutes, without a single word, the Spartan soldier had been defeated by an Athenian peasant.

On the way back to the house, dragging the remains: breastplate, sword, knife, helmet, shield - the Spartan's warlike junk, Theo, still nervous and incredulous, recovering from that episode that had taken only a few minutes, wondered how it all happened, and what they would do with the man, whom some of the other servants he had called were taking, astonished, to the barn.

The house was in an uproar. The women, initially very frightened, gradually realized that they were out of danger, and even went to look at the wounded soldier, trapped in the barn: they had never seen a Spartan. He was a strong boy, barely older than Theo. Ganymede decided to take him the next morning to Athens, and turn him over to the authorities.

"And stop feeding this man with mazza!" he said to Iphigenia and Calypso, who were already treating him like a sick child.

In the barn, the wounded and humiliated soldier had a whirlwind of thought in his mind. His life had been spared by an enemy peasant. He was alive; with effort he could break free, and kill these people, but he could not go back to camp: how would he explain what had happened? He could not lie, he would have to say that he had had his life preserved by the Athenian, and that he returned stripped of his clothes, his horse, his shield, his weapons, his honor. A pussy. He would be expelled from the army, and his family would be dishonored. Before he had been killed by the peasant. And yet, he could not get that look on him out of his memory at the moment when, knife raised, the Athenian had failed to strike the fatal blow. What he saw in each other's eyes in those tense seconds when they both saw, each on one side, life hanging on a thread, had thrown down everything he believed in, everything he had learned as the sole and absolute truth in all his years of military life.

Before dawn, with the sky still dark, and everyone in the house still sleeping, including the farm slaves, the soldier used his last strength to try to free himself. With great effort he dragged himself to the kitchen and, groping in the dark, staggering, feverish and desperate, found a knife.

And the family woke up startled by the cry of the slave who had risen first to go and prepare breakfast.

On the kitchen floor, in a pool of blood, he had found the Spartan dead, knife thrust into his chest.

"Why did you do this, my son?"

Standing there, hands clasped, tears running down her face,

Iphigenia, dismayed, watched the grave being covered at last by the shovels of earth thrown by the servants.

With the Spartan's suicide, they had been left at a loss for what to do with the body, not finding it convenient to cremate it and take the remains to Athens. They also didn't like the idea of burying him anyway, without the funeral rites. Furthermore, Ganymede and Iphigenia both had mixed feelings towards the boy. They felt the presence of Helios throughout that episode. Together they came to the decision to offer the dead a dignified burial, and they ordered the servants to open a grave where the fight had taken place, and where Theo, just the afternoon before, had found the soldier's horse grazing.

Iphigenia poured libations and tears over the grave as she prayed to Apollo and Hermes. He had placed a coin between the dead man's lips, a custom of the ancestors, as "payment of passage" to the underworld. She was freed from a painful weight by mourning the death of that enemy soldier, not out of revenge for her son's death, but because she was finally able to vent all the pain she had felt years before when she lost Helios, and which still oppressed her soul. When we cried for the Spartan, it was for the son that we cried.

After the burial, they purified the tomb, the house and the barn, through fumigation and water spraying, in order to rid the property of that mìasma, that serious contamination, where a person had infected the sacred home by taking his own life . With the purification rituals, they brought the house back to the purity demanded by civilization. The maids threw some pots and amphoras out of the windows, which broke with a loud crash outside, thus contributing to the noise to chase away the evil spirits.

In Sparta, the boy's mother, who had said goodbye to him with the words repeated by mothers and wives to the Spartan soldiers who went out to war: "Return, with your shield, or on it!", did not see her son return from the war one way or the other.

And Theo got a horse.

Ganymede took the Spartan's equipment to the Assembly, the Assembly headquarters building, where the five hundred councilors met, and recounted to a thousand eager ears all the details of the episode between his slave and the enemy.

"Your house produces good Athenians," says one of the Advisers, marveling at the feat, and referring to the heroic death of Helios.

Since his son's death, Ganymede came less to the city, not even for the Assemblies, and when he did, he was always greeted with honor: everyone rose and fell into a respectful silence; some nodded, others called him by name and welcomed him in wonder. All those killed in war were heroes, and families were admired for a long time.

But Theo's achievement went further, it had an epic connotation, it took people to the ecstasy of stories told and retold and where the protagonists were venerated almost like gods.

Theo, meanwhile, oblivious to the harassment of admirers, strolled around the city waiting for Ganymede, who said he had important business to take care of at the Market.

Athens had no special attraction for Theo. Now he often came to the city, accompanying Ganymede, getting to know better the details of the business, the sale of produce; the purchase of grains and seeds; the fluctuation of prices at the port, fines and government taxes. He also knew the merchants, the less dishonest and those who couldn't trust a hair. Aside from these matters related to farming, nothing else in the city interested him. He had become an even quieter man than he had been as a teenager. He rarely laughed. His face was not quite serious, but his face was always at least serious. Only when he was with Calliope did his smile open.

In fact, under his unreadable emotionless face, he was still shaken by the Spartan's suicide. Called by the slaves who ran first with the maid's cry that fateful morning, he found Ganymede beside the boy's body, perplexed, asking him what to do. And Theo, who hadn't stabbed him in the fight, bent down to take the deadly knife from his chest and close his eyes. He felt suddenly helpless. He couldn't understand that death.

At first he wandered through the city, ascending to the Acropolis, at a rare moment when he was allowed to do so. He stopped in front of the statue of Athena, the great statue thirty feet tall, imposing, holding the spear and wearing the armor and helmet. Looking at her, so many questions he asked, finding no comfort for the soul. He didn't quite understand everything that had happened. Sometimes he wondered if he had somehow killed the Spartan. Other times he wondered if he should, out of obligation, have done it. All he remembered and was sure of was the magnanimous strength that had held his fist when he was about to deliver the blow. And the boy's gaze, surrendered at his feet. And the voice of Iphigenia, "They are brothers". Athena didn't give him the answers he so desperately needed, but he felt as if she understood, and supported him.

Walking through the Market, looking at the stalls, he didn't let himself stop at any of them. The anecdotes and profanity of the men around him did not make him laugh: he did not find that kind of verbiage amusing. He was not seduced by the fallacy of the city, nor the calls of the sellers, the goods, the different instruments and the madness of shopping. Only at the stalls that sold women's paraphernalia did he stop, admiring those things, thinking of Calliope, who she would certainly like to take in her hands and buy them, and he smiled inside imagining her with those trinkets hanging from her ears, adorning her neck, decorating her hair, coloring her face and eyes.

Among the tents, people were already commenting on the story of his achievement, from the simplest of them to the most distinguished citizens. The appearance of the Spartan, the details of the attack, the wounds, the kicked helmet, the heroic gesture of saving him, the theatrical suicide, it was all told by word of mouth, and people were amazed and proud. He heard, incognito, his name pronounced here and there.

"The Athenian peasant faced the entire Spartan army alone!" told Pan, who didn't lose the habit of making things a little bigger, to a group of stunned baggers who had just arrived in the city.

The offenses meant nothing to him either, and he left quietly, without speaking to anyone, indifferent to his own fame.

The credit, however, was going to Ganymede, since the hero was a simple slave.

Tired of wandering aimlessly, he looked for a place in the Pecilus portico, in the shade, sitting next to a bald and bearded man, the two of them standing side by side, quiet and thoughtful.

Theo looked even more circumspect than usual. Hearing the people talk about what he had done confused him, only adding more doubt to his thoughts. Little by little, a circle of very talkative citizens began to form around the bearded man, and everyone began to discuss the episode of the Spartan's attack on the countryside as well. Gesturing, talking loudly, some said that the peasant should have killed the Spartan, others said that his act had been full of bravery and nobility. All talking at the same time, giving disparate opinions, each wanting to know more than the other, finally a man asks Theo:

"What do you think? Do you think the peasant was brave?"

Everyone is silent to hear that boy so quiet. Theo thought for a moment before speaking. He felt shy in front of these well-dressed and verbose citizens. He, who sometimes spent whole days without saying more than two or three words.

"What do I know, sir... I don't even know if I know the meaning of the word bravery..."

The men continued talking, not giving any importance to his answer.

But the bearded man, who had watched intently with searching eyes as Theo spoke, noticing his country robes, takes up his words again:

"Yes... the meaning of the word bravery... What is it, anyway? Who can tell me?"

The long sentences, the definitions, the discussions begin again, until a very tall man, a military man, approaches, also wanting to participate in the debate."

"Tell me, General, you who are a strategist must know what bravery is. I am very interested in clarifying this concept - asks the bearded man."

"Well, bravery consists simply in not running away from the adversary."

The bearded man scratches his chin with a funny air of doubt and, after a moment, he asks again:

"And if you have to carry out, for reasons of strategic convenience, a retreat, in order to attack the enemy on the other hand or to defeat him in better conditions, would that be cowardice?"

"Not at all," says the general. "How will this be a cowardice?"

The bearded man scratches his chin again and then responds:

"However, you told me before that bravery consists in not withdrawing from the enemy."

"Yes," replies the general, exasperated, "I said that, but I should have added that withdrawing doesn't always mean cowardice."

"Oh!" exclaims the bearded man, "So, it means that your first definition was not entirely accurate."

Some of the citizens smile, and little by little the wheel is unraveling.

When Theo saw Ganymede approaching him, he got up to meet him.

"Boy!" called the bearded one.

"Sir?" Theo answered, turning around.

"I praise you for what happened in the field. And by your words, here in town."

When Ganymede finally finds Theo, they go to that part of the Market where the bankers stood, installed side by side on their stalls, counting and stacking their coins.

"Ah... my dear Ganymede! How are you? And how is your wife doing? And those wonderful lands, which Demeter blesses? Come, sit down, sit down, my dear!"

"We're all very well, thank you, Pásion.

Pásion was an ex-slave who had made his fortune both as a banker and in the arms business, owning a workshop where shields were made. He knew the lands of Ganymede well; for the rest, like all bankers, he knew almost all the citizens well, and especially the citizens' affairs . He always spoke with a studied formality, along with a measured friendliness and a soft voice, whatever the content of the conversation or the inflammation of the speaker.

"And she... pardon me, Miss Calliope? What a beauty of a girl, what an excellent marriage you found for her! Cassandro is progressing a lot! He has made transactions in Piraeus that make all producers envious, even on the islands they know about him!"

"Cassandro, Cassandro," thinks Theo, standing beside the table, suddenly getting annoyed.

"But what business brings you to me? Can I guide you in something? Maybe you want... some advice, or something like that?

Ganymede decides to cut to the chase:

"I am thinking of planting new seeds that arrived this week, I think we will have a special production, and we will be able to reach a price much higher than the average for wheat, as these seeds are of much better quality wheat."

"Yes?"

"I just haven't had a top crop this year... and I'd like to get a loan to buy the seeds, and the equipment that will lead to a much faster harvest."

" I see."

"Anyway, I see an excellent harvest for next year. There will be a surplus, we will even be able to export, as the harvest will far exceed the quota established for Piraeus.

Pásion knew very well how things were going in the countryside. All he had picked up from the news of Theo's achievement was that the Spartans were prowling Athenian lands, and that there was no guarantee in agricultural activities. There never had been. As a man of finance, he had learned never to trust the changing of the seasons. But he saw in Ganymede's intentions a great opportunity... for himself.

"But, as I see it, Demeter decided this time to reward this house of heroes!" He says, looking at Theo, then to Ganymede: "Farming has always been, in my opinion, the safest business. People were wrong to flee the countryside, come to the city; we need men like you, Ganymede! Who work hard and see the product of their sweat! Afterwards, the envious ones hang around the corners lamenting their own ignominy, watching you count the drachmas!"

Theo doesn't like this babble. But Ganymede perks up and sees that he's going to get the loan.

"My dear, I make a point of counting these coins and giving you all! The metal of today is the bread that will feed many mouths tomorrow!"

At the next table, the conversation, which at first was very low, begins to swell, and Theo can't help drawing attention to what was going on between them. Apparently, the banker had taken out a loan to a maritime merchant who had pledged the ship as collateral. The loan would be repaid at the end of the trip. But something wasn't going well between those two.

Once the value and term of the loan was settled, the painful moment came for Ganymede to learn at what interest it would be granted.

"Let's see… it's an agricultural credit… The preparation of the land… the first months of sowing, then the wait… the harvest and the result… – Pásion was doing his calculations – you receive this amount and he will return it to me in twenty-four months, at the end of the harvest, with the addition of twelve percent. What about? It's the lowest interest ever!"

Turning his attention to Pásion, Theo gets a bit lost in this part of the transaction. But Ganymede, confident of his investment, does his math in turn, and concludes that the interest rate is fair, and will still give him great results.

"Sounds good," he says.

At the next table, things were definitely not going well for the banker who, speaking loudly, was pounding the stall.

Ganymede didn't even notice, he was already dreaming of his wheat, bagged, the city's quota in the Market, the surplus shipping to other lands, at prices free of government inspectors.

"I just need a little something, my dear Ganymede,' said Pásion, making the coins he'd counted to pass into the farmer's hands jingle.

"Yes?"

"I have this paper here, I need you to sign it; it's just a formality, understand, it's part of transactions of this type – says the banker, taking a pile of papers from under his desk, taking one out, already with several things written on it, and starting to fill in some spaces.

"What it is?" asked Ganymede.

"It's… the guarantee…" says Pásion, adding a few sentences to the end of the document.

"Guarantee?"

"Ganymede, whose eyesight had never been good, took the paper when it was finished, squinting to read it, the letters shuffling while Theo, standing behind him, tried to peek at the text.

"My dear Ganymede, you see, everyone has their business and seeks the best for themselves, and I'm no different... This is just a guarantee... although I know I'll have you here as agreed, with the sum and the interest, and maybe I'll get a small sack of wheat!"

"But here the guarantee is all my lands!"

That part Theo understands.

"Now, dear Ganymede, my brother. It's just a paper, nothing more! That I'll give it back to you in two years' time, I'm sure!"

And Ganymede then signed the mortgage, while at the next table the situation came to a climax, with the borrower getting up and walking away, and the banker punching more violently than anyone else at the bank, turning it over. , making the coins roll all over the floor, shouting from someone beside him:

"He knocked down the table! Broke the bank! Made bankrupt!"

"Ganymede, my husband, don't you think it's risky?"

"Nêna, Nêna, there comes a time when you have to risk a little!"

"A little? It's all you have! Doesn't it seem like an exaggeration, a much bigger guarantee than the loan?"

"Don't worry, woman! Soon you will be gathering the best wheat in the world, making bread worthy of the gods! Remember what the ancients said: we are bread eaters!"

"I remember you as one who advised never to ask for loans!"

Calliope wakes up in the early morning, still dark, and is surprised to find Cassandro lying beside her, sleeping soundly – he was always one of the first to get up every day, especially at harvest time, his favorite time, when he got excited , rubbing his hands full of joy, watching the production finally happen. On those days Calliope hardly saw him, as he left early for the country and spent most of the day with the employees, helping himself with several of the heaviest jobs. He would return home at night still very excited, but wanting to eat and go to bed soon, calling Calliope to him, because he would not fall asleep without her at his side. This morning, lying there, he seemed to be still in a deep sleep. He must have been tired of the previous night's love affair.

"Sandro! Good morning…" she said, touching him on the back and pulling the blanket over him, who seemed to be cold.

But Cassandro didn't move.

Calliope, lying on her side, looking at her husband's back turned to her, inert, shivers.

"Cassandro!" She spoke louder, already with her voice changed, touching him again, pulling him to turn around.

And jumped out of bed, horrified. Cassandro was dead.

Calling the foreman and the slave, Calliope, wrapped in a blanket, sitting on a kitchen chair, stares into space, as if she doesn't understand anything around her.

"Lady Callíope…" said the foreman, also taken by shock, "what are we going to do?"

Calliope didn't seem to hear. Kept looking at the void.

"What do you want me to do?" follows the foreman, while the slave signaled him to be quiet.

After a few minutes in this stupor, in which a world of thoughts passed through her head – memories of the last few years, the last conversations, and especially the last night, still so vivid and warm in Callíope's memory, when Cassandro had let go of her after he left. they loved and fell heavily to the side, immediately falling into that deep and icy sleep - Callíope struggles to start giving some orders, without exactly knowing if she was doing the right thing, without anyone to count on to make decisions, without anyone to guide her or supported. The head of the house had died. The decisions were up to her at that difficult time. She had seen a few funerals at this point in her life, but organizing them was something else.

"Laerte" she begins, her voice coming out weak, "have some servants dig a grave, next to his mother."

"Yes ma'am."

"Syra, you have the courage, call someone to help us prepare and dress him… Then, Laerte, we need to carry him to the living room."

"Yes ma'am."

"Send someone to my father's house, to let me know...." A lump in her throat choked her words.

"Madam, I think it is also necessary... to go to town to call an officer, to note down the mor... the passing of... the... of him."

"Yes, you're right."

"And ma'am, sorry to say, but what about the harvest? If the employees don't go to work, it won't be good for the wheat."

"That they continue the normal work... no problem... It's what Cassandro would want... Just call a few to help us..."

And Calliope was silent for a few more minutes, several thoughts taking over her head, mixed with fear, dizziness, the pit in her stomach. Her body felt like it wouldn't respond to her commands when she got up and tried to walk. She was thinking of one of the last things that Cassandro had mentioned to her, the night before, in those conversations they had when alone, in the bedroom. And she made a decision that surprises the two employees. She was going to Athens right now, taking Syra and another slave.

"Laerte, pay attention. Wait until we get back, and only then send a messenger to town to announce what happened."

"But, ma'am?"

"Do not worry. In the meantime, go ahead and take the steps I mentioned: my parents, the grave and the preparation of... his... We'll be back later this afternoon."

"Madam, are you sure?"

"Come on, Syra, we have to leave soon. Laerte, send an employee to prepare the carriage!

"Lady, do I get your brown tunic?" asks Syra.

After a short silence:

"No not yet. I will go in my gown."

Then Calliope and the two slaves left, the day wanting to dawn, the city beginning to rise as soon as they arrived. Callíope, circumspect and without exchanging words, tells the employees nothing about what she had gone to do. She just asked them to wait while she makes a visit and then make their way back. The employees understood nothing.

The return to the house had Calliope still quiet, but feeling bad, her face upset, struggling with the memory of Cassandro's frozen body beside her in the morning, as well as her words and caresses the night before.

Ganymede and Iphigenia were already waiting for her when she got off the carriage. The mother immediately took her in her arms, and Callíope started to cry, nervous.

"She didn't feel well when she came back, Lady Iphigenia," said the slave.

"We had to stop twice for her to vomit."

"We were scared when we arrived and we didn't see you here, my dear..." said Iphigenia, hugging her as she accompanied her to one of the bedrooms, so that she could change her clothes. Calliope did not want to go into her room, as she still had the memory of the morning. "Are you feeling better now? Come on, drink this water."

"But, my daughter... What were you doing in the city?" Ganymede asked, after giving some orders to the other employees who, somewhat dazed, were waiting for someone to tell them what to do.

Recomposing herself, Calliope tried to start talking and explaining herself.

"I had something to do, Dad."

"What thing, my daughter? At a time like this!"

Although overwhelmed by the grief of Cassandro's sudden death, Calliope had the strength of spirit to go to the city to do something unusual, and that she didn't even know how it could end. In a flash of unexpected lucidity for a moment like that, she thought of such practical things, in which few would have thought, let alone acted.

She found herself alone, widowed and childless. More than lucidity, she was cold-blooded.

She had climbed into the well-groomed and bejeweled carriage, determined to carry out what she had in mind. They arrived in town when people were starting to leave the house. They went first to the market, where Calliope had given some orders to the employees about the occasional purchase to be made. Then, with instructions not to mention Cassandro's death to anyone, she asked them to drop her off at the house of the kapelos – retail merchant – that Cassandro had mentioned the night before. Her husband had told her, laughing in his carefree way, that this rascal owed him a very large sum, a debt long overdue, and that he would certainly have headaches to see debt honored. Calliope knew him vaguely, having passed with Cassandro close to him on some festive occasion.

"Lady Calliope! But what an unexpected visit!" said the kapelos upon receiving her.

"Sometimes even I need to come to the city" - she said, with a polite smile and kind manner, "and I take the opportunity to make my visits!"

"Let's go to the living room. You are tired from the trip, for sure! Bring some figs and honey water!"

"No, thank you! It's not even necessary."

"But... what makes you so, so... so..."

"So undesirably," completes Calliope in thought, keeping her polite smile on her lips.

"I had some shopping to do. I let the employees take care of it..."

"And how's Cassandro doing?"

Calliope felt a chill down her spine.

"It's... precisely Cassandro who brings me here, so... strangely..."

In fact, it was an unusual visit to say the least. The wife of a wealthy citizen did not go out alone like that, nor did she go to visit a man alone...

"I understand..."

"You see, talking to my husband – you know how husbands are: in the privacy of our rooms, they tell some things about their lives..."

"Some do."

"And he just told me the other day, about a, a certain business, a business transaction, that he had done with you, I don't know."

She knew very well. Just like him.

"Yes..."

"And I saw my husband, let's say, quite changed.... Well, you know, harvest time, he is naturally nervous..."

It was when Cassandro was happiest and in a good mood!

"Yes..."

"And I saw him screaming, as I had never seen him... He even scared me... He spat when he spoke..."

Cassandro's laughter.

"I understand."

"I said I would come here to see you."

Cassandro closed the subject without further details.

The kapelos starts to straighten up in the seat, closing in on the rear.

"And I certainly thought that attitude was extremely exaggerated... I tried to reason with him: "But, my husband, how can you say that, he is an honorable man, on which all homes depend, because he is the one where we acquire our food."

"Appreciate!"

"But Cassandro was... unrecognizable... and said things I didn't quite understand...It wasn't exactly commerce that my husband was talking about at that hour."

"Such as?"

"That he would come to town to have a conversation in the Assembly, that he had a series of things to say, which would make you regret..."

"What things?" the voice of kapelos is already a tone above normal.

"Ah, you know how husbands are... they never say things entirely to women... they say they're 'men's affairs'... Just ask, and they refuse to talk any more..."

"I know,"

"Anyway, thinking of all the things I just told you, how much the tables of all homes depend on men like you, and seeing my husband about to take such an untimely attitude, I decided to take advantage of my visit to the city to come and see you, thus anticipating my husband, who does not leave the house today – Calliope has another chill – to come and place me like this, as a sort of intermediary, on a mission of peace, so that you are carrying out now the payment for me, I can take that amount back, thus preventing my husband... let's say... carry out his words..."

The kapelos looks at her in silence for a moment, then gets up, going into another room, returning several minutes later with a bag that jingled many coins.

"Behold here...."

"Oh!"

"Please tell me."

"What is it, not at all!"

And the return home was then the way it was. The memory of the night before; of cold Cassandro in the morning; from the face of the kapelos; the bad feeling of having left home at that moment; the impulse for that petty enterprise; the unknown and uncertain world that awaited her henceforth.

"My daughter! What have you been doing?" said Ganymede, at the end of the report.

"That money belonged to Cassandro, father, and maybe it's the only one I can count on. Dead Cassandro, dead the debt. The kapelos would still do well!"

"But how could you be thinking about that at a time like this, my dear?"

"My little girl, how nervous you were... – Iphigenia took the empty glass from her hands.

"But what you did was... threaten... and that's illegal..." Ganymede is dumbfounded.

"Why, father! Illegal! How illegal, what what! How illegal? Will someone sue me for what I did? How could I? First, the money belonged to Cassandro itself; second, there was already the tradition of coins; and third, I am a woman, and women have no rights, how can they be prosecuted? It would be like suing a slave!"

"It's not like that..."

"Papa, it's done. What could that rascal do now? Go to the magistrate and say you were deceived? And he has the courage to go near a magistrate?"

"What was it that kapelos did, that could be taken to the Assembly?

"Cassandro never told me about it."

"But then how did you know what he did?"

"I didn't know anything, but the kapelos certainly must have known! If you saw what he looked like!"

The employees were almost all gone.

The few were hired specially for the harvest, Calliope paid and fired them as soon as they finished what they had come to do. The slaves, almost all of them, after the master had died, thus receiving their freedom, left at once. Even Syra, who had accompanied Calliope all those years, stayed only a week, and then left, as she had friends already freed in Calcis, with whom she was going to live.

In that desolation, Calliope did not know exactly what she was waiting for. That house was no longer hers. In fact, it never had been.

"Daughter..." Ganymede had told her, right after the funerals "Let's go home, come..."

"Home, father...? What is my house?"

"You don't have to stay here."

What he really meant was that she couldn't stay here.

"I don't know, Dad, I still have a few things to close. The employees."

"They no longer have anything to do in these lands... They're free... Didn't you see, they'd barely finished opening the grave, they were already leaving... If it weren't for the foreman to hold some, the grave wouldn't have been closed."

Slaves could never have expected their fortunes to turn that way: a young master like Cassandro, at the age of forty-six, dying thus, and without heirs, ended their slavery. They were free men and women overnight. Along with the hired employees, they took to the road even before finishing their prayers at the coffin.

The government agent had come to do the normal inquiries for a case like this. Although the family knew that this was not a murder but a natural death, and therefore there was no point in reporting what had happened, Ganymede thought it best to call an officer. Cassandro's death was announced at the next Assembly, and his name revered as one of the most notorious farmers in Attica.

The widow, however, would be stripped of everything. If the law did not give her the right to succeed her father, even less did it in relation to her husband.

A little less than a month had passed when Callíope saw a cart arrive at the house, bringing some government men.

"Are you Lady Calliope, widow of Cassandro, who died twenty-five days ago?"

"Yes."

"Lady, we came to take possession of the lands... Is the harvest gathered in the granaries?"

"Yes."

"Are the equipment, objects, documents stored?"

"Yes."

"Here's the notice, ma'am. As of today, these lands and their production officially belong to the treasure of the city of Athens."

Calliope pales. Of course, he'd been waiting for this moment, but hearing the words like that was a stab.

"From now on, you are invited to leave..."

"Lady Calliope, are you sure you know how to go alone?" asked a freed slave who stayed, and who ended up being hired by government agents as a housekeeper.

"Yes I have. I've done this route a few times."

Alone, carrying her personal things to the carriage, wrapped in a himation to shelter from the cold, Calliope started her return to her parents' house.

The path was already easier to go, with the road smoothed by the servants Ganymede brought on his visits. The lost thought, a deep sadness taking over her soul, the feeling of an era that was ending, a depth of revolt turning her insides, Calliope could not define what she felt. The beautiful lands of Cassandro, of his family, which Pelopia had suffered so much to see, now being held by the State. Under the carelessness of uninterested officers. Even the instruments, Cassandro's inventions, the well-preserved harvest, everything.

Not everything. The coins of the kapelos, these were already with Ganymede.

From the top of his tower, Theo sees the carriage approaching the foot of the slope, far down the road.

Chapter VI
Hera – Protector of women and marriage.

Not that she didn't grieve over Cassandro's death. It had been nine years together, and so much had happened in those summers and winters. She had gone from a carefree girl to a woman on whose shoulders so many people's expectations rested. She had witnessed the changes in her mother-in-law, who had turned out to be a woman with her past, her motives, her anxieties. She had followed her husband's painful path, in his relationship with his mother, in his quest to rescue his father's memory, in his loneliness, his regrets, his guilt. Certainly a strong bond had been created between Calliope and Cassandro. Especially lately, in the struggle to get a baby. But life with him was nothing more than a reflection of the patrimonial needs of the two men – the father and the husband. As, moreover, were practically all the citizen's marriages.

Back at her parents' house, it felt like those years had been much shorter, as if they had been a dream. She missed Cassandro, of course. But it was just a physical lack, not exactly her company, her affection. He had been the husband her father had chosen, and she had adapted to him as she could, and quite well, given the circumstances. Because not only had her mother-in-law been a problem in the early years, but Cassandro wasn't exactly someone she had kinship with. The age difference between them was too great. She was a child when she got married. She was a stranger in her mother-in-law's lifetime, with her hostilities over the lack of grandchildren. Later, alone with him, she did not come to form that couple full of complicity that she saw between her father and mother.

Ganymede and Iphigenia also had the same age difference, but for them the goddess Hera had reserved a gift called Calypso.

Calypso was older than Iphigenia, and younger than Ganymede. He was right between the two of them in age, and in so many other ways. Only in bed did she not appear to mediate them. She had always been a counterbalance, a friend, a sister. She bridged the gap between the couple when things got controversial. She was pondering with a young Iphigenia; it showed the youthful side of life to an austere Ganymede. It was that source of prudence and common sense that both of them sometimes lacked. Thus, Calliope's parents were able to create an affinity, a great relationship, a deep affection, as they had to guide and unite them that creature illuminated by the gods of goodness, understanding, tolerance and joy. Not all homes had this light.

Over so many years, Calypso did not age. She always kept her docile gestures, her elegant bearing, her slender body, her straight spine. She had managed to teach Calliope that same way of behaving, and both then seemed mother and daughter – if not in features, at least in posture. As a young girl, she had not been an exceptional beauty, but her candor made her pleasant, and there were those who took a real interest in her. It was her only love story, and it should have given her painful memories, as she didn't like to talk about it. It had been before Ganymede and Iphigenia were married. Once when Ganymede's father had given a party, inviting several friends from the city, one of them brought his two sons: the eldest, whose marriage would take place in a few days, and the youngest, to whom no one paid much attention , although he was a serious soldier, esteemed by his companions and superiors. He fell in love with Calypso as soon as he laid his blue eyes on her. She, very embarrassed, was not indifferent to those looks. They talked a lot, strolling through the gardens of the house, which was still the old house, while the men drank the wine mixed with water in the crater, served by the employees, at the symposium that followed the meal, and the women, attentive to everything, joked between giggles that would come out of more than one marriage in that family.

The women played only because they considered the chances of marriage between the son of a citizen and a slave to be small.

They underestimated Calypso's charms, however. Because the romance evolved, and the boy decided to buy her freedom and take her in marriage, facing the father's denials, and getting support from the whole family of Ganymede, who esteemed the girl for all her attributes. But loving happiness didn't seem to be in Calypso's favor. A cousin of the boy's father died childless, and in the line of succession that followed to find an heir, Calypso's fiancé was arrived at. A small problem posed, however: he was to marry the deceased's daughter, who had left a will to that effect. In the flurry of exits he thought of to avoid such a marriage, even suicide occurred to him. He spoke with knowledgeable of the law, consulted with famous speakers and even an oracle. He wanted to run away and take Calypso; set up scandals; threatened to move to Persia. But nothing can go against the force of the father's customs and authority. Ten kilos thinner, his face pale, his eyes sunken and lifeless, he married his cousin and went to live in the lands of that distant relative. He did not go to the city again until he was summoned to some position. He had never stopped loving Calypso.

Ganymede had to divide his attention between farming and the issue of his daughter returning home. It was a different situation, one he didn't quite know what to think about. I would have to go into town to talk to someone who was more knowledgeable about the laws on the subject. If before he worried about the situation of his lands, now it was also the future of his daughter that tormented him.

Your poor daughter. When he found her that husband, how could he have known that Cassandro would be barren, that he would have no relatives, and that he would still "package" so soon? Cassandro could have made a will, disposing of the assets and determining Calliope's situation vis-a-vis a legatee heir. Surely that had even crossed his mind.

"But who would have thought that the man would "stretch his shins" overnight?" Ganymede asked himself.

It pained him to see his daughter as if lost on that immense property, from whose possession she would soon be dispossessed, when he and Iphigenia arrived for the funerals. And it hurt even more to see her little face, arriving that afternoon, in a carriage, alone, a few changes of clothes and a few objects like her cargo.

111

Widow, not subordinate to any agnate of the deceased, could she go back to being his epiclesis? If she could, he would marry her to some citizen, a widower with children, warning him of the situation: she gave him that girl who had no siblings in marriage, and the child born to them would be her heir, continuator of her maternal grandfather, inheriting from that grandfather as his own son. Of course, this citizen would want a good dowry in exchange for such a nuptial agreement. But about that Ganymede had no worries.

The crop he had staked so much on was doing very well, as he had never seen it, in all the years he had cultivated the land. He and Theo walked proudly through the fields, watching the seedlings grow, the weather helping, the animals getting fatter, an unprecedented crop sprouting from the earth and swelling. It was really a connoisseur's stroke that he had risked, buying those special seeds, thus perhaps radically changing from then onwards the type of planting and harvesting in those lands, so difficult to work and produce. He would sit with Theo in the late afternoons to talk about it, discussing harvesting methods, the next fields, the best time to buy new seeds, hiring helpers. Theo had innovative ideas, he wanted to diversify the plantations. He knew the land even better than Ganymede, for he knelt personally on it, feeling its quality in his hands, its moisture, its color, its smell. He knew which production was best in every corner of the property, he knew the cycles of the year, the winds, the rains. He knew how to make the most of everything the land had to offer: from wheat, the biggest crop, to goat's milk cheeses, whose production he had organized in an addendum to the granary, and he handed them over to Ganymede to sell at the Market. Ganymede rubbed his hands together proudly.

"The banker will be amazed to see how production will be much greater than we had anticipated!"

"What banker, papa?"

Calliope did not know about the loan. Upon hearing the story and the amount, she immediately intervenes:

"But dad, you don't need to wait until the harvest and sale! You can pay off this loan now!"

"Already? How?"

"Well, take those drachmas I gave you, remember? From kapelos?"

"But, daughter, that money is yours…"

"If so, this is what I intend to spend it on! Could there be a better job? Money goes out of the hand of one rascal to go into the hands of another!"

"That's life!" Calypso, who was lately very quiet, comments.

"My dear Ganymede! I see that you are indeed one of the best connoisseurs of the agricultural business in Attica! - says the banker, with a certain barb in his voice, making him sit down in front of him, at his bench.

"Are you aware that the crop is going well?" Ganymede asks, unable to hide the joy of a successful peasant.

"You did well, choosing to change seeds."

Theo didn't like him. Again he was standing behind Ganymede, pretending to be scattering and dispersed, but his ears missed nothing of those conversations.

"The joy that brings me here is immense, and I believe that it will be for you too!!" says Ganymede!

"Let's hear it!"

Hardly anyone can guess what will be joy or sadness for a banker. They, on the contrary, know the ins and outs of successes, and above all failures, of others.

"Here is all the amount I had taken as a loan, plus the interest as agreed!" Ganymede places on the bench a leather bag loaded with the coins that the kapelos had given, weeks before, to Calliope.

"But, my dear… - the banker doesn't change the position of his eyebrows. "I think you're too hasty… It's not yet time to pay me."

"It's not, I know, but I can do it now, and why should I wait?"

"Because that's how the contract determines."

"And even so?"

Theo doesn't like this at all.

"I have it here... - the banker takes a box, among several that he has under the table, and after rummaging, takes a paper - Look... Read here... you owe me this amount at the end of this term, with the production of that specific crop... You still have time, don't you think?"

"But I would like to pay off this debt now."

"My dear, unfortunately that was not what was agreed upon. It is not necessary to have this value at this time. Let's wait for the term the contract says. I'll be waiting for you then!"

Ganymede returned home a bit confused. For some reason, he didn't feel that this conversation was a good omen, even if he came back with a bag full of coins. Theo didn't feel good about that deal either. Though he considered himself a mere ignorant slave, a creditor who did not want to receive payment of the debt seemed very strange to him. He didn't like it at all. But the arrival back at home makes them forget about the banker a little.

The women were grappling with Calypso, who was feeling bad.

Calliope had already taken action, with her little recipes, her broths and infusions.

As the weeks went by, Calliope was engaging herself and getting used to the calm joy of her father's home, now added to that expectation full of enthusiasm for successful farming. She helped her mother and maids with the housework and kitchen. She scolded Calypso who insisted on saying she was good for work. She spent hours sitting with her parents, recounting things about her late husband's house, funny passages with her mother-in-law and servants; observed the differences between the two homes. Little by little, the resentment she had felt at her precarious situation as a widow passed away, and she hardly thought about it anymore. She looked forward to the years to come yet to take her down new paths.

Above all, with the greatest of joy, she had resumed her childhood friendship with Theo. In all those years she'd been married, he'd barely been to see her at her house. He had avoided as much as he could to accompany Ganymede, Iphigenia and Calypso when they went to visit her, but when he would come across her, it was always with a broken heart that he saw her approach him, wanting to know the news about her father's house, about the others. slaves, of their common affairs, with her manner and presence that bewitched him. They had had so many experiences, one and the other, throughout that decade. Both twenty-four years old, they were adults now. He had become a strong, robust young man. But he kept his face clean-shaven and his hair cut in the same way she'd had it as teenagers. To her, he was the same old Theo. And she, although she had become an even prettier woman than she had been as a girl, thinner and a little taller, elegant, with finer facial features, her eyes were still the same ones he liked to stare in, in silence , scrutinizing them, drawing from them the sap of his life, the light of his soul, losing himself in them, and ending up plunging in them, as in a sea, his sea. As before, Theo's gaze, in which she saw herself, still made her smile first, then blush, lowering her eyes.

It soon seemed to them that not one day had separated them. Like teenagers, they walked around the countryside, laughing, talking about everything, giving opinions and, above all, wanting to hear each other's opinions. Everything was a matter of conversation, from a branch of a different plant to doubts about death. The smile came back to Theo's face. And Calliope's too.

"What is on your mind?"

"I won't say!"

"So I'll guess!"

One day when the crop did not require him to spend every hour since morning in the field, Theo took her to see the place where the Spartan had been buried. The parents spoke little or nothing about that episode, which enveloped the dead man in an aura of mystery, almost a myth. It was a complicated matter , for the whole family. And she, who had not witnessed, but had only heard the stories of the story, also had her share of grief for what had happened.

"What a thing..." she exclaims, standing still, looking at the grave. "How paradoxical, that mother has recovered from the death of Helios, through this death..."

"Not just her. Lypso too. And the father, in a way."

For Theo, Ganymede had always been "the father". Ganymede, moreover, was very fond of the boy calling him that. He, as well as Iphigenia and Calypso, had a deep affection for the boy, like a true son. And Theo, on the other hand, if he had to explain the love he felt for his father, he would not be able to do so, because in addition to not having the parameters, he felt even more for that man who had come to get him, at the moment, when he it was so small, immediately introducing him to the bosom and affection of the family.

"I think Father and Mother see Helios's tomb in this one… It's like he's here… But I think Calypso felt for the soldier, even. She always comes here to pray for him."

Calliope looked at the tomb and the surrounding bush. She knew this was where Theo had faced the Spartan. She tried to imagine that scene his father had described to her at the time.

"How difficult it must have been for you, all of this, Theo."

He was silent, unable to even agree to those words. He hadn't had the opportunity to talk to anyone about the turmoil of feelings that swept through him at the time of the episode.

"I didn't know what to do… It was just instinct…"

"But your strength helped you, instinct was not enough."

"He wasn't that strong. He fell to the ground, he didn't even have time to retrieve his sword. I could have killed him."

"But you didn't…."

"I don't know, I don't know if I was the one who didn't kill him. At the time, it seemed to me that someone, a force, held my hand. You know, like the decision not to kill him wasn't mine. So I feel as if, with him dead, it was after all I killed him."

"Do you think that sparing him was not enough? Somebody should, perhaps, have stayed by his side, to avoid the…"

"I do not know…"

"Theo, I think you didn't kill him… Even if a force held your hand, if you wanted to kill him, it would have been easy to overcome that force. As for what he did afterwards, maybe the same force tried to stop him, but he wanted to be stronger than her…"

After nearly two years, Theo had finally managed to breathe out the things inside him, hear words that soothed his soul, and look at that grave without feeling responsible for that death. He finally seemed to understand what had happened. Breathed deeply again.

Calypso did not improve. Not even Calliope's care was helping her, and the girl felt insecure caring for the one she loved like a mother.

"I get nervous and anxious, I lost my gifts" she said, distressed, seeing that no effect resulted from her soups, broths and compresses.

So, after talking a lot, Ganymede decided to allow Calliope's suggestion to take Calypso to Epidaurus, for a more modern treatment, with the assistance of specialists who were there to help the patients who sought that sanctuary city in search for a cure. They were going to use Calliope's bag of drachmas, who thanked heaven for having the money to take Calypso and her mother for a season in that city, with the comfort they both deserved. From the hands of the kapelos, the money was finally going to a good and necessary cause.

Calypso was getting weaker. Staying in Epidaurus was the right way to lift her spirits and cure her bodily ailments. With its temples, colonnades, hospitals, hotels, baths and gymnasiums, Epidaurus was the place where patients from all over went to spend a few days to recover their health. The god Apollo, god of medicine, who had transmitted his knowledge to his son Asclepius – whose most famous sanctuary was in that city – would certainly find the answer to the disease that afflicted her. The doctors who were there understood that with baths, rest, massages and simple foods, the body would heal itself. Calliope and Iphigenia would go along. Iphigenia would take the opportunity to rest. And Calliope, to learn a little more about healing the sick.

Couldn't have done better. The two women, who had not left the house for years, were delighted as soon as they arrived at the sanctuary. They thought they would find a dreary city, with sick people crawling dying in its corners, and an air of disease and death hovering between the columns. On the contrary, they found a place full of joy and optimism, where both the patients and their companions and the doctors were always happy, and even groups of friends were formed who went together for walks and talks, to drink the medicinal waters, to sit in the shade for conversation, and attend some lectures organized by doctors and wise men.

When they returned home, at the end of their stay in Epidaurus, with Calypso fully recovered, they found things somewhat out of place. Of course, Ganymede was not made for domestic administration. He said, throughout the journey back, that he could no longer bear the absence of women, and the three of them confirmed, as they entered the house, that it was their services he was referring to. But they too were already wanting to go back, and it was with joy that they began to put everything back on track.

It had been more than a year since Calliope had been widowed and returned to her paternal home. She no longer remembered that she had once had her own home, a husband, a life so different from that, with her family. She enjoyed life at her parents' house very much. But she feared that Ganymede would soon give her another direction, arrange some marriage, always with a view to having a grandson. It was just a matter of the harvest being over, the wheat being sold, things getting back to normal, and he was going to get her married again. Again she would have to move in with a stranger.

One winter's night, when her parents and Calypso had retired to their rooms, she and Theo went into the living room, as they did with children, sitting on the floor in front of the brazier, curled up on pillows and wrapped in blankets, roasting grain. pouting, warming up and talking softly, Calliope picking up a note or two from the lyre, in a song she had learned to play, a very fine snow covering the ground outside in white.

"I wish this wheat took a lifetime to sprout!" she said.

"Why?"

"That way, I could stay here longer."

"But what does wheat have to do with it?"

He knew very well what she meant. And he also wanted the wheat not even to be born that year. But they both knew that the day was approaching when their lives would be separated again.

"I'm going to have to go, right..." she says, stopping playing.

"Calliope..."

So, in the dim glow of the brazier, with only the noise of the ember interrupting the silence, she didn't blush under his gaze, or at least she didn't lower her eyes. This time, he was the one who had to turn his face away, disturbed, and move a little away from her, because he no longer trusted himself.

Chapter VII
Zeus – king of gods and men

"Let's go, children! I want to get to town early and unload all that wheat right away!" Ganymede says, rubbing his hands.

He couldn't be happier. Throughout his life, he had seen the production of the countryside year after year, sometimes many sacks, sometimes a few stunted grains that were not even suitable for the family's consumption. This time, with his vision of an experienced farmer and the work, knowledge and commitment of Theo and the other employees, as well as those extras he had hired for the occasion, he watched the carts being loaded one by one with the best wheat he had ever seen. , of an unprecedented quality, surpassing even that coming from Thrace and Egypt. He was proud of himself, of his lands, of Theo, of everyone anyway. It had been weeks of intense work...

"Demeter be praised!" Iphigenia had said, thanking the land's fertility goddess, on the afternoon when Ganymede informed the family that the next day the best harvest of their lives would begin.

And so off indeed. Once the hired servants from the city arrived, Theo showed them the lodging for those days, followed them into the fields, carrying the necessary equipment, instructing them in the way of work and the rules of the house, and returned to the barn, tumbling exhausted. .

"Do you know where Theo is, Mom?" Calliope asked, biting a loquat.

"He is sleeping, Calliope.

"Sleeping? At this time? Is he sick?"

"No, tired, I believe."

"I'll go get him."

"No, leave him, dear. He worked harder than the animals all these months. Quiet as he is, doesn't like to let it look like he gets tired, but we're not blind, are we?

120

Although he didn't go to work in the harvest or on the threshing floor where the wheat would be threshed, Theo couldn't stop going to help the contractors, and he also quickly rushed to get on with the other crops, which were smaller in importance and size. The grapes would soon be harvested and expressed in the domes and presses, followed by the olives, which would have to be shaken from the olive trees and then pressed into the gutter. And all those fields had to be prepared by sickle and plow, some for fallow, others for new sowing. While Ganymede had eyes only for wheat, Theo was careful with every pod on his father's land.

"Good morning, Lypso! Have you seen Theo?"

"He got up and went to the field, my dear!"

"What a thing! Looks like he is avoiding me!

Calliope was not far from the truth.

Theo was no longer a child, and the presence of the girl he loved so much, with those eyes of hers, her hair, her scent, her charms, left him too upset. He avoided being alone with her. He was no longer sure of being the master of his actions. And he could never betray his father's trust, much less in this abject way.

Finally, the day came to take the entire production to Athens. Workers bagged all the wheat the day before, Ganymede had decided that he would take Theo with him and as many servants as needed to drive the carts, which were many. He would talk to several people when he get to town. He knew the sytopoleis – wholesellers who bought the grain in the Market, and also some bakers to whom he sold directly. He could barely contain himself as he anticipated the admiration with which everyone would look at his product. And the quantity was such that there would certainly be a surplus, once the city's quota was guaranteed, and he would then go to Piraeus to export his wheat!

"What a beautiful day, children!"

It was another sunny day in Athens. The line of carriages entered the Dipilo Gate into the waking city, with merchants setting up their tents, citizens going about their business, maids out shopping for their ladies, slaves and beggers walking lazily at sunrise. Other farmers were also arriving with their carts, greeting each other, some exchanging information, others looking a little distressed.

And Ganymede soon realized that something was different. Something was in the air at this early hour of the morning that didn't seem normal. Something sinister seemed to be happening.

Approaching the Market, Ganymede saw several merchants and producers with their carts already assembled, gesticulating, talking loudly, irritation in their voices. Centering the hubbub was the group of fifteen sytophylakes – inspectors who controlled the sale of wheat and bread, and who seemed unwilling to talk. Ganymede was soon reached by a friend from the city:

"Ganymede, my dear! At what point do you reach me! It's the end! It's the end of us all!"

"But what is happening, Tearion?"

Tearion was a famous Athenian baker, to whom Ganymede was used to selling his wheat, and from whom he bought such tasty breads, cakes and pies."

"It is not a good day for any of us, my brother! The government has just confiscated all the wheat from Attica!"

"What... ?!"

All the color the sun has put on Theo's face over the months drains from him the instant he hears the news, the blood from all over his body draining to his feet.

"It's that damned war, Ganymede," Tearion continues. "One hour they sign a peace agreement, and then let it break out again. And they come and tell us that such and such soldiers' encampments are in need of food, and there goes all our wheat, and also barley, and even wine – especially wine! What am I going to live on, Ganymede? Than? Bread is my life…"

"But what about the people, what are we going to eat?"

"They've already set aside a quota for the city. The big part goes to supply the army and certainly to raise more funds for this war. Our families will have to live on leftovers for a while…"

"Those… those bastards in the Assembly!"

Ganymede cannot even articulate the words.

"Ganymede, Ganymede! In which hands is our city? My friend… if we were the ones taking the decisions, instead of war, we would be selling wheat and bread to the Spartans, instead of fattening our soldiers to go there and be killed by them… " the baker laments, tears in her eyes, taking a handful of Ganymede's wheat in his hand. Knowing that inhospitable land from which it was a miracle to make some food grow, he felt the excellent quality of the grain, looked at the carts one after the other and, with a catch in his throat, bowed his head, ashamed of his own political leaders.

The whole family was in shock for a few days. Calliope and Theo didn't know what to say. Iphigenia and Callypso would retire to the kitchen and talk quietly so as not to disturb. The other employees were even afraid to speak. But to none of them the episode shook as much as Ganymede. I didn't even talk to anyone. Not that the government couldn't have done what it did. They could, and this wasn't the first time. Confiscation was nothing new. What devastated Ganymede was that it had happened precisely in that exceptional harvest. He was a farmer, anyway. He was proud to be one, and that year he had seen the biggest and best, the best-kept crop, with the weather helping in every way: there had been rain and sun in the exact measure. All his precious wheat. The memory of that sad morning continued to bring a bitter taste to her mouth. The bags, unloaded, scattered around the Market, the inspector taking notes indifferently, and his colleague randomly throwing other producers' bags on top, mixing everything up. While everyone in the family was revolted, unhappy with this fate, with the disobedience of the government, and called the City Administrators by all names, Ganymede entered a lethargic state of complete amazement.

"I'm sorry, sir," the inspector had said, in front of his despondent gaze, at the Market.

With the money that remained, he paid the hired workers, who were almost as sad as the family, and some left immediately. Ganymede had even lost his appetite. His torpor was such that he had not yet stopped to think about the sequence of events.

One afternoon when work had given him a break, Theo walked across the field with Calliope, who was trying to lift her head and spirit, not thinking about the latest events. But Theo couldn't take his eyes off her face. He was worried. Very worried. He didn't like Ganymede's apathy and despondency at all. He thought about the serious consequences of that confiscation. And in the document signed by Ganymede, committing him to the banker. And in Calliope, at her side, wearing the tunic as she had been used to doing it since she was married: she would pass a long thin strip of leather behind the nape of her neck, crossing it between her breasts, going to cross it again on her back, and finally tying it around her waist, thus outlining her slender figure.

"Soon, I'll be leaving here soon, won't I..." She said, a little sadly, while the bright sun was hitting her face.

"Why do you say that... ?"

"Well... the father is certainly already thinking about what to do with me, he must already have some man from the city in mind, to marry me again..."

His face didn't exactly look stunned by the idea. She was resigned to whatever her father might decide. But she was sad. Theo, for his part, felt powerless at those words – for her, and for himself. He knew that as a slave – ex-slave, having been freed some years before – he would only have to see her marry some other citizen, he could not even think of joining her. Both surrendered to their fates, overwhelmed.

But each other's company was too pleasant for them to indulge in grief. A few minutes passed together without soon starting to smile, joke, look at things around, talk about their common affairs, and feel life renewing in their hearts.

"I think it's going to rain," she said, looking up at the dark clouds in the sky.

"It was good, because the land needs irrigation."

"What are you thinking about?"

"Nothing... in all this..."

Thunder erupts, startling them.

"I don't think we'll have time to get home."

"Let's get going, before this rain starts."

Despite quickening their pace, the drops begin to fall, thick, and the thunder and lightning were intensifying. It was really going to be a summer storm.

"Run!"

"I slipped!"

The two of them start to run laughing, as if they were children.

"We won't make home!"

"Let's go to the tower!"

They aproached Theo's Tower, when the rain was already heavy and merciless.

"Let's see who gets there first!"

"I'm going to slip!" her hair coming loose, Calliope runs, laughs, stumbles, with Theo helping her to her feet.

"We're here!"

"Oh."

They climbed soaking into the tower, just as the rain begins to fall harder, as they have never seen it before. Lightning and frightening thunder in a dark night sky, in the middle of the afternoon. Still laughing, but already a little scared, Calliope runs her hands on her arms, taking the water that runs from them. Theo brushes back the wet hair that has stuck to his forehead. And after a few seconds of calm, a strong lightning strikes right beside the tower, immediately followed by thunder, throwing Calliope into Theo's arms. With her face buried in his chest, her arms instinctively encircling his waist, their bodies touching, her hair, soft, damp, flowing down her back, Theo felt all his strength drain away. He wasn't going to be able to hold back any longer, he wasn't going to try, and he didn't even want to think about anything else. The impulse to kiss her had already taken him completely, he felt the blood rushing through every vein. He would be expelled from there, maybe killed, but whatever! Nothing else mattered! His unsteady heart prevented prudence from reaching his thoughts. He holds her a little tighter in his arms and their eyes meet, silently. And then Calliope turns away from him, looking away down the side of the road. A carriage was coming up to the house in the storm, the driver trying to quicken the mule's pace. Annoyed, at the same time saved, Theo descends from the tower, going to help this person who was arriving.

It was the agent of Pásion, the banker.

"Lord Ganymede, understand, we know what happened, but here in this contract it is written in all letters."

"But it wasn't my fault... You see that the harvest was exceptional! Exceeding all expectations..."

The rain continued, with even stronger thunder.

"I know, I know, but the contract is lawful."

"I can't pay now…" Ganymede had a hard time formulating the reasoning.

"That's really a pity, sir."

In the kitchen, the women and Theo didn't know what to do. They were eagerly awaiting the end of that conversation, from which they could only hear a sentence or two. Theo would like to intervene and say that the next harvests of grapes and olives would be enough to cover the debt. He hoped Ganymede would remember that.

"But in a few months I will be able to pay off this debt; we will have more products then!"

"I'm sorry, sir, but your contract says you owe this amount now, at the end of this wheat harvest," says the agent, stretching out the paper where Pásion has scrawled the mortgage clauses.

"Now! And when I went to pay, months ago… he didn't want to get paid."

"I can't say anything about that, sir."

"But what should I do? What should I do?"

"Well… according to this legal instrument, by not paying off this debt, you now lose these lands, which you had given as guarantee. You see, foreclosure on this mortgage is very easy, it's a matter of days just for the officers to come and ask you to leave the property."

From the kitchen, everyone hears this part, and a black cloud covers their faces. Calliope feels a shiver run through her body. Her parents' entire lives; the mother's joy in that house; the father's pride in his farming; the stories and efforts of grandparents and ancestors; his father's agony at having an heir to run the estate. Generations and generations of their family, everything, on the verge of disappearing from the face of the Earth. In a split second, Calliope reflects on her own life. And without saying anything, soft and decisive, she goes to her room where she closes herself, and quickly comes back all dressed up and coiffed.

"Mom! Tell Dad I need to talk to him now. I have the solution for that."

"But, daughter, I can't go there…"

"I'll go myself, then."

And with slow, elegant steps, her posture haughty and resolute, she enters the room where the two men were, with Ganymede speechless and inert, looking out the window, not knowing what to say. She greets the banker's agent and, turning to her father:

"Dad…"

Ganymede raises his downcast face to his daughter, his eyes lost in anguish.

"Yes, daughter… what do you want? We don't want to be interrupted…"

"Father, calm your heart. You won't lose your land. It's all very simple."

"What…

"I will be the payment of this debt."

"But I don't think that…" the agent begins to say.

Ganymede still hadn't come to terms with his daughter's proposal.

"Yes, it is possible, yes" Calliope continues, Papa's lands given as guarantee are worth infinitely more than the loan. The debt amount, I know what it is. And I know I can be sold at a higher price. Dad's debt is paid, sir. Let's go. I'm ready. We can still catch slave merchants at the Market this afternoon.

The agent, equally unsure of what to do, gets up and goes to the door that opened onto the patio, and goes out to it, leaving father and daughter alone.

"Daughter, what is this?" His voice came out in a different tone, taken by agony, unable to contain the sobs. "No way! Go back to your mother, what an idea! I am dealing with a serious matter!"

"Dad! Dad! Listen to me!" Calliope crouches down in front of him, taking his hands. "Dad, don't be like that… it doesn't make any difference, after all… It's a way out, for the good of all! I'm a burden to you, I know. I wouldn't stay here anyway… We'd be splitting up soon, wouldn't we…"

"How can you think of such a thing, my daughter. You don't know what you're saying…"

"Dad… There's nothing else to do… That's it, or the government officials will come to tell you to leave the house, like I did…

Papa, don't cry... It's not a thing of the other world. You see, slaves are treated well, they live a normal life, like any of us..."

"How can you say that!"

"And what would we do, then, tell me, Dad... Where would we live... you, Mom, Lypso... I... Theo... In the streets of Athens? Huh, dad?" her voice chokes too, at the simple visualization of the image of her parents in the most inhospitable misery.

Ganymede cried, looking away from his daughter, his thoughts completely dulled by pain. There really was no way out. Iphigenia had come in and had heard most of the conversation.

"Daughter, no..."

"Mom, don't cry too. This is our family home, and you won't be kicked out of here! No way!"

With her parents transfixed, tears running down their faces, Calliope calls the banker's agent.

"Let's go? I'm ready."

"Well I..."

The agent didn't expect this. He saw, however, that citizen's daughter, sold into slavery, would cover the debt and still make a profit for the boss. Going soon, he would be able to sell it that very afternoon. He hands the girl the document – the mortgage – and she, in turn, places the paper in the hands of her father who, in a despondent torpor, no longer had a sense of anything around him.

Theo, completely beside himself, tries to stop her from going, holding her by the arms and dragging her into the house, saying that it didn't make any sense, that he would go in her place, which soon the agent was he hastened to say that he would not reach the amount of the debt, that the girl was indeed valuable. Theo tries to assault the agent, but is caught in time by Calypso, who takes him to the kitchen before the man hears him say he would kill him.

"Don't make any more problems, Theo..."

Calliope goes to say goodbye to her parents who, sitting side by side in the room, inert, couldn't figure out what was going on.

"Mom, don't be like that. I'll keep living the same, you know!" She tried to put a happy tone in her voice. "With the same tasks... The kitchen... The loom... What women do, anyway... only in another house! How it would be if I married again! I won't suffer... We've already split up once... and we'd split up again, wouldn't we?"

Iphigenia holds her hands and is unable to say anything, just looking at her intensely so as not to waste those last few minutes with her little face in front of her.

Calliope looks at her father.

"Papa... I'm on my way, Papa." She runs her hand over her face, trying to smile. "Do not Cry..."

Ganymede had two thick tears that did not fall from his eyes, and it seemed that they would stay there forever, clouding his vision and his soul. Calliope kisses her parents and leaves.

"What will I do? What will I do?" Ganymede says, in a breath of despairing voice, because there was nothing to do.

The storm was beginning to abate, the thunder and lightning less strong.

Calypso, as if maddened, with gestures that were not hers, not believing that this was happening, running a cloak to place over her little girl's shoulders.

"Let's wait for the rain to pass..." says the agent.

Calliope looks at her parents, sitting in the living room, like two lifeless statues. He hears Theo's screams and punches shattering everything in the barn, where three servants, who still hadn't left, had taken him and had a lot of trouble holding him down. And he sees Calypso in front of him, trying to be strong. The two hug each other tight.

"No. Let's go anyway. The rain is already subsiding." Calliope said to the banker's agent.

Pulling her hood over her head, she climbed into the carriage, and the two of them set off for the city, leaving the desolate family behind, in silent and helpless tears, with the bleak and uncertain future awaiting them all.

At the Market, Calliope was sold for a very high price, given her circumstance as the ex-daughter of a wealthy citizen, and the slave trader, taking his commission, handed over the money from the sale to Pásion's agent, who before going to see his boss stops at an inn to have a glass of wine, as the day has been very tiring for him.

In the tower, Theo, sitting on the ground, leaning against the wall, sobbing, crying, screams into the air, out of control, a searing pain breaking his heart:

"Zeus! Zeus! Why did you make me a miserable slave, unable to accomplish anything, to help in anything, a man's rapture, a useless piece of meat? Huh? Answer me! Zeus! Why do you one moment, with your rays, throw this woman into my arms, and then with those same rays you take her away, away from me? Huh?! Huh?! And how do you expect me to live, now, without her? How can I live? Calliope... Calliope... I can't live... if my life is without you..."

With his head bowed, stinging tears streaming down his face, he feels Calypso's hand touch his shoulder.

"Come on, come inside, honey. It's no use crying, is it?" she says, holding back her own tears.

When they entered the house, the rain was already giving way, the sky opening, the sun shining again, the smell of wet plants filling the air with the sweet scent of nature that renews itself, oblivious to the excesses and despair of men. Theo looks out the window, sunlight filling the garden and brightening life, but his heart is in darkness. He remembered his brother's death, and how much he had suffered. And now Calliope was gone too. Helios was his brother, but she was his sun.

Chapter VIII
Hephaestus – god of fire, artisans and blacksmiths.

In the house where she went to work, Calliope was immediately paired with a male slave to be his companion. She'd come to town to be sold on the very day he'd gotten into a fight over one of another's female slaves. The houses where a reasonable number of slaves worked had already learned from experience that the area where they slept tended to become the scene of fights, confusions and fierce sexual encounters, which led masters and administrators to the conclusion that the ideal was to form couples , in order to dampen everyone's spirits, making men more settled and calming the rage of women.

"What is this shouting?" asked the boss, hearing the confusion coming from downstairs from the room.

"It's Demetrios, sir, again..."

"Call Tartaros right here! Let him now go to the Market to buy a woman for Demetrios and get it over with!"

Tartaros, the foreman, had then rushed to the Market to buy a slave to put an end to Demetrios's problem, and when he got there, the only woman for sale was Calliope, and for a very high price. Wanting to solve the employer's problem, he bought it anyway, to the great delight of the agent of Pásion, who took to the banker a sum much greater than that which was owed to him by Ganymede.

The foreman knew that his master would not like the amount he paid for a slave. And in fact, the boss frowned when he found out, but he knew how the market worked: you paid high when the urgency was great. The banker's agent, on the other hand, thought he would receive the highest pay for bringing that unexpected sum to the boss. But he was wrong. The banker also frowned. In fact, Pásion was furious, and instantly dismissed him, screaming and cursing.

He didn't want to receive the money. He already had a lot of money. But it had within himself that same frustration of all the metecs and ex-slaves who had managed to get rich with trade: they were rich, very rich, but they had no citizenship, no rights – and above all, no land. If, on the one hand, men like Ganymede had place, vote and word in the assembly; honor and respect among other citizens, and property, land, on the other hand, had no cash. This one, who had it, were the successful merchants and bankers, like Pasion. And eventually honorary citizens had to borrow, as Ganymede had done. Upon receiving the large sum from the sale of Calliope, Pásion lost the chance to seize those lands and become the owner, which was all he wanted and for what he had engendered and wagered on that hoax in which Ganymede had involved.

Only a banker could have such a value in his hands and still feel dissatisfied.

Tartaros felt indebted to his master for having bought a slave at such a high price. The acquisition of Calliope had become a personal burden for him, and he would come to torment the life of the new slave because he felt bad about his actions at the Market. He wanted to "compensate" the boss for that exaggerated expense. As soon as they arrived at the house, he himself had roughly cut Calliope's long, soft hair close to the nape of her neck to sell at the Market to rich women for braiding. The other slaves watched the scene where the fledgling, still half frightened, was humiliated by the foreman who brutally grabbed her hair with one hand, hurting her, and with the other passed a machete in a straight line, pushing her then.

"Come... I'll help you..." an older slave had said, taking pity on the girl who, lying on the floor, dazed, could barely get up.

It had been right on her arrival the first clear demonstration of what she would live, of what it meant to be a slave, of what life was like for those people deprived of any right, even to feel humiliated.

But Calliope quickly composed herself: she was doing what needed to be done, what was right. Her heart, her eyes and her conscience were at peace. She wouldn't give up or be frightened. Her parents were safe and well, and that was the most important thing, that was enough for her. And the hair, it will grow back.

The other slaves had a hostile attitude towards Calliope from the start.

"Rich girl," they said, with disdain and anger.

"Full of habits and tastes."

"She will cry all the time and refuse to work hard."

"Poor girl… What a fate… Besides becoming a slave, she also had to marry Demetrios!"

The Demetrius.

Calliope hardly knew what awaited her. She would still miss her mother-in-law's times…

Demetrius was not a handsome man, but he thought he was. Son of a slave who had gotten involved with a meteco, he never got to know his father, from whom he had inherited his name. He learned the potter's trade but, with a foreign slave, he had learned to master the art of making small pieces of colored pottery, which he knew how to put on walls and floors, in adornments much appreciated by architects and rich lords of Athens, and he was beginning to become fashion. He was in fact an excellent technician at what he was working on, and he did it with responsibility and a love of art. Often called upon to do this work in state buildings and other homes, its owner kept most of the salary he received, and Demetrios spent his share on cheap wine and gifts for women, not thinking of saving to buy his freedom.

"Freedom? For what?" he asked himself, and with reason, because he already had enough freedom in the way he lived, according to some women who knew him.

Demetrios, moreover, saw nothing of freedom in the way of life of citizens or metecos. Everything they did or didn't do was a function of the State! They were always dealing with wars, with civic duties, with obligations to the gods. The citizen had to go to work today in this government function, tomorrow in another one; having to eat this and not eat that; having to marry this woman and not being able to marry that one. The State was an almost divine authority! The city and its gods ruled everything the citizen did! And all his "rights" could be taken away from him, if the State thought that the citizen was dangerous to the interests of the motherland! It could turn out to be exiled, and then ... lost even the right to have to submit to the gods! Why would he want such freedom? Demetrios had seen a lot in his life. And he thought that cities were all the same: they could be headed by kings, tyrants, aristocrats, or even democrats; citizens could sue in court, vote in assemblies, be appointed magistrates and even archons: deep down, they were slaves as slaves. They were slaves of the state.

That's why he lived his life in that kind of braggart way, which made men laugh and exasperated women.

The other men sought his company, perhaps because they liked to hear his stories, his jokes and anecdotes, his loud, mocking laughter, and reports of his amorous conquests. Because Demetrios could not see a tail in a skirt, whoever she was, slave or rich lady, foreigner or Athenian, married or unmarried, beautiful or ugly: he did not lose sight of any woman who passed his way. And if given the opportunity, he would attack, sometimes successfully, sometimes not, sometimes coming back with a curse or even a slap, which he told his friends, chuckling. What to do with Demetrios?

Calliope had come prepared to surrender herself to whatever her fate as a slave might be. On the trip she had taken from her parents' house to the city, she had come silently, despite the banker's agent's attempts to start a conversation. She knew it wouldn't be easy, that she would have to work hard, obey all sorts of orders, sleep uncomfortably and maybe fall ill easily. But none of that tormented her. Her soul was calm, knowing that this had been the only way to guarantee her parents housing, the continuity of their lives and, above all, the property, history and honor of the family.

When she was told that she would be made a partner to a slave, it didn't shake her. When the other slaves told her about Demetrios, she didn't care. Why would she care? What difference did it make?

Calliope was adapting to life in the city, to living with so many people together, to pettiness, to gossip, to nights full of noise and laughter in the slave quarters. And it became more urban, less rural, more intimate with the things of group life, and a very tumultuous group, by the way. Although living with Demetrios only on behalf of her employer, Calliope had decided that they were a couple, and that she should seek to transform their lives as much as possible into a "home". Each morning, by the kitchen fire, she threw a tiny handful of grain as an offering, making a prayer to Athena, concluding that she would be their protector. She had also introduced a novelty in Demetrios' life, by making a mattress, gathering the straw that was piled up on the floor, on which the slaves were used to sleeping, and with great effort and bruised hands, she had tied everything up very well, finally doing a lining, with old sheets he'd gotten from the house. She found it strange that the other slaves had never thought of it. She always kept the small cubicle that served as their bed/room/dwelling room clean. In the end, she had managed, with great difficulty, to convince Demetrios not to have children: of course he had to use tricks to advocate this cause, which required of him certain maneuvers to which he was certainly not used.

"This is difficult, this is very difficult..." he said at the time, all confused.

Surprisingly, the idea of not putting more slaves in the world made him stop to think and, even if he tried to tell her that it would be enough to expose the child to come, she dissuaded him from this practice, without needing to go into detail about the experience of her family. This part about not getting pregnant was especially difficult for Calliope, who had spent her entire life with Cassandro tormented with the desire and need to have children.

At first indifferent to the man with whom she was forced to live, Calliope gradually came to understand the opinion of other women about him. Accustomed to Cassandro's calm and the tranquility of the countryside, Demetrios' comings and goings initially meant nothing to her. But there was a limit. Demetrios pissed her off.

Demetrios made a point of praising in front of Calliope the feminine hips that passed in front of his eyes. At the Market, she heard his name in the mouths of several women, in tents next to hers, sometimes in the same. In conversations with other slaves, Demetrios would raise his voice to tell the spicy stories of the day.

There was always a woman's name in his mouth. Was there a whistle in the air? It was Demetrios, enchanted by some lingering.

"What's the problem with that? What does it matter to me? " Calliope would say to herself, not without a hint of anger in her voice.

Anger she couldn't hide when she met him at bedtime, when she saw him approach her with greed in his eyes and making an innocent face.

"Not tired enough today?" she asked with malice.

Their fights were full of verbal violence.

Separated in their cubicles by thin plaster walls, which did not reach the ceiling, the intimate life of each slave couple was heard by everyone, kisses and hugs, shouts and curses. And when Calliope and Demetrios quarreled, the other slaves would get nervous and asked them to be quiet, or else they would make fun of it, laugh, bet on how the argument would end, the bet worth a loaf of bread, heavy work, sometimes even a coin.

"Who do you think you are? What do you think it is? All-all strutting around town, full of himself, never saw a mirror! She spoke loudly, enraged, her voice altered, trying to get away from him. Calliope barely recognized herself at those times.

"Is that you? With those airs of a rich girl! She's a slave's wife, really! Come here now!"

"Look how you talk to me, you think I'm one of yours...!"

"You're jealous! Do You like me!"

"I hate you!!!"

"Shut up, I want to sleep!"

The slaves' routine could be tiring, but it was by no means tedious.

Once, Demetrios took too much risk and almost got a vase on his head: Calliope had brought the small pot of oil mixed with essences to her bed, massaging her body with this mixture and removing the excess with a cloth, then going to wash. The discussion began and only too late did Demetrios noticed the pot. When Calliope threw it in his direction, he luckily averted his head, the pot going to crash hard against the wall, as she had shot to kill. Demetrios pissed her off.

In fact, although he was in fact very fond of the opposite sex, Demetrios had never seen a woman as beautiful as Calliope, and the coldness she had shown when she arrived made him exaggerate in his advances with the others, always deliberately making the provocations that so tormented her. He wanted to get her attention and make her at least jealous. The more indifferent she was, the more he raised his voice to speak of other women. Seeing her enraged was, for him, the only hint of love he could manage.

Almost always, however, when the fights actually turned to the fore, and the two began to grapple, perhaps because the space was so small, they ended up in each other's arms, with Demetrios finally defeating the prey and dedicating himself to his favorite activity.

"This is difficult..."

Then they fell asleep in each other's arms, and night at last fell on Athens. What to do with Demetrios?

One night, as sometimes happened, they didn't go to sleep right away, but stayed that way, silently cuddling, after a fight and reconciliation, and Demetrios realized she was crying. Softening his voice, he said softly:

"Calliope... stop crying... I didn't mean that..."

"It's nothing. Sleep, it's not you."

It was just that she would sometimes find herself thinking of her parents, the house, Calypso, Theo... She missed everyone; She wondered what they would be like, and ached to imagine that she would probably never see them again. It also happened that, during the day, she stared at infinity, thinking about her family, Cassandro, even her mother-in-law. The other slaves watched her pain without saying anything.

Demetrios then embraced her in silence, feeling a tear fall on his arm where she rested her head, mute and overcome by that pain in Calliope's soul, which his love could not alleviate.

Phocion, Calliope's employer, immediately realized that he had acquired a special maid, of remarkable intelligence and wit, not to mention her gifts with the sick. It was he who resorted most to his work. A widower, having lost his beloved wife to the plague more than ten years ago, being left alone with two small children, he did not want to marry again, and now Calliope came to fill that void in his daily life. His children, aged fifteen and sixteen, spent more time with their friends at the school than at home, preparing to become soldiers. One of them would still give him a famous grandson, with the same name as his grandfather. Famous orator - a democrat of aristocratic origin, as well as Pericles had been - eloquent and possessed of great moral authority, always sought after by citizens who looked to him for advice and support, he often called Calliope when he was going out and had urgent things to do , and asked her to take care of receiving people he was waiting for, running messages and listening to important messages. He always counted on her for that, since she was able to understand everything men said, whatever the subject. He even asked her opinion.

"He said it, right? What face was he looking like? Do you think this will work?"

Or:

"Give this message, but make it look like I didn't say it; which is something that 'is known through the air.' Let's not make a fuss about anything.

He particularly protected her from the start, especially after a rather unpleasant episode starring Tartaros, the foreman, which had taken place in the first few months she had come to work there.

The money for the braids made with Calliope's hair had been little, and Tartaros was not satisfied. Then he had another idea to make the girl's presence surrender, this time at a party that Fócion would give at the house, receiving his friends, some members of the assembly, and even some other less habitual citizens.

Phocion was not used to organizing symposiums since, like Pericles in the past, he considered them typical of extreme aristocrats, who found a form of political manipulation there. Tartarus, however, had seen this party as his unique opportunity, and had called Calliope, then still a novice as a slave, giving her some instructions, along with some clothes, telling her that she should serve the men during the symposium that would follow the dinner . He went in person to the barracks before the party, to make sure she had dressed as he'd ordered, giving even more instructions on how to walk swaying her hips, smiling all the time, doing whatever was asked of her, pleasing everyone. In this way he intended to "gift" to one or more of the men invited, with her obeying what they wanted on their couches, and to bring him, the foreman, the merits with the boss.

When the time came, when Fócion and his friends went to the room where the divans were and the craters where the wine would be mixed with water were taken , Calliope, very awkwardly, appears among the guests, half naked, her slender body wearing only a small piece. of sheer fabric tied around the breasts; the same fabric, in pleats, serving as a skirt, held below the navel by a string of colored beads, her hair in an exaggerated way, full of ribbons and bows, her cheeks and eyes painted, and wearing dancer's sandals. . Little by little, the men gathered there turned their eyes to her, the silence taking over the room. Connoisseurs of Phocion's sobriety, whose discretion and moderation were notorious, never associating him with an excess of wine, music, and libidinous women, they stared open-mouthed at that spectacle, beautiful by the way, but so unexpected.

"Calliope! What is it? Cover up now!" shouted Phocion, irritated, throwing at her the cloak of one of the guests, the first one she had seen, and which she had picked up at random.

"Sir... I..." she starts to say, full of shame, covering herself, to the sadness of many of those present.

"What does that mean?" Phocion was exasperated.

"Sir... it was Tartarus... he ordered me to dress like that... and come and serve them the wine..."

Phocion left the room and immediately went to speak to the foreman, followed by Calliope, wrapped in her cloak, her head bowed.

"Tartarus! What kind of a joke is this? Don't you by any chance know this house, where you've been working for so long?"

"I thought..."

"Well, don't think anymore! You've got more shit on your head than the whole Pnix on Assembly Day!

All the servants were close by and they listened in silence to the rebuke that Tartarus was carrying. None of them had ever heard the boss raise his voice, or say heavier words."

"Don't you know I don't share these dubious tastes? That I don't turn my house into a brothel, as some out there are known to like to do? You don't know that I hate Manichaeism, that I don't use this kind of vile subterfuge in my private life, much less in public, like certain citizens, who use wine and lust, putting vulgar women on opponents' couches to get their graces. , and the approval in the Assembly?

Calliope, at her side, covered by her cloak, begins to tear up.

"My daughter, go get dressed; it's not you I'm talking about," Phocion tells her, his voice softer.

"Sir, I didn't want to go…" Calliope said, holding back her tears.

"Don't worry, go. Don't forget to return the cloak."

And turning to Tartarus:

"Do you want to bury my reputation, bringing to my home everything I've been fighting for years? Go! Go serve the wine in the crater! "

It all helped to break the ice between Calliope and the other slaves, who had gathered in the barracks when they heard the master's yells and curses, and were then reunited, somewhat vindicated with the foreman, whom obviously no one liked. Sitting in a circle, listening to Calliope tell the story, describing everything, especially the face of Tartarus, each one of them begins to tell other stories, laughing and drinking zurrapa, realizing at that moment that Calliope was one of them and was suffering like them, after all.

Phocion, a great orator, deftly undoes the bad impact of the entire scene when called upon to speak, reminding guests of his stance on wine and behavior at the symposium, ending his speech by paraphrasing a comic poet :

"Only three craters I mix for the warned: one for health, which they drink first; the second for love and pleasure; and the third for sleep. After this, the invited guests go home. For the fourth no longer belongs to us, but to insolence; the fifth, screaming; the sixth, to the orgy; the seventh, to black eyes; the eighth, to the bailiff; the ninth, bile; and the tenth, to madness and to furniture thrown into the street".

One guest, however, regretted more than all that Calliope had left the room: it was Alcibíades, whose cloak was precisely what Fócion had taken to cover her, and that she, very embarrassed, had come later, quickly and timidly, to return to the owner.

At the age of thirty-four, a famous orator, rich, powerful and seductive, yet arrogant and unscrupulous, Alcibiades was considered the most handsome man in Athens. By women, and by some men too. Not since Pericles, her uncle, Athens had seen such a charismatic politician. Not even his confused speech, due to a defect in his pronunciation, robbed him of his charms. On the contrary, it gave him even more charm. Rich, handsome and famous, everything about him was allowed and admired. Of course, such popularity fueled the pent-up anger of their political antagonists. Suddenly enchanted by the beauty of Calliope – he whom a woman rarely bewitched – he can no longer pay attention to the speeches other men were making around him. Since then, this unusual politician at Phocion's house has been making unexpected visits, holding Phocion in long conversations without beginning, middle and end, hoping to catch a glimpse of her, or enigmatically withdrawing, without even telling the who had come, upon discovering that she was not there.

The slaves gradually got to know Calliope better and, with the exception of a few, still spiteful and envious, they really grew fond of her, who told them things they had never heard of.

"It must be difficult, girl. Get out of life as a lady and end up here, in the middle of this dirt, with all this work."

"You know, work is no problem... I already had this job in my house, even before I got married... Every woman does the same things, in the end..."

"Yes, but the ladies are tidy, they are respected and well treated... The husbands honor them..."

"But Tata," Callíope said. "There's so much we do that rich ladies don't do...."

"But we have to 'marry' like that, with whoever we are told."

"And isn't that exactly what parents of rich girls do? They don't choose their husbands either."

Although she had been assigned housework, Calliope was sometimes called to go to the Market, to shop for vegetables, fish, meat, etc. She also sometimes went to the house of a friend or friend of her employers, when they got sick, because they knew she had healing gifts. At first she was embarrassed, and even fearful, for she didn't want the city's doctors, in their offices and clinics where they took patients, to consider her a charlatan. But that had never happened, and she was going to visit the sick who called her, walking all over town, meeting more people. And at those times she felt so happy that she almost forgot the pangs of longing. She walked alone, going through the streets of the affluent neighborhoods of Athens, cleaned and paved.

Rich women didn't walk around town. They stayed at home, or at a friend's house, protected from the sun and the sight of men. One or the other, here and there, was seen in the street, always in the company of a slave, or another older lady, or finally with her husband. The poor women, the wives of metecos, and the slaves, came and went alone or accompanied, to the market or anywhere else. And that was the greatest joy for Calliope, who had always loved that city.

She was enchanted by the gardens, the flowers, the colors. The statues adorning the squares. The fountains, the monuments. The cheerful and gaudy people; the sellers; citizens making excited speeches. She was not insulted by the things some men would say to her as she passed, which was the great fear of rich ladies. She just blushed, and laughed a lot, to herself, not caring. She liked to hear the language spoken in the streets, to learn new words. This was her city.

When she would return from these walks, happy, smiling, his skin pink, it was Demetrios' turn to be furious. And his jealous attacks were far more virulent than hers.

"Why that face? What have you been doing in town?"

"Nothing that involved my lower abdomen, as it happens to you!" Calliope had already adopted the jargon of the populace.

"Let's take that smile off your mouth!" he makes a gesture with his hand.

"As for that, you don't need to bother: just look at you and my smile disappears!"

"Good, Calliope!" screams a slave, on the side.

"Come back here!"

"Let go of my arm!"

"Woe if I find out that some meteco touched you!"

"Fret!"

"Who did you talk to? In which stall did you go shopping?"

"Let me go!"

"Tell me who did it!"

"Who did what?"

"Who spoke to you, who heard you, who wanted you! Tell me now, I'll go there and kill this bastard!"

"Me..."

And finally, pressing her against the wall, he covers her mouth with a kiss, and the other slaves finally turn aside to sleep, while the two end the colloquy in the same way as usual.

"Calliope..."

"Hmm?"

"You piss me off..."

One day Calliope was interrupted in her duties and urgently called by other employees:

Calliope, Calliope! Drop everything, go to the barracks, they're bringing Demetrios! Run there, he looks like he's going to die!

Calliope barely has time to realize what she had been told, she runs to the entrance to the slave quarters. Demetrius was being brought in by some men, completely bloodied, unconscious, with wounds all over his body, looking half-dead. At first glance, terrified, Calliope thought that he must have fallen from above, having lost his balance on some scaffolding, but she heard someone speak of a "fight", and imagined that he had gotten into a fight again because of some woman, and felt less sorry. But when they took him to their bed, they were telling her what had really happened.

Demetrius had been hired, along with a good number of other men, to work on a project. Slaves, metecs, and even some poor citizens were there together, working stone, clay and wood, for equal wages and on equal terms. No one could say how, but suddenly what seemed like an everyday conversation turned into an argument, involving Demetrios and a citizen, the latter insulting Demetrios' origins and abilities, perhaps with envy. Demetrios, who for his part was not used to taking shit home, joined the fray outright, insulting the man as well, and quickly kicked and punched despite the metecos' attempts to separate them. They called some

143

guards, who took the citizen's side and instead of admonishing Demetrios, they beat him too, beating him angrily, almost to death.

Calliope, frightened, did not know where to start. He had deep cuts, bruises that were already taking color, spitting blood, vomiting and contorting his face, full of pain. Leaning back, his eyes could not open, already swollen, and his breath made an appalling wheeze.

"Tata, please bring me an amphora of cold water; put a pan on the fire to heat another amount of water, do me a favor my friend! Get me some clean cloths too! There!"

The main thing was to check for fractures, and she fearfully verified that Demetrios' right arm appeared to be broken. She wasn't sure, however, and decided to tie him up and paralyze him as she had seen being done on Epidaurus, because she wanted to ensure that he regained that arm that was, after all, fundamental in his profession.

"Apollo, Asklepios, Hephaestus, help me!" She said, to herself, distressed, carefully bandaging Demetrios' arm with the cloths she had cut into strips, after putting a wooden splint wrapped in fine fabric to make it straight and firm."

And she began to clean the wounds and put the ointments she always had ready. She bandaged the major wounds. She gave him water to rinse his mouth and clean the blood out of it, put clay on his chest to staunch internal damage, made cold compresses, alternating with hot, on her forehead, abdomen, and feet. He made an infusion that she gave him to drink slowly to calm his stomach. She called some of the employees and asked them to bring the tub where they bathed, filled it with cold water, and asked the men to very carefully place him in it, legs out, abdomen immersed, a kind of bath. sit for a few minutes to alleviate general malaise and lower fever. Demetrios, half awake, was barely aware of what was being done to him as he was put in and then taken out of the tub.

When his breathing improved, his chest stopped wheezing, and he seemed at last to sleep, Calliope sat beside him, watched him in silence for a few minutes and, seeing that he was asleep, covered her face with her hands and burst into tears. affliction. She had been so afraid he wouldn't recover, that she wouldn't be able to help him survive. But he seemed to be out of harm's way anyway. Silently, Callíope prayed to the gods to intervene and help him heal. Turning his head towards her, Demetrios opened his eyes a little, as if to see who it was, and seeing her beside him, distressed, he reached out to take her hand and went back to sleep. During the night, she was serving him a ptisane – stew of pounded barley – to lower the fever, which was coming with force.

The next morning Phocion told Calliope to stay and look after Demetrios, while he would personally try to verify who the guards were who had done it, for a fair redress under the law, as he was very fond of the slave, he considered him a great technician. But he had said this only to appease the tempers of the other employees, who were angry. He knew beforehand that he would not be able to obtain anything, since he was a simple slave, and they had no right, no access to justice. He could, at best, in his own name, bring an action for damages for himself, given that his employee would not work – and would not earn a salary – during the recovery. For the slave, nothing could ask. A slave was a person who did not exist. No magistrate would even accept to assess whether it was a graphè – a lawsuit having an offense to the State, or a díke – a civil lawsuit with an individual offense, between private individuals, much less receiving the complaint and opening the process. There was no "cause" to be sought there.

One day, another slave, passing by Calliope on his way to his chores, interrupts his taciturn pace and his own languor, to comment to himself, with his empty eyes:

"I was the one who wanted to be in Demetrios' place, and lie down doing nothing for so many days."

"How can you say that... He was in Hades' arms, who almost took him with him..."

"And?"

Such was the detachment of slaves to life that it offered them nothing to urge them to fight to preserve it.

A few days later, having resumed her responsibilities in the kitchen with the other maids, with Demetrios recovering and out of harm's way, Calliope brought him a dish of mazza.

"Oh, I already ate; Nikkipa brought me a dish just now," he said, taking up the old, familiar tone he assumed when saying another woman's name.

Calliope was about to burst, but she just glanced at him in the corner, arching her eyebrows over a withering glare. Demetrios pissed her off again.

Chapter IX

Athena – goddess of wisdom and peace.

Despite all the changes in her life, only Demetrios could drive her mad. In the rest, Calliope maintained the elegance of attitude and posture that had always distinguished her.

It was still the same slender girl, with a smooth walk, straight back, and elongated gestures. And it was this elegance that, on a day when she was walking at the Market, caught Danilos' attention.

"Look there! The Athena of my life!! What a bearing, what a look, what a presence! Bring this woman here, I need her here now! Quickly! Before she's gone!"

Danilos had been appointed by the Council to organize the Panateneas that year, and he walked around town collecting ideas, gathering volunteers, bringing together the women and children who would make the procession, talking in schools with teachers who would rehearse choirs with students , ordering fabrics, etc. He had some innovative and controversial ideas that he wanted to see carried out. When Calliope was brought close to him, not understanding anything, his jaw dropped:

"I can't believe it! It was Athena herself who helped me, I have to run and sacrifice a sheep for her!"

Calliope was smiling, still not understanding.

"My daughter, what is your name?"

"Calliope, sir."

"She's Phocion's slave, from what this rascal here told me," says Danilo's servant.

"Yes sir."

"Formisium! Write down these names: "Calliope, from the house of Phocion. Climbing to Athena"

"But, sir..."

"Where were you?" he yells at a woman who is approaching, "I was almost leaving, and you weren't coming back with these samples! Did you talk to the florist?"

"I said yes. He said he doesn't think it will."

"How is that possible? Let's see if it won't work! Formisium! Write down: "florist: threaten him and his family" – and turning to Calliope – My daughter, be at the Parthenon tomorrow at sunset. You came to save my life! The Athena of my dreams!"

"Sir, I..."

But he was already going in another direction, talking to other people who were arriving loaded with papyrus. She manages to hold Formísio:

"What is all this anyway?"

"It's for this year's festival; from what I see he liked you, and he wants you to take part in the procession... See, it's to be at the Parthenon tomorrow, rehearsals are about to begin."

Formísio finally explained to her what all that was about.

Danilos had been chosen as organizer of the event, among other reasons, due to his experience as an organizer at the last Dionysian feasts, when playwrights presented their latest works in the theater, and the plays were submitted to a jury vote. Danilos had received a handsome award along with the author of the play he had sponsored. It is true that playwrights did not always get along so well. They tried at least not to let the same thing happen with Phrynicus who, more than fifty years earlier, with his tragedy "The Conquest of Miletus", had made the audience cry so much that not only did he not receive any awards, but was also fined in a thousand drachmas for the pain inflicted on the people.

With his innovative ideas, Danilos had imagined a party a little different for that year: the first days, with songs and games, torch, horse and car races, would be relatively the same as all previous festivals, like the last , four years earlier. But the last day, that of the procession, would have something new: a woman dressed as Palas Athena, as if incarnating the goddess, being carried through the city by the entire procession of the inhabitants! He had submitted the idea to the Assembly Council, and the latter had approved everything. The Council thought that this would be an excellent opportunity to put an end to a negative legend that had swelled in the people's minds from one of the anecdotes told by Herodotus. The late historian had told that the Athenian tyrant Pisistratus, in the previous century, would have used a stratagem to regain power, disguising a girl as the goddess Athena and sending her by car to the Acropolis, preceded by heralds, summoning the people to welcome him back to Athens under the protection of the goddess herself. The naivety of the people of the time in believing this to such an extent had so impressed the historian's listeners that the legend stuck like a shame in their memories. The Council saw in Danilos' idea an opportunity to show the people that everything was just a fantasy, freeing popular thinking from the historian's exaggerations. There would be a contest between the girls of the noble families of the city, to choose who would be Athena, but Danilos seemed to have no more doubts. He had found his goddess.

"But what about my boss? If he doesn't let me?" Calliope asked Formísio.

"Oh, I don't know that!"

"A woman dressed as Athena? But this Danilos is really looking for trouble!!" laughs Phocion, upon hearing Calliope who had come to ask permission to go to the Parthenon the following day.

"Do you believe that I should not go?"

"Not at all, quite the opposite! Yes, go! He has good taste, this boy! I just think some older gentlemen will find in all this a reason to trample him on! Ah, the guardians of religion, my daughter! Those, yes, hinder the life of this city...."

"Anyway, I imagine that the number of girls in the contest is quite high..."

"I think we will have unforgettable Panateneas!" said Phocion.

And he went on his way, hurriedly.

The next day, Calliope was walking through the city on her way to the Acropolis, thinking about the whole story, a little anxious about what awaited her. Surely she would find all the rich girls of Athens, the daughters of important citizens, gathered there for the contest, each trying harder than the other to be the chosen one.

She thought these girls would resent the mere presence of a slave among them. The city, however, did not seem to be aware of the preparations for the party, although many were in charge of the various phases of the games and races, the cleaning and preparation of the temples and public buildings that would be used for the banquets and awards. The heat and the sun were strong, as they were in Skirophorión, which preceded the Hekatombaión, month in which the Panateneas were held.

Arriving at the foot of the Acropolis, she was surprised to see no one there, just a guard, in the exact spot where, twenty years before, she and Theo had held hands with a guard in full dress, waiting for her mother and Calypso reappear at the opening party of the Parthenon.

He always saw the Parthenon from below, it was a sight he was used to. I had gone up once to see him up close, on the occasion of another smaller party. Today it was all quiet, empty and mysterious.

"No, you can't go up," said the guard, who was in charge of the place.

Nobody could go up on the Acropolis, only a few people connected with the party were allowed to go there.

But when he hears Calliope's name and what she had come to do, he said:

"Oh, is that you? Go ahead, Danilos is upstairs waiting."

And the guard watched as Calliope slowly climbs the very white stairs, a single speck climbing that immensity of marble, flanked by statues. Going through the zigzag, approaching the Propyleus, Calliope stopped before passing through the six Doric columns of the grand entrance, which was even more imposing thus deserted, with the light of the setting sun giving it a golden-yellow color. sumptuous marble cluster of columns and steps.

To her right, the graceful little temple of Nike, where Athena was worshiped as the goddess of victory. On the left, the Pinacoteca.

At 156 meters above sea level, the harmony and symmetry of the temples on the Acropolis, with the magnificent view of the city at their feet, the sea in the distance, caused admiration not only to the Athenians but also to all those who arrived there.

Crossing at last the Propyleus, on her left, the statue of Athena awaited her – the one that was already a familiar image of hers, as she visualized it in her prayers every morning. And in front of her, on the highest point of the Acropolis, the Parthenon.

Perhaps because of the effect of the sunlight that was setting, perhaps because there was no one but her, giving the place and the moment a mysterious aspect, the fact is that emotion suddenly begins to take over Calliope, in front of those temples that represented everything what was the Hellenic world, all that the city preserved with pride and devotion, all the things that the ancestors had lived and whose difficulties and victories one would not want to forget.

With her heart suddenly pounding, as if it wanted to break out of her chest, she approached the entrance to the Parthenon, shy, and even a little afraid. An infinite silence filled the air, stagnating his thought, the city, his life. Looking up, his eyes slowly traveled over all the details of the frieze, where Phidias, the sculptor, had depicted, in vivid colors, the various stages of the Panateneas. She felt a force pulling her into the temple, a force she could not fight, an irresistible and seductive force. As he was about to break down and carry the steps, he saw Danilos approaching, walking along the side of the Parthenon, saying goodbye to a bald boy of the same age, thirty or so.

"Didn't I say?" he comments with his friend, pointing to Calliope.

Returning from the world of the gods, Calliope waits for the boy to leave.

"Sir, that contest, to choose the girl," she said, approaching Danilos.

"There won't be any more! One less job!"

"But...."

"I've already decided: Athena is you!"

"Lord, forgive the intrusion, but having chosen me, a slave, over all the others, can't you bring a problem with the vanities of the girls of the richest families in Athens?"

Danilos thought for a minute and said slowly:

"My daughter, having chosen you, a slave, solves the problem of vanities among the girls of the wealthy families of Athens!"

They were all gathered at the Odeon: Danilos, his assistants, workers, girls, boys, curious people, all somehow participating in the organization of the party. Calliope had arrived early as requested. Everyone in Phocion's house – slaves and family – was thrilled with her choice for the "role" of Athena, and she had been freed to go to rehearsals whenever Danilos called her.

Some women have finished taking their measurements, to make the tunic, armor, helmet, shield, in short, all of Palas Athena's attire. Calliope, with her arm outstretched, trying to get used to the idea of holding an owl tied to an olive branch, was getting to know the girls and boys who were part of the procession, and who laughed at everything around her.

"Formisium! Didn't they say the owl was trained?" shouts Danilos.

"They said yes, my boss!"

"Well, it seems that this grumpy owl wants to get into trouble with me!"

"What if we used a terracotta owl?" Calliope suggests, afraid of the bird, which kept flapping and opening its wings menacingly, wanting to take flight.

"If Athena is real, the owl must also be! Are we ready?" – he asked the six boys who would lead Calliope – Athena – raised on a fence, in the procession.

"We are!"

"Calliope, you stay here. Yes, climb on the siding. You are going to lift the siding on your shoulder and take it, walking at a pace, do you understand? One step, stop. Another step, stop. Otherwise you'll drop it! You, always holding the shield in one hand, and the branch with the owl in the other! Ah! Ari! – Danilos interrupts, seeing his friend approaching, that same boy Calliope had seen with him in the Parthenon.

"Good afternoon friend! I came to bring my bald man to see how this boast is going!" says Aristophanes, laughing.

"Come on!" shouts Danilos.

"One two... ! Go up!"

The six boys put the siding over their shoulders, with Callíope balancing, holding on to the nail nailed to the wood that served as both an olive branch and a support for her, the angry owl flapping its wings.

"I will fall!" Callíope says, half laughing, half afraid.

"Drop here, I'll catch you!" Shouts one of the boys, laughing too.

"Heads up! Like that!" shouts Danilos. "Now, the first step, with the right foot. Watch out! Always look to the sides to see if they are aligned! WE won't let the goddess drop in the procession! One step, stop! That! Left foot! Left!!!"

But the owl showed no signs of cooperating, and fluttered its wings desperately, while Calliope, definitely afraid, losing her balance, let go of the wooden board that served as a shield.

As the six boys lowered the siding, and Formísio untied the hysterical owl from Callíope's fist, a yell began to form at the entrance to the Odeon. A man with a thick voice and very angry came in, out of breath, yelling at everyone, throwing his cloak over his shoulders theatrically.

"Who is responsible? Where is it?"

"Oh!" says Danilos, ironically, seeing approaching the one who was one of the strictest priests in the city. "It didn't take too long for him to show up!"

"But then it's true!" shouts the old man looking at Danilos, Callíope and Aristophanes. "End it now! Transfiguring a woman into Athena! Inspired by Herodotus' stories, certainly! Whose is this preposterous idea? Such a thing has never been done!"

"There's always a first time!!" Danilos answers.

"Sacrilege! The gods will be angry with the city! Athena will no longer protect us!" and recognizing Aristophanes, the comedian – "Aaah, but that could only be it! They're all from the same bunch! They had to be behind this story, these joking dramatists who mock everything that is most sacred! They make fun of beliefs and traditions! All virtues are thrown into the latrine! They incite the people to debauchery with their shameful pranks! And they still win prizes!"

Calliope, Aristophanes and Danilos, side by side, watch, perplexed, the man getting redder and redder, gesturing and jumping up and down, alternating standing on tiptoes and then on heels, on the faces of the three young people the same smile disguising the laugh that almost they couldn't control it. Formisius continued to struggle with the owl.

"Sir, would you excuse us," Danilos said at last.

"And I even think I heard that they will choose her in a female beauty contest, in Lesbos fashion!! shouts the old man indignantly, his cloak slipping off again."

"There will be no more! She has already been chosen!" Danilos says triumphantly, looking at Calliope.

"A... a... - enraged, the old man measures Calliope from head to toe - a slave in place of the virgin goddess! I will not let this happen!" he yells, almost touching his nose to Danilos. "I'm going to the Council personally to alert them to ban this infamy!"

"You waste your time! The Council has already allowed it!" Danilos shouts at the old man, nose to nose, annoyed too.

This information catches the priest by surprise, who falls silent, his face completely turning purple. The owl screams, flaps its wings and makes a fuss.

"Formisium! Take away this useless old owl now!" shouts Danilos, losing his patience.

"Which one?" asks Aristophanes.

"I won't allow it! I will not allow it! Damn Democrats! It's all their fault!" shouts the old man, furious, leaving, throwing the cloak over his shoulders again, leaving the scene like a tragic character.

"Let Hades take him!!!" said Danilos.

And Aristophanes finally bursts out laughing, turning to Calliope, who was already smiling.

"My dear, I hope you were not offended by what he said! You saw that nothing he says has any value at all..."

"Oh no! I do not care! I've seen so much in my life!"

In two or three sentences, she tells him quickly how she married and became a widow without children, ending up becoming a slave, ending up there in those rehearsals, and Aristophanes' smile gives way to an expression of introspective reflection, thinking about the story of that woman, in the detours in his life, and with his eyes he follows her as she walks away with Danilos, to continue the rehearsals.

Of all the religious festivals – and there were many, every month there was at least one in honor of some god – the Panateneas were certainly the most important in Athens. They were the ones that brought together the largest number of people, as everyone was allowed to participate, even metecos with their wives and daughters. The procession was huge, the entire city going up to the Acropolis and passing in front of the statue of the goddess, leaving offerings and all sorts of thanks. The Parthenon frieze itself bore a reproduction of this procession. The festival took place in the month that bore the name of the most solemn of sacrifices – Hecatombeon – with the sun and heat contributing to increase the joy and colors that took over the polis during the twelve days that the festival lasted. The Eucharist ordered 100 oxen to be sacrificed, in addition to all other minor sacrifices. All citizens were offered a piece of meat, after having been offered the best parts to Palas Athena. There were musical shows at Odeon; poems were recited; there were horse and chariot races at the racecourse; torch races; athletic games; fights; regattas in Piraeus, and the winners received a wreath of olive branches and an amphora containing oil extracted from the fruits of the sacred olive trees. And the last day was the one where the great procession took place, departing from the Ceramics district towards the Acropolis, crossing the entire city, carrying a cloak embroidered by young Athenians to cover the statue of the goddess.

"Come on, everyone!" shouts Danilos. "Heads up! Be very careful at each step! Calliope, serious face, please! No laughs! If Athena roars through the city, we will all be thrown from the Bárathron.

Danilos was beginning to regret it all. But the population by now was already aware of Athena that would pass loaded, in flesh and blood, and everyone was looking forward to this moment. He'd spent the entire month rehearsing, he was exhausted, a lot of things hadn't gone his way, he'd fought with a lot of people, he'd made new enemies, and he wasn't sure what it all turned out to be in the end. Backstage theater nervousness. He should be used to it by now.

His entire group was waiting at the Leocorium, in the Cerâmico neighborhood, from where the procession started. The boys who carried the goddess Athena's dais in their white tunics kept talking nonsense to each other, were it not for the fear of the owl – another owl, this time trained and quiet, but still a real owl, trapped in the olive branch – Callíope would certainly have succumbed to the urge to laugh. They were part of one of the first groups, coming right behind the magistrates and priests, and were followed by the sacrificers bringing the oxen and small animals, which came decorated with wreaths of flowers. Then came the elders bearing olive branches; the girls with baskets of offerings on their heads, accompanying the robe of the goddess made by them especially for the occasion; behind them, a group of women continued to throw flower petals. And here came the mass of the population, the citizens and their families; the metecs bringing as an offering small ships that symbolized their foreign origin; the women of the metecos bringing water vessels, and their daughters bringing stools and umbrellas. Then came the delegations of the clerics (33) and allied cities. At the end of the march came the Athenian cavalry in traveling uniform. The entire population was involved with the party. Prisoners were released for the twelve days it lasted.

Leaving the Ceramics, the procession went towards the temple of Demeter, on the way to Eleusis, and from there along the Pelasgic wall on the Pnix, and finally to the Acropolis, where the statue of Athena was covered with the mantle, and the offerings are placed at his feet, as well as wherever there was room.

Obviously, this year's Panateneas had all their attention on Calliope. And when she passed, suspended by the boys who finally fell silent, there was no one who wasn't thrilled to see her. Danilos had really been right. Calliope personified in her posture, features, and countenance exactly what the popular imagination conceived of as the goddess of her city. They all looked at her in wonder, respect, as if they were actually seeing her protector there, before them, proud of them, honoring them with her enigmatic presence. In a mixture of haughtiness and serenity, with the blue tunic made in special fabric, thin, a little shiny, edged in gold, the cloak in the same shade thrown to the side, falling off one shoulder; the goatskin shield, made by one of the city's most renowned shield and armor makers; and the plume helmet, made especially for her head, much smaller than the smallest of soldiers' heads; her black hair sticking out from the sides of her helmet; the olive branch in her right hand, where the owl calmly alighted, she still had her captivating and mysterious gaze, always looking straight ahead, as if she were in fact the goddess descended from Olympus for her party and her protégés. Even the priests were moved. How beautiful was their goddess! People didn't fit in with joy and emotion. They couldn't get it out of their eyes.

A pair of eyes, however, taken by her uneven heartbeat, was not content just to look at her. He would have to have her closer.

After passing through the Propyleus, and revering the statue of Athena, the group finally ended their passage. Gradually, slowly, the entire mob began to disperse, tired, but still with the excitement of the party to liven up their conversations.

When she was going home, coming down from the Acropolis, walking through the Perípathos, carrying the helmet, her hair loose on her shoulders, Calliope was stopped by a slave she knew. He worked at Alcibiades' house.

"My master sends me to call you to his home, Calliope!"

"But...."

"He said to come with me right now, before returning to your house."

Calliope had no desire to go. She had known how to evade him when he came to look for her at Phocion's house. How many times, while serving wine and dried fruit to the two men, passing by Alcibiades, had Alcibiades held her by the arm, trying to breathe a word, some suggestion, some invitation, and Calliope, discreetly disentangling herself, pretended not to hear or not understand .

"My dear Alcibiades, leave this girl alone..." Phocion had told him on one occasion, who, besides, knew very well that he was not the reason for the visit of the notorious young man.

But Calliope did not know what to expect from Alcibiades, in his own home.

Annoyed, not knowing if she was doing the right thing, whether or not to obey that order of a citizen who was not her master - Fócion had always made it clear that she did not want to get into friction outside the Assembly with her opponents as well as with his allies - she went, distressed , with the slave through the paved streets of the rich neighborhoods, approaching the place where the general lived. She even had an impulse to run away when she reached the door.

"The boss is waiting. Please follow me" said the slave.

The house was dangerously empty. Certainly everyone – women, servants and children – were still at the party. Calliope followed the servant who leads her through large sumptuous rooms, looking like palaces or government buildings, or even temples. On a wall she recognized the work of Demetrios, the colored stones forming harmonious drawings referring to the city, the struggles, the beautiful women. When introduced into a room, she did not see that Alcibiades was already there, and she was startled, turning towards the voice that was suddenly speaking to her, seeing him standing near a chair.

"What an honor to receive a visit from the goddess herself…"

Alcibiades wasn't exactly an ardent worshiper of the gods. Those words, in his mouth, might have sounded sarcastic, were it not for his slurred speech and his awkwardly flirtatious yet sincere tone, which confirmed to Calliope his intentions.

At thirty-five, in the splendor of youth, health, and vigor, he was even more handsome than he had ever been. The scandals involving his private as well as public life made him even more charismatic. He was one of the most heard politicians in town, at the height of his strategist career. He had power and influence in the most important decisions – especially those related to the war against Sparta, a war that he supported and encouraged. His courage in battle and his speeches in the Assembly earned him the title of general at age thirty. His tumultuous life in politics, diplomacy, and war had brought him many ups and downs, and now his popularity had re-established itself on account of his victories in car racing at the Olympics the year before. Nothing was denied to him, and he was too used to all the perks.

"Sir, they told me you had called me…"

At Fócion's house, Calliope had been used to treating her boss, by his order, in the most informal language, as with servants and free men, without the hierarchical barriers. With the other gentlemen, however, she knew that treatment should always be respectful.

He takes a step towards her, who in turn takes a step away.

"I couldn't help calling you... to say that you are as stunning as Athena."

Calliope lowers her eyes.

"Thank you, sir."

What was it that most caught his attention about her? Her beauty? Her intelligence? Her delicacy? Her indifference? The fact is that Alcibiades had fallen in love with that woman in the same overwhelming way that his uncle Pericles had fallen in love with Aspasia.

"Calliope... Will you never understand what I want?" he said, approaching her, softening his voice as much as he could, used to giving orders, and almost always rudely.

"Sir..." Calliope once more walks away.

"So many times over these months I tried to get close to you..."

Alcibiades was amazed at the slave's firmness and indifference. How could she not succumb to his power, his charisma, his beauty? She takes a few more steps away from him.

"But I want to stay still, please! – he said, losing some of the softness in his voice.

Calliope stands on the ground and looks him straight in the eye, head bowed.

Alcibiades trembles under that gaze before which his haughtiness shrank.

"By my side" he continues, soft again, "you could be very happy."

He gets even closer, almost touching her body. She averts her face and eyes, saying nothing.

"I could get you out of slavery... You would live in a house I would buy, just for you, with employees, with jewelry..."

Calliope keeps her eyes fixed on a spot on the wall. He wanted to turn her into his mistress. Alcibiades sees her like this, in profile, as close to him as she's ever been, and alone. He felt her scent, her heat, saw her skin, her hair, the shape of her slender, elegant body. With his mouth dry, feeling dizzy, his heart wanting to leave his chest, he is on the point of losing control, taking her in his arms, kissing her mouth, her neck, and finally subduing her. She remains silent.

"I know your dignity, I know that I do not offer what is up to you." He is lost in his own words, in his own desire, and in the intoxicating presence of the girl.

The room seems to be getting darker.

"Ah, Calliope! I don't know if I can stand another minute seeing you so close to me... I need you now." He puts one hand on her shoulder, while the other holds her arm.

Mute and impassive, she knew he would not be defeated. If in his voice he showed tenderness, his hand on her shoulder already made a pressure with which he showed possession. The crucial moment of this conversation had arrived, the outcome of which she dreaded.

"What do you say?" he asks.

Calliope was silent for a few more seconds before speaking.

"Sir," finally she begins, slowly but firmly, "What do you want my word for? What can I say, a simple slave? I know, as you know, that I must obey orders... I, a maid, and you, an honorary citizen... What is my word? You have power as a citizen, as well as strength as a man. If that one I oppose with my vain word, this one I will also oppose, as I can, with my arms."

That was it, then. If he wanted her, he would have to take her by force. Alcibiades is perplexed, not letting go of her arm and eyes. He wanted to cover her with kisses and tell her how much he loved her. He felt his strength slipping away at the beauty, honor, and courage of that woman.

"Why do you condemn me, you too... to love without being reciprocated?... They leave me alone, with this feeling I carry... which I can't control... I can't help feeling... I will have to remain like this, seeing you from afar, admiring and loving you... from a distance..." He spoke like a defeated boy.

Calliope was not impressed. She knew that despite those words, she could be taken by force at any moment. And yet, with all her senses alert, she hears that someone is entering the house and talking loudly. His silence takes the general to the last consequences, speaking in a mixture of pain and breathlessness, as if about to cry:

"Tell me... what you want... tell me what you need... I'll do everything, anything you want... I'll abandon everything. I'll walk away from everything. From home, from the army, from politics, even from the city. I'll give you what you want. Give me the order, and I will, whatever it is!"

A noise is heard and the employee enters, followed by Andocides, a friend of Alcibíades, who doesn't wait to be announced and starts talking in a rush:

"General! They are after us! Some members of the Council are coming here, we need to make a decision! We may have to flee!"

"What happened? asks Alcibíades, returning to his normal voice, impatiently, annoyed by such an inopportune interruption, but noticing in his friend's tone that it was something serious.

"There was an act of barbarism, the Hermas were all capped! All across town! None of the pedestals are left intact! Some drunken hubbub, certainly. But they're attributing it to you, and me too! – Andocides didn't even stop to breathe – "Everything that goes wrong in this city is our fault! They will say that we have hurled the god Hermes at Athens, destroying all his statues! My friend, if this understanding is established, it will be the end of us! We will be judged, ostracized, or perhaps even sentenced to death!"

The news had darkened the face of Alcibiades, who saw the fact as a probable obstacle to his bold strategic plans against Sparta, which had already been practically accepted and approved in the Assembly. Calliope takes the opportunity to leave.

Which of the two had been saved by Andocides? She, faced with the general's imminent onslaught, or he, who had put his word and such radical promises to the test?

When she arrived home, tense and nervous that turmoil her feelings, Calliope was surrounded by slaves who admired their friend, still in her elegant Pallas Atena costume. Demetrios, also fascinated by his wife's notoriety, welcomed her into his arms, in which she finally cries in distress, finding in them the security and familiarity that make her surrender to her husband, when alone, with a voluptuousness as unexpected as well. coming to Demetrius.

And in the excitement, they both forget about the care they should have taken in those days of the month.

That afternoon, it was not only Alcibiades who was delighted to see the beautiful Calliope pass by with the procession, transformed into Palas Athena. In the midst of the crowd, incredulous and marveling at the sight, Theo saw his goddess pass by, whose whereabouts he had not known since she had left two years before, that day when Zeus had punished the land.

"Ateninha... Atenika... what's wrong with you?"

Demetrios had been used to calling Calliope that since the night of the Panateneas. He had come to treat her with special deference. But that hadn't made him less interested in other women's skirts. He just recognized that the one he had by his side deserved a lot of respect – within his conception of respect, of course. And for days she had been feeling sick, tired, unwell. Clumsy, he didn't know what to do to see her better.

"Sir, I must speak to you..." Callíope says to Phocion one morning.

"What is it, my daughter? Is something not going well?"

"It's just that I... I'm expecting a baby."

Phocion looks at her for a minute, saying nothing, more watching the girl's reaction than occupied with his own.

"Did it happen, anyway?" he asks.

"Yes..."

"And what do you intend to do?" His voice showed the affection he felt for her.

A father-to-daughter relationship had sprung up between them. Calliope was looking to her boss, at that moment, for more than advice or a word: she wanted support.

"Lord, you know my thoughts about the children of slaves... During this time I tried to avoid them."

"There is always the option to expose it. Or until..."

Calliope had seen that in those years at the house. Some slaves abandoned their babies. A maid from another house had an abortion. None of them had such decisions been easy or indifferent.

"Sir, I want, I would like to have the baby..."

Phocion smiled. She knew Callíope's story so well, her efforts to have a child with Cassandro, and then for not having one with Demetrios. But above all he knew her will as a woman.

"I know" she continues, "that I didn't want to put a child in the world to live and grow up in underprivileged conditions…"

"Callíope, my daughter, does not need to justify or leave your heart in doubt. Know that here in this house, your child will always be very well cared for and well liked! Have it, yes. It's been a while since I've seen children around here, it'll be good," said the boss, smiling, "They're the future, after all!"

All the slaves already knew, and they only needed to see the symptoms that were so common, which almost all of them had already gone through just before their wombs began to grow. Only Demetrios still had no idea that Calliope had gotten pregnant. How could he not notice? Of women, he only understood what interested him. From then on, the subject was none of his business. If any woman had a child by him, he had never known. Pregnant, by the way, was something he shied away from, not even knowing what.

"Are you feeling well today, Ateninha?"

"Yes…"

"You'd better have some of those soups you make when one of us gets sick."

"Demetrios, I'm not sick, I'm pregnant…" she finally reveals to him.

"Like this?"

"I'm having your baby."

Demetrios kept looking at the woman as if not understanding. He had never heard that words before. "I'm having your baby." So many friends had told him that they ran away at this news. He found himself not wanting to.

"It was Ateninha's night, wasn't it…?"

"It was… I actually knew from that moment… And now I'm sure…"

"Forgive me, Atenika… it was my fault…"

"Demetrios…"

"That's why you didn't feel well these days!" He spoke, with the triumphant voice of someone who unravels a great mystery.

"But I'm already fine, just take care of me."

Calliope did not know how to tell Demetrios that she had already decided she was going to have the baby. It seemed strange to her that she had little or nothing to say on the subject, the conversation with the boss being much more decisive. It seemed to her that for the first time in her life she was making a decision on her own. She didn't realize that she had already done it so many times, contrary to the prevailing rules that put women under the yoke of a man - be it the father, the husband, the boss, the lover - never taking a step without their permission.

"And how will it be...? You didn't want to have children..." asked Demetrios, who also didn't know how to deal with the matter, "Are you going to abandon him?"

She takes courage, and responds, looking him straight in the eye:

"No, I'm going to have him, Demetrios... Once inside my belly, I want him... very much... My baby... I want and I'm going to have our child..."

He's quiet, his face serious, maybe mulling over the news, maybe wanting to start a fight, maybe just missing a beat. Calliope, however, prepares for the usual clashes.

"Ateninha... you'll have... a little god!"

Calliope smiles and the two lie in the dark, talking softly about the pregnancy, about Athena's night, about childbirth, about bigger tunics and baby crying.

"Hey... Calliope! And then? What did he say?..." whispers a slave approaching the cubicle, since that conversation so important had not occurred in the usual screams shared by all slaves.

"I'm pregnant! I'm having a baby!" He shouts, laughing, hugging Calliope.

Demetrios pissed her off.

The first few months were easy for Demetrios. It didn't even look like she was pregnant for the first time. It seemed that an aura of motherhood enveloped her and gave her an air of honor and dignity. She was already used to the nausea, which incidentally had stopped after a few weeks. She caressed his still-flat belly in her spare time. And she especially liked the enlarged breasts.

"Are we okay today, mommy?" he asked.

Around the sixth month, however, Demetrios began to feel uncomfortable with her growing belly. He couldn't find a position, didn't know which way to turn. And he finally found the right side: beside other women, with no protruding babies filling their wombs. For Calliope that was neither news nor sadness. On the contrary, she could then sprawl at will without him coming looking for a leg, a thigh, a hip. Not that he had given up completely, but at least he was already relatively satisfied and – that, yes, new – with a certain amount of guilt. In fact, he had never been so happy. He continued to live his usual life, he had a woman who was the envy of slaves, metecs and citizens, he was going to have a child, and he was increasingly in demand for the services in which he was so skillful and refined. The works he did on the floors and walls of public buildings, with the pieces of colored pottery forming harmonious figures, had become the sensation of architectural works.

And it was this ability that one day brought him a change that, in other times, would have made him even happier, in his spirit of adventure. But now they left him stunned, not knowing what to feel, and just having to obey.

"Go get your things ready," said Tartaros. "You leave tomorrow on the ship that leaves early for Ephesus, together with a group of artisans."

Demetrios' fame had crossed the seas. Phocion had been summoned by the Council to sell the slave to the State to be sent to that city in Asia Minor to carry out his work in local buildings. The inhabitants of Ephesus were known for their taste for fancy, sumptuous buildings designed to dazzle the eyes. The famous Artemision, Temple of Artemis, the hunting goddess, was a work that people all over the world would like to see. Demetrios must have been excited by the idea of going to such a place. But that had not happened. Nor did the expectation of meeting other women cheer him up.

"I need you to know that there was nothing I could do to prevent this," Phocion said, frustrated and saddened, having called the two of them into his presence to talk about Demetrius' departure.

He didn't want to see one of his best employees go. And she thought that Calliope, after all, was fine with that man, whose child she was carrying. He had tried to convince the Pritans that he needed the services of that artisan, but the Pritans were already convinced that they needed him even more. Phocion didn't know if it was because she didn't love Demetrios, or because she had already suffered so much, but she saw in Calliope's face that she didn't really suffer from the separation. He could no longer say the same about Demetrios. His desolation was evident. He wished he could tell the couple of employees that the separation would be temporary, but he knew the most likely thing was that, after that venture in Ephesus, Demetrius would be sent to some other place even farther away, at the behest of the State.

For the first time in his life, Demetrios knew what it meant to be a slave, to have no voice or rights. Taking a ship, crossing the seas, discovering other lands, gaining fame and money, meant for him at that moment the most poignant lack of freedom.

"Little Athenian…"

Being separated from Calliope caused him a pain he had never imagined he would feel. He looked at her face and belly, and felt a lump in his throat, for he knew he would probably never see her again, would not even see his child born, and he would certainly never get to know him. It was the goddess Aphrodite who was taking revenge on him at last. At his doorstep, with the sun rising that morning, carrying a bag containing a few tools and a few personal effects, he took one last look at her, saying goodbye to the woman in his life."

"Mom… If it's a girl, would you name her Athena?"

"Yes, yes. And I will call her Atenika."

Demetrios smiles.

"And if it's a boy, have you already chosen a name?" he asked.

"Yes. If it's a boy, he'll be called Demetrios."

His eyes water. And Calliope hugs him tightly, her eyes also full of tears, for the one whom, if she had not loved, had respected and even obeyed as she had been taught as a girl, what wives should do, and whose son, kicking in her womb, she already loved with all the strength of her heart.

Had she been given a choice, Calliope might not have wanted Demetrios to leave. Together with that man she had not loved, and to whom she had been united through work, she had built what most resembled a "life for two", where the common goal, rather than the perpetuation of family and property real estate, was simply the pursuit of survival and everyday well-being, day after day. Somehow this goal seemed to make more sense to her than the other. And with all the reserves she harbored for Demetrius's exasperating behavior, they had managed to achieve some edge of that common goal.

The last months of the pregnancy had Calliope almost all the time indoors. Phocion definitely treated her like a member of the family, and as such, preferred that she not go out into the street too much. In fact, he had never been able to stop seeing her as a "citizen," and he treated her that way, preserving her from the eyes of the people, as citizens did to their wives and daughters. Had it not been for her already heavy belly, Calliope would have resented it, as she enjoyed walking around the city a lot. She had always been a great admirer of the polis. Athens appeared to her like a large sunny garden, the scent of summer flowers scenting the air. It was a pleasure to go shopping in the Market on a sunny morning, amidst the colors and screams and all the life that that open space contained. The buildings, the gardens, the statues, the harmony of forms, everything enchanted her eyes. She liked to walk along the paved streets, especially those in the more structured neighborhoods, in a checkered layout in accordance with the recent invention of Hipódamus, who sought to give the entire city an order, gradually ending the lack of symmetry and paving of the narrow old streets , where the houses were small and uncomfortable, out of line with one another, among which loose animals wallowed in the mud splashing the tunics of passersby. Calliope loved her Athena.

There were two months of quiet at home, helping the maids with their tasks, and advising Fócion in their jobs, writing the speeches he dictated, giving her opinion here and there about a phrase or an idea, taking messages, imagining strategic solutions for situations the delicate ones that the boss eventually got involved. On one of these days, in the midst of a dictation, she felt her first pang. Phocion immediately called the other maids and set the house in an uproar, nervous as a true grandfather. The thing looked like it was going to be too fast. Someone must have been on duty, because immediately a midwife arrived from town.

And so, on a spring day in that month of Mounichíon, Demetrios was born.

They finally had a baby in the house.

Phocion, whose two sons were in the army grappling with war and easy women, did not see the prospect of having grandchildren around so soon. Calliope, being like a daughter, it was with naturalness that she let that child and her cute little ones take care of everything and everyone. It was Calliope who saw to it that her son grew up knowing the limits of the employer's house and the servants' quarters. With her practical and objective way of seeing life, she knew that it was no use harboring illusions: she and her son were slaves.

Being a mother was a joy in her life that she didn't expect. She was simply in love with the boy. In the first few months of his life, she had been a little distressed, because she thought he was too small. But the other maids soothed her, saying it was just like that. As he grew and grew stronger, his afflictions passed. She looked at him all the time, as if she were seeing a miracle. Each smile of his, each attempt to speak, each new gesture, put a light in Calliope's eyes that didn't exist before.

The experience of seeing her belly grow with a new human being forming inside had given Calliope the opportunity to observe and learn more about pregnancy. Then, with her little boy in her arms, night and day, she also learned about children, their peculiarities, their fragility and also their ease in recovering. And soon the mothers of Athens turned to that girl who was already used to tending to various patients, citizens and slaves, rich and poor, old and young, men and women. Now it was almost daily the search for help from Calliope for the little Athenians, from babies to teenage boys and girls. What most impressed Calliope was to see how mothers did not get their children used to healthy eating from an early age, sometimes letting them eat whatever they wanted on their own, thus making them grow without the necessary nutrients and, what is worse, without the habit of eating what could save their lives one day. How the food in the countryside was better! There was never any lack of food, as they planted everything they needed. Neither drought nor war made life difficult for the peasants who, in the absence of grain, due to a whim of Demeter, the goddess of the fertility of the land, had the resource of always easy hunting. No wonder the country people had the fame they had! Of course, they were averse to the city, which robbed men of their time and health, without giving them peace and tranquility in return for their hearts!

So children flocked to Calliope like horse-drawn carriages in sporting competitions, and it was a stomachache here, an unexplained fever there, an earache there, a little bruised foot further on, a broken arm further on. In the beginning, Calliope felt sorry for each one of the little ones that appeared in the arms of the mother or nurse, their little eyes filled with tears or else dimmed with weakness. But little by little, she learned that sympathy not only did not help with the cure, but also hindered his contact with the little patient: all sick people need to know that their doctor has, first of all, control of himself, and that he is capable of analyzing the case coldly, in order to better be able to direct your thoughts towards the solution for each case. And even children have this instinctive perception.

When she wasn't attending to a sick person or taking down Fócion's speeches and messages, Calliope would stay with her little Demetrios – Dimitriki, as she affectionately called him, and everyone started to call him too – watching him grow and gain weight, and begin to walk and wanting to talk.

Pan was on his way back to the hostel where he slept on winter nights when he saw Calliope pass by, carrying the boy in her arms.

"But... if it is not the little Calliope, daughter of Ganymede... the one who dressed as Athena..."

He had just received some change from Theo a day or two earlier. He knew the family of Ganymede – as, moreover, he knew the entire population. I saw the boy quite often, but it had been a long time since I saw Calliope. And now she appeared with a child in her arms! How many things he was not aware of! Also, the girl had not appeared for a long time now. Was it really her?"

Pan no longer had the same memory as before. In his late 70s, not even he knew how he survived all those winters, living on the streets, living on alms. No, it was her yes. It's just that he has not seen her in a while, that's all. And Theo, too, had his right days to show up. I would inform both and put them in contact.

But that was an exceptionally cold night. And Pan stopped on the way, feeling great pain in his mangled limbs. No longer able to drag himself to the hostel, he ended up spending the night in the street, hungry, covering himself with some rags. And he dawned dead.

Chapter X
Apollo – god of poetry, music, sports, hunting, and the art of healing

"Calliope! The boss is calling you, inside! Let me watch over Dimitriki!"

All the women liked the boy, now almost three years old.

"Sir... Did you send for me?"

"Yes my dear. Here is someone who came especially to meet you!" said Phocion, having beside him a very dignified man that Calliope had never seen.

"What a joy to meet you," said the man, bowing his head a little. "I found out about you just yesterday, at the Market. I hear you excel at curing the sick! Children especially!"

"Calliope, come closer to us. This is Hippocrates. He came to meet and talk to you."

Calliope feels her face turn red.

"Meet me, sir!"

Everyone in Athens knew this famous doctor, who used to travel around the Hellenic cities, helping people while teaching and learning even more.

"I was interested in you when I heard the things said in the city" continues the doctor. "It seemed to me that we have similar methods of treating the sick."

Calliope didn't know what to say. She was still amazed to hear that notorious citizen tearing up the praise for her.

"Sir, I just follow my instinct and observation."

"Well, it's the way you start, my dear... And that should never be put aside..."

"I'm actually just collecting information here and there, watching people, their reactions, their food."

"Ah, the food! Yes, we really agree on this point and certainly on so many others!"

"Sir, what do I know..."

"Calliope, I am organizing in Cos, the island where I live, at the medical school, a study group to teach what I know to those who want to learn, and also to study health issues even more deeply... I want to spread this one study, expand the number of men – and women – able to help other people recover from their bodily ailments. Would you like to spend a few months with us there?"

Calliope widens her eyes. She could never have expected a proposal like this. Get out of Athens, discover an island! Learn from this master, who had revolutionized the entire study of medicine, making it an organized science! To be admitted to a circle where practically no woman had ever entered! She didn't know what to say. Phocion, who had left the room, returns just as his jaw has just dropped.

"I think you already told her," he said, as he knew beforehand the proposal that would be made.

"Sir..."

"Much joy would bring me if you joined our group."

Calliope looks at Phocion.

"Well, as for me..." he said, "I'm happy and proud - I'm not the one who has to decide, honey..."

"But, sir, I'm your maid..."

"But it's not your service I'll miss while you are away, but the company, the intelligence, the candor! Not to mention these pains in my knees, which only you can treat with your clay compresses!

"Want to go? " Asks the doctor, anxious for the answer. "It will only be a few months. Then you go back to tending Phocion's knees."

"But what about my little boy?"

"Well, he's coming too, of course! The island air will do him a lot of good!" he continues, realizing that she would finally acquiesce. "Have you ever been outside Athens? Get to know the most beautiful island in the Dodecanese! A huge floating garden! My family will be delighted to meet you!"

She smiles, imagining all that, hardly believing what she heard, the opportunity that was opening up for her, everything she could learn, the joy of little Demetrios, how life could bring surprises, bad and good too.

Calliope and Dimitriki were out of Athens just when the reaction of the aristocrats, who, for a short period, imposed their government of four hundred members on the people, trying to assert their views above all in relation to the war against Sparta, which they always opposed. But the army, occupying the island of Samos, managed to put the Democrats back in power, choosing Alcibiades as its leader. Alcibiades who, at the age of thirty-nine, had seen and done everything in his life. Four years earlier, he had fled because of the scandal at Hermas and, again, sentenced to death for such sacrilege, had joined the Spartans in the Peloponnese and had even seduced the wife of Agis, the king of Sparta, later falling under the suspicion of the Spartans when they were defeated at Miletus, going then to try to negotiate peace between Athens and the Persians. He didn't seem to get tired. Now he was back again at the highest point of the Athenian army.

But Calliope and her little son saw nothing of these things. They spent almost a year on the beautiful island of Cos.

There, she could learn even more about people's birth, life, health, and death. She couldn't spend full time at school, as she had little Dimitriki to look after, and she was so happily received by the family of Hippocrates, with whom she stayed during her time on the island, that they didn't want to let her leave the house. But she helped the master by taking care of the sick. She heard explanations and theories from various students everywhere. She made several notes to Hippocrates, who dictated to her a series of actual treatises, of which she made some copies for herself. She studied plants and foods. She accompanied the group in studies carried out directly on the bodies of the sick – and sometimes on the bodies of the dead. Learned more about bones and joints; she took a liver in her hands; she saw lungs and even a heart. She got used to seeing a lot of blood. She studied urine and feces. She often left the study room to vomit – but she could not be accused of female frailty, as she was not the only one to have such a reaction.

The other students were astonished to see this girl so well versed in subjects they themselves knew very vaguely. She talked to them about those new religious theories, those alternative rebel

groups who disowned the religion of the gods—things she still remembered from the time when the late Cassandro had immersed
himself in the question of soul salvation. For them, it was unprecedented to have a woman in the group, and still bringing coherent
and well-exposed points of view about life and about such profound things. One or another guy fell in love with her. But Calliope had no eyes for any of them. Her little boy, and that world of
information and study, took up her time entirely. Hippocrates'
family provided her with the affection and companionship his affable nature required. And the doctor's wife, who had her two teenage boys, Thessalus and Draco, and her daughter already getting
married, found in Calliope in those months an inseparable friend.

By the time she returned, however, she had already missed
Athens very much – it almost ached in her chest to see the Market
again, its colors, its bustle, its people, the temples, the squares, the
Parthenon. And it was with a hug party that she and Dimitriki
were welcomed by friends and friends at Fócion's house, who, with
tears in his eyes when he saw her, said that his knees would not
bear another minute of pain. The only one with a frown was Tartaros, the foreman, whom the popularity of that slave – first with the
master, then with the other servants, then throughout the city of
Athens, and now even on the islands – always exasperated to an
unbearable limit.

It was a feast day in Athens. All the people had come to the
streets to celebrate the victory of Alcibiades, the great general, who
had made his triumphant entry into the city after the successes at
Cyzicus and Byzantium. Great victories always lifted the spirits of
the Athenians, who were always ready to leave whatever they were
doing to go celebrate great deeds and honor the gods. Nobody noticed that the weather was cloudy and rainy, and that otherwise,
the day would even be considered sad. Only Calliope lived a day of
sadness – the greatest sadness of her life – and it wasn't the rain
that blackened her soul.

She was going about his business when he heard the foreman
calling her name, in his usual gruff voice.

"Yes? You called me?" She asked, getting up.

"Go prepare your son, I'm taking him."

"Taking him? Where?

"He was sold; and don't ask me any more questions. Go prepare it as I said, and bring me the boy, the buyer is waiting."

"And I? Will I go with you?"

"No of course not! Only he was sold!"

Her heart stops beating, her vision blurs, and the ground opens up under Calliope's feet. She wanted to think that the foreman was joking with her, but realizes it was true when she saw the maids who were close by immediately surrounding her, their eyes bulging, waiting for her reaction, which they knew would be heavy and painful. Calliope puts her hand over her mouth, feels nauseous and her knees bend. A slave holds her and leads her to a chair, while another runs to fetch a glass of water.

"Calm down, my dear" said the one who was supporting her.

"This is normal to happen, dear. We all know, don't we? You yourself already knew…" says the oldest one, maternally.

"It's just that no one is ever prepared for this... – said another.

"This foreman doesn't deceive me…" said yet another.

"Drink this, come on. Breathe deeply."

"Dimitriki…"

"They're bringing the boy."

Calliope could barely speak. She wanted to react and scream, she wanted to get up and go punch the foreman, she wanted to take her son and run away with him, she wanted to die right there. But she knew the slaves were right. This was the fate and fate of slaves: they had no control over their lives, nor the lives of their children. It would do no good to rebel. When the boy is brought in, she looks at him and hugs him, her eyes full of tears, kissing his little face, telling him she loves him, trying to explain that he would be taken away from her, trying to give advice, arranging the strength to ask him never to forget about your little mother, that she would never stop thinking about him for a minute, the world collapsing in her heart as she watched him walk away with his foreman.

Praying to the goddesses Hestia and Athena to protect her little son, Calliope sees the foreman catch Dimitriki, leading him out of the house, and her legs refuse to hold the weight of her body. She felt that not only was she inert and unresponsive, but that she was going to collapse right there. Suddenly, however, an idea strikes her in the midst of her despair and, overcoming the stupor that took hold of her movements and thoughts, taking a decision, she turns to the slave who was at her side:

"Nikippa, help me quickly to get ready, to look beautiful!"

"But where are you going?"

"Help me, my friend, I'm seeing my life come to an end."

The city was still partying, but Calliope was unaware of the riots and singing. The enthusiasm of the people was indifferent to her Groomed like a rich lady, her face lightly painted, her hair tied back and decorated with a blue ribbon, a belt in the same color marking her waist, outlining her thin silhouette, a little perfume following her movements, she walks at a step one so hurried – the only sign of her distress – as she struggled to maintain her usual elegance. She finally arrives at the point in the city where she had already been years before, where the richest residences were located. She was going to talk to Alcibiades, the great general.

More than seven years had passed since she had been here, at his house, still wearing the robes of Pallas Athena. Would he remember her?

"But what do you want?" Asked an employee who was at the door, taking care of visitors.

"I would like to be received by Mr. Alcibiades."

"This is good! As if he was going to receive everyone who wants to talk to him!"

"Please say it's Calliope, by Mr. Fócion; he knows who I am..."

"Look, ma'am, I can't bother the general..."

"I beg you, please. Tell him Calliope is here..."

Faced with the woman's distress, the servant goes inside, at least with some intention of talking about her to the general. To his surprise, however, he jumped up from his chair when he heard her name, and sent for her immediately.

"Calliope" thinks Alcibiades, his heart pounding as he waits. "How long...".

He is thus absorbed, looking at the courtyard where a light rain is falling again, a series of memories coming to his mind and taking the place of all the most recent events – the battles, the victories, the recognition of the Athenians, the prestige – when he hears a voice behind him:

"Sir..."

"Athena ..." he says, turning and seeing before him a Calliope even more beautiful than any of his memories.

"Sir..." She lowers her head, unable to control the tears and the lump in her throat. He soon realizes that something isn't right with her.

"What happened? What's wrong with you?" he asks, approaching, using the tenderest voice he can manage, after so many months used to shouting at soldiers, as well as the absence of delicate women.

"I have a son... a little boy... Dimitriki..." and the tears begin to fall, at the same time she tries to find strength in the midst of the pain to finally explain why she came to him, finally there in the house of the general giving in to despair, talking in spurts, between crying and sobbing, one sentence after another, without pausing for breath – "He's six years old, and the foreman sold him... the foreman sold him, now they just took him I don't know where they took my son! They sold my son! Help me please! I want my child! Only you can help me! Bring me back my son! Because I'm going to die!"

"A son? But...". Alcibiades was confused, faced with Calliope's anguish, and also with the news of this son he didn't know. Was it his? He asks himself, stunned, forgetting all past events, still overwhelmed by the thrill of having her there, so close to him again. "But we don't... we don't even...". No, the boy was not his; he remembered well now – what had not happened.

"But how, sold? Did the foreman do this? And was Phocion consulted?"

"Phocion isn't in town... Help me..." Stopping crying, she recomposes her face and her voice. "Sir... I know I have no right to be here asking for this... I beg your help... I'm willing... for anything..."

The allusion was clear to what had passed between them. An employee enters, interrupting:

"Sir, there are some gentlemen from the Council."

"I can not now; I'm taking care of an important matter. Let them come back another time; maybe tomorrow! Don't interrupt me anymore!" and turning to Callíope, returning to the soft tone and voice, "Do you know where they went with the boy?"

"I think for the market."

"Arato! Run here! Quickly! Quickly!! Don't be slow!" He shouts, calling the servant, now again with the same haste from the battlefield. "Gather two more, three, as many men as possible; call some guards, go to the market and Phocion's house. Try to find out about the sale of a slave boy of about six years old, called Demetrios, from Phocion's house. Say that I oppose this sale, that you bring the buyer to me so that I can undo the deal. Run! Is it urgent!"

When the men leave, Alcibiades sends for an amphora of wine and goblets. Calliope was going to deny it, as she rarely drank, but she is already starting to say "yes", as part of the deal. Alcibiades, moreover, immediately notices this attitude.

"It's not to get you drunk, it's to calm you down a little, just a little sip, let's go..." His voice is calm again. – "Let's wait for them to come back..."

"Thanks."

"Callíope, I want to tell you that when you said you would do anything..."

"Yes it's true."

"Let me talk..."

"Sir..." Callíope begins speaking slowly, but goes on growing, with emotion—"If anything happens to me, I don't care. Isn't that what we're subjected to, women? So, throughout my life, I was deprived of my opinion, my will, my family; that I have to lie down on men's beds according to the order and convenience of others; to work on whatever it is; let them hear what they want their ears to hear; that they make me speak or be silent according to the will of others, that they do what they want of me, but that they don't take my son away from me! Don't take my son away from me!"

"Callíope... let me talk... calm down... don't cry... I want you to know, that you don't have to, you don't even have to think that I want you... I want you to know... .that I don't expect any "favors" from you. That all I want is to see your eyes dry and your face smile again. Don't even think about it, then. You can rest easy. I'll never touch you, if you don't want to..."

They stayed like that, in silence, for what seemed like hours to Calliope. Sitting on a chair, her back straight, not touching the back, her knees together, her hands in her lap, she stared at the floor without seeing him, her head spinning. Only the noise of the fine rain filled the emptiness. Alcibiades watched her, noticing that she felt bad, seeing in her eyes, when she caught a glimpse of them, that they glowed too much, and that her face was red. Going to her, who did not repel him, perhaps not even noticing his proximity, he felt with the palm of his hand that she was burning with fever. Then he went to his rooms, and brought her his himation - the mantle with which he had entered the city, under the praises of the people - placing it on Calliope's shoulders, as he had done with his himation, years before, at the symposium na Phocion's house when he first saw her.

It took the men a good two or three hours to return, and by the time they did, Calliope had calmed down a little.

"And then? What news do you bring me?" Asked the general.

"We're sorry, sir."

"Ah..." Calliope sits down again.

"Like this? Sorry for what?"

"We went to the market and got informed; we also went to Fócion's house, we spoke with the foreman. We asked around the city."

"And then? Speak up faster!"

"The merchant has already left town, and the buyer is unknown; we inquired about all the houses, to find out which ones had purchased slaves. Nobody knew, nobody could inform. We learned that some outside buyers had been shopping, but we looked in taverns and hostels. Nothing. It must be gone by now. Nobody knows anything.

Callíope started to cry again.

"Incompetent! Get out of my way! Get lost! You don't work for me anymore! Outside! Already!"

The great general had been unable to do anything, and Calliope rose to leave as well.

"I'll accompany you..." he said turning to Calliope, vexed by the failure of his orders.

"No, no, I'm on my way, no... I'm leaving." She stands up, wanting to take off her cloak, but Alcibiades forces her to keep it.

She leaves then without even saying goodbye, disoriented, having lost track of where she was and not knowing where she was going.

At nightfall, she walks without seeing, her whole body wanting to succumb, her internal organs refusing to function. Among all the things she had gone through in her life – the struggle to get pregnant; the deaths of his brother, in the war, of his mother-in-law, to illness, of Cassandro, full of anguish; the dismay in her father's eyes when she was gone as a slave; the separation from her loved ones – this was, without a doubt, the greatest pain she had ever felt, which she could not understand and had no strength to bear. In vain she seeks to pray a prayer to the gods, through whose representations she passes along the way. None of them could offer her comfort, give her an answer, show her a light. They were, after all, just frozen statues in the face of facts and their pain. At the crossroads of her feelings, Calliope brought her orphaned soul.

At a distance, Alcibiades sees her entering Phocion's house. He had followed the girl from afar, so as not to disturb her, and to make sure she got home safely in the darkness of that hideous night, and his eyes fill with tears as he sees her closing the door behind her. He had cried before, in his life. But this was the first time he had done it for someone else's suffering, not for his own. On his own, he felt only contempt at that moment, at the futility of his power to help this woman he had not ceased to love, in contrast to the recent victories of the Athenian army under his command. Meager victories, he saw them now, still being celebrated all over the city, on that sinister and unfortunate rainy day.

"How sad is this life... If it's not the war, it's the money that brings our children..." said one of the slaves, hugging Calliope who, mute, sat on the floor in her cubicle, leaning against the wall , arms around the knees. The other slaves, next door, don't know what to say.

"Tartars – said one of them at last – he never forgot that symposium, in which he got that violent scolding from his boss, in front of everyone, because of Calliope."

When Phocion returned and learned of what had happened, he dismissed the foreman summarily, filled with an unspeakable rage, screaming and cursing, hiring another man to take his place. And ever since, he's been feeling sorely missed by Calliope, because in addition to not having been able to avoid selling the boy, he now saw his maid, for whom he had so much affection, go into a kind of torpor, speechless, the absent spirit, the look distant, always mute and inert in a corner, life passing her by, she indifferent to life, life indifferent to her. Everyone tried to spare her, but actually they knew that what she was living was hell on earth, it was the god Hades bringing her and imposing on her the world of darkness, in full life."

"Come, Callíope, come help me prepare this salad, come on, dear" calls one of the slaves, trying to distract her a little.

Little by little, she started to talk again, and people were able to talk to her, just one sentence or another, trying to console her, showing that life, finally, had to go on.

"That..." Phocion told her one day, trying to console her, "would be a natural path... I know that for a mother it is always difficult to accept, but you see, even in the richest families, boys leave home and they are separated from their mothers, going to study in gyms, preparing for life, then going to war... One thing you can know, honey: he won't be mistreated. He will be learning a trade. If he drew on his father's skill and his mother's intelligence, he will be a great professional!"

After a few weeks, Calliope was slowly recovering her will to live. The words of affection and encouragement that everyone addressed to her – especially the slaves, who one day, years and years before, had treated her with such hostility, but who now loved her so well – ended up making her see that, of In fact, life went on.

Without ever mentioning her pain or remembering the episode of her son's farewell, she was adapting that blow to her daily life, fitting those memories into the compartment of her mind that joined her heart. She raised his face bravely, struggling to silently accept what life had in store for her.

Phocion has finished eating a frugal lunch when the new foreman comes to announce a visit.

Phocion was used to receiving visitors. Many people came to talk to him, with all kinds of situations, problems, complaints. He received them all. He listened to them. He understood them, or at least he strove to do so. Today, however, the visit affected him personally.

Alone and thoughtful, then, after that person has left, he finally calls the foreman, who is waiting at the door of the room.

"Well, bring Calliope here, so I can talk to her."

It was an afternoon like any other – with no new facts to stir the people, who, by the way, seemed to be taking their siesta, so calm and silent was the air throughout the city.

"Did you call me?"

"Yes, daughter. We need to talk. Sit here."

"They sit side by side on a couch."

"You know that since you arrived at my house, years ago, I took for you an affection like a daughter. And you also know how I blame and suffer with you for what happened."

"Sir… it wasn't your fault."

"Anyway, all these years you have been here occupying a fundamental position in my house, in my life. There were countless occasions that I counted on you and I had your help in things that were very important to me... Several were the times when you alerted me and opened my eyes to facts and details that I would not have noticed."

"Calliope did not understand where he was going."

"For these reasons, as well as for your delicacy, your education, your gentleness, it is that all this time it has never crossed my mind to deprive myself of you... you are part of this house, this family... Knowledgeable of your history , I know well of everything that goes on in your heart, of the difficult times that you have already gone through and are still going through... That's why I would never imagine seeing you far away from here."

Overcome with emotion, Phocion, for the first time in his life, had difficulty in exposing his own thoughts.

"But I want you well, and I know what is best for you. So, I authorized it and I have just completed your sale."

Calliope's jaw drops.

"I would never do that, were it not for the circumstances."

"But, sir, I don't..."

"I know, honey, I know... But believe me... I know you, and what's best for you..."

"I really have to go...?"

"A man came by and wanted to buy you, he's taking her out of town. I think the change of air will do you good."

"Sir..."

"I'm sure what I did, honey... Go... Get your things... and go..."

"I'm going to miss it here..." she says, looking lost.

"I'll miss you too, my daughter... But I want the best for you..."

"After saying goodbye to her friends – so many real friends she had made among the slaves! – Calliope picked up a package where she had put her things, and went out of the house, saying goodbye to every corner, every piece of furniture, every memory, looking back, keeping everything in her memory, a feeling of emptiness taking hold of her. Another painful farewell in her life that she would have to carry in her heart. With the sunny daylight momentarily blinding her, she arrived at the door where a carriage waits, and the foreman points out her buyer. Calliope at first does not distinguish that silhouette. But he finally manages to identify it, and her heart leaps inside his chest. It was Theodoros.

For a moment the two look at each other in disbelief, just a few feet away from each other. He smiles at her with those eyes in which, even from a distance, Callíope sees her own reflection, as she always had, as she had never seen herself in anyone else's eyes. And a small smile begins to play on her saddened lips.

She looks back and sees Phocion at the door, who has come to accompany her.

"You didn't think I'd let her go with just anyone, did you?" he said, smiling, his eyes full of tears.

Calliope runs to Theo, and throws herself into his arms, emotion preventing her from speaking.

"Theo... Theo... They took my son, Theo... They took my little son...' she says, finding her voice through her sobs, finally letting out all the pain that was embedded in her soul."

"Let's go?" He gives her his hand, to help her.

Climbing into the carriage beside Theo, Calliope can hardly believe she'll see her father and mother again. Seeing Theo had already been a surprise and a thrill that had brought so much joy back to her heart. Theo's familiar face. His gaze, his gestures, his voice that she had so long thought she would never hear again. At thirty-four, like her, apart from a few gray hairs at the temples, he was still the same Theo who had hugged her that fateful rainy day in the tower.

Beyond the city walls, on her way to the lands of Ganymede, after telling her all about the sale of little Demetrios and some things that had happened to her over the years, she notices the road, smooth as a carpet.

"And where are the holes of the father?"

"They disappeared, little by little..."

"How is everyone at home, Theo? The father? The mother? Lypso?"

Calliope didn't know where to start her questions. She still didn't believe what was happening. Her joy in returning home was immense, it was like a dream, she still couldn't figure out that she was really there with Theo, and that she was returning to her parents, back to her childhood home, to her roots. Although she hadn't been mistreated in those years of slavery, it was actually like a long, bad dream coming to an end.

"Mom and Dad won't believe their eyes when they see you... They can't even imagine..."

"How are they? And Lypso?"

Theo gets serious.

"Calypso... Calypso died, Calliope..."

The smile faded from her face.

"That day," he continues. – On that damn day, she was the only one who managed to keep better... Because her father and mother were very bad... I didn't help much either... She held us all, she was the one who took care of the house for several days... So I went back to work, and she continued alone with the chores until the mother got better, started talking and everything... The mother got better little by little... And then, about two months after that you went, Lypso fell sick again, same thing she had, remember? But much worse... And in three days she died..."

"Lypso!"

"I think she died of grief."

"And the father?"

Theo lowers his face.

"The papa was very bad, Callíope... Very bad. He stopped talking."

"... Like this... ? He got quiet?"

"Spoke a word or another.... Remember when the wheat harvest was taken, in the Market? I saw that in those days the father was very dejected... Too dejected... He wasn't well anymore... When the banker's agent came that day, he couldn't react because he couldn't think straight. And after you left, since that very day, he... he hardly said anything else..."

Theo's voice chokes and his eyes water. It was very difficult for him to talk about the illness of his father, whom he loved so much.

"I tried everything" he continued, "But he didn't react... He stood there all day looking out the window, not talking to anyone, and sometimes it seemed like he wasn't even able to see... He never went to town again... Nor he would get out of that chair... At night, if we didn't take him, he wouldn't go to bed. He lay there, inert, the only movement we saw him having was shaking his head, as if in disbelief. It seemed... like it had slipped into itself... I took care of the land as best I could, Calliope... I wanted him to come to town to talk to someone, about you, about the banker, because I thought that that loan story, the mortgage story, hadn't been true. I even tried to talk to some people, but no one listens to a slave. And with the sick father, nothing could be done. Neither the mother nor I could do anything, she as a woman, I as an ex-slave... Our hands were tied..Because only he has decision-making power...

"Is he better now?"

"Almost nothing... The first two years without you were the worst. And as much as I looked, I hadn't heard of you... Until that day of the party. The Panateneas..."

"You were there?!" she was surprised.

"I was, and I saw you, and I found out where you lived..." he continues, getting happy. "When I told Father and Mother that I had seen you, and how beautiful you looked in Palas Athena, that everyone was looking at you with their jaws dropped, that you were the success of the procession, he smiled for the first time in so long."

"But then, did you find out where I lived?"

"I did, and I went there whenever I came to town, to try to see you, talk to you, and buy you back, but that foreman..."

"Tartars..." Calliope frowns again, full of pain, thinking of Demetrios.

"That... He always kept me from seeing you. I tried to talk to the guards to help me, but Tartaros also talked to them, told them that I was some bandit, that I was putting that family in danger, and so I couldn't even go near the house anymore... I tried at the door of the Pnix, on Assembly days, but no one ever listened to me, they always said that the father should come and talk to them, that my word was worthless. Same thing in tholos, trying to talk to some pritane. That's how it was all these years. But I never gave up... Until today, without waiting for this to happen... It was another foreman... And he soon told me to wait, that he was going to talk to the boss. And it was like this..."

"Theo..."

"Yes?"

"Thanks..."

"Not..."

"Thank you, thank you, thank you very, very much..." she repeats, her eyes filling with tears.

Continuing the journey in silence, Calliope thinks about her son again, and finally, after so many sleepless nights, she is taken by sleep, managing to fall asleep, her head resting on Theo's shoulder – just like him one day, daydreaming, carrying. back to Cassandro's house, he had imagined her doing. He wanted to finally feel the intensity of affection between them, her leaning against him. But Calliope's sadness prevented him from savoring that moment.

When they reached the foot of the slope, Calliope and Theo climbed out of the carriage to go up on foot, as she had always done, every time she returned home as a child. What a sight, that landscape in front of her again, like a picture that had never been hung from the wall of her memory! So from a distance, at the moment they arrived, the house seemed empty and silent, no one could be seen around. No one had come to look out the window, attracted by the noise of the carriage. The two enter and go straight to the kitchen – that same kitchen where, thirty years before, Theo had entered, led by Ganymede's hand – and where Iphigenia was now preparing a dish, with Ganymede sitting quietly beside her. And their hearts come to their mouths when they look up and see Calliope, standing at the door, looking at them, as if in an incantation. Iphigenia, changed with emotion and disbelief, brings her hands to her face, holding back the tears, and finally stretches them out, taking her daughter in her arms.

"Mom! Papa!"

"Calliope... Calliope...."

The light returned to Ganymede's eyes, along with the tears, looking at her daughter in disbelief, reaching out to take her who, also moved, smiles without being able to speak.

The three cry, embracing, standing, shaken by sobs, while Ganymede gently strokes Calliope's hair.

"Calliope... My little daughter, my little daughter, you're back!"

It was the first full sentence he'd spoken in over eight years.

Calliope had woken up that morning after sleeping for many hours, regaining sleep and health in her girl's room. Iphigenia was waiting for her with cakes and cheeses in the kitchen, tidying the house and talking nonstop about her daughter to the maids who didn't know her.

"Good morning mom!"

"Good morning, my dear! How did you sleep? Come eat!"

"And the father?"

Iphigenia opens a smile:

"He snored all night, in a good, heavy sleep like I hadn't seen for a long time! Woke up and asked about you; baby, I was so thrilled! He, who no longer spoke! It had been a long time since we heard his voice like that! When I said you were sleeping, he told us to be silent so as not to wake you up, he ate with a lot of appetite and went to sleep himself some more!" her eyes fill with tears.

"Good, mom! Appetite is the best sign of health!"

"I agree, my dear!"

"And Theo?"

"He left early…"

"What a thing! He remains the same! I can't say good morning to him!"

"He said he had to go back to the city, because many things he had gone to do yesterday were not done; I even said that maybe it will take many days, that we shouldn't worry! He takes care of everything here on the land, my dear."

Iphigenia looked at her daughter's face as if not believing she was at her side again. All those years she'd spent her days struggling with homesickness and despair, working her own thoughts so as not to make things worse at home with Ganymede, whose apathy was then her and Theo's greatest concern. After eating a little, the two go out for a walk through the gardens and fields, arm in arm, eager to be together and talk about everything that came to them. There were so many things Calliope had to tell her, but most of all, she wanted to tell him about Dimitriki, the little grandson they had and would not see. She wanted to share with his mother the pain that the tragedy of separation between her and her son was causing her. She had avoided going into details the night before, so as not to sadden his parents in that moment of joy that had been his return. And she didn't want to undo the positive effect on Ganymede's health, who had recovered significantly in a few minutes just in the company of his daughter. Calliope had been very sad to hear Theo's account of her father on the way back from Athens.

"Is that what Theo told you?"

"Yes… why do you ask, mother? Didn't things turn out like that?"

"Darling, Theo spared you by telling you things like that… After Calypso died…" Her voice breaks a little.

188

Iphigenia also had many things in her heart that she needed to talk about, to vent to someone.

"Theo, who had been terribly shaken by your departure as a slave" she continues, "resumed her work, drawing strength from within himself, certainly seeing that his father and I still showed no signs of improving. Your father, my dear... Since the death of our Helios, your father was already different... When he seemed to recover, you became widowed... It was difficult for him, at that time; I know him well. Then that... the harvest... do you remember?"

"If I remember..."

"The day he came back from the city and told us about the confiscation, I could tell by his voice that that blow had been very strong, added to the sadness it already brought... And so, you went, Callíope, and he stayed ... very, very sick..."

"Sick how, Mom? Did he have discomfort? Did you feel palpitations? Couldn't walk? What symptoms did he have?"

"None of these, my dear... He, besides not speaking, just a word here and there, would stand still, he sometimes seemed to have lost his mind... Then Theo, in addition to taking everything in the fields under his responsibility , he even took his father to himself... Because his father didn't even want to eat, only Theo could force him, and Theo then got up, as you know, very early, before daylight, went to the countryside, went back to the time for our breakfast, he made the father eat; he went to the country again, but managed to come back two or three more times throughout the day to feed his father. Sometimes Ganymede didn't want to leave at all, turning his face, pressing his lips together, and Theo, with Apollo's patience, fed him in his mouth, his eyes filled with tears, sometimes taking more than two hours to make his own. father eating a small dish. This, every day! Every day, over the years, cold or rainy, Theo came to feed his father in his mouth... He also bathed him, and put him in the carriage to force him out of the house, to walk, to sunbathe, to wander the lands, although Ganymede always seemed to be absent, not even understanding where he was... Sometimes Ganymede got up at night. Theo had already come to sleep at the house, in Helios' room, as you saw. I don't think Theo slept a whole night with good sleep, as he was always

taking care of his father.... And yet, he had everything in the fields
to look at, and he had to go to town, instead of his father...

"He told me he was trying to get someone in town to help
him."

"Yes... But nobody listened to him. They said that he should
bring his father so that they could see him... Several times he wanted to take him there, so that the prítanes could assess him, and they
could take action in your favor, Calliope... But every time the moment arrived, that Theo brought the cart to the door of the house,
his father had the worst reaction possible... He was terrified of the
idea of getting on the cart, he realized when to go into town, and
he was shivering, cold from fear. The servants suggested to Theo
that he force him on, but Theo didn't want to do it, he was very
sorry for his father... The only thing Theo forced was that he eat
well... Calliope... Theo actually carried his father in his arms... He
never let himself be carried away by what some doctors he brought
from the city said, that his father had lost his mind. He never believed in that diagnosis. He said he was sure his father was there,
inside himself. She made him sit beside him at night, and kept telling him about the fields, so that his father wouldn't at least listen,
even though the words didn't seem to make any sense to him.
Sometimes a lump rose in Theo's throat, making his voice trail off
in the middle of a word, and then he couldn't hold back the tears."

Iphigenia had never been a fearless woman, like Calliope, or
some of the women of the city. Like most citizens' wives, she had
not been raised to take the initiative, but to live totally under her
husband's protection and guidance, being able to do nothing but
take care of trivial household chores, out of sight of the world.
When Ganymede had fallen ill and been incapable of any action or
decision, she also seemed incapacitated. She even tried to do something, going into town, talking to someone, finding some solution
for those setbacks that befell his family. But she feared not knowing how to express herself, and she lacked courage and persever-
ance. Theo, too, tried everything he could, but it was too little: he
lacked the necessary legal powers. If they had been able to go together, he and Iphigenia, to the city, perhaps they would have
achieved something. But Ganymede could not be alone without at
least one of them watching: once Theo and his mother were in the

field, looking at some crops, they were hurriedly summoned by the servants and arrived in time to prevent Ganymede from falling from the tower, where he had climbed and sat on the parapet. Since then, they took turns, not letting go of their father for a single minute, afraid of the impulses that his father showed he might have.

"I even went to town twice," said Iphigenia. "I went with another employee, I came close to the house where you... worked. The first time, I didn't have the courage to do anything... And the second time, I went there, but you were out."

"I was probably shopping, Mom..."

"No... You were outside Athens..."

"Ah... it was when I was in Cos for a few months."

"In Kos? What were you doing in Kos?"

"Oh, it's a long story..." Calliope smiles.

Walking through the countryside, Calliope tells all about her experience taking care of the sick, and when she met Hippocrates, and her facility in taking care of children; tells her about that very beautiful island where the famous doctor was opening a school to teach other doctors how to take care of people's health. As she spoke, she looked around, and she couldn't help noticing how different things were in the house and in the fields. Everything looked much more organized; there wasn't a piece of land where a foot of something wasn't planted. The barn was renovated; the domas and lagars, where the grapes and olives were squeezed, were new and seemed to function more efficiently; the house was painted and tidy, with flower pots and a well-kept garden. Iphigenia tells her that it was all the result of Theo's hard and tireless work.

"But what about the money...?" Calliope asked Iphigenia.

"You know that Ganymede was paying Theo since he was eighteen. Not being used to things in the city, not liking to drink, or hanging out with whores, he didn't have much to spend, and he saved the money all these years... He always brought me all the sales results, so I could checked and kept it, and showed me that it was taking his share, in proportion that Ganymede used to pay him.... And so, he was able to go to the city to look for your... boss... to buy you back... These lands prospered, Callíope... After that, with wheat, Theo decided not to take any more chances... He

191

started to increase the planting of olive trees, and so the biggest production today is oil... He continued with wheat and barley, but not enough that, if caught by surprise, we're in a difficult situation again... And he increased the production of goat cheese, you haven't seen it yet! The goats, which you two were so fond of as children! There are so many! He learned how to make this cheese, the one you just ate, and he sells it in town to merchants. The employee says that he goes with him to the Market where women slap each other to buy this cheese first!

Calliope smiles, her eyes watering, thinking about it all, how grateful she was to Theo for everything he had done and was still doing, for that great love he felt for his father and mother, and for being there, next to them, faithful to the family, another member of the family.

Although Calliope was immensely happy to be back at her parents' house, it was very difficult for her to keep that shadow from her eyes, the shadow of the memory of her son Demetrios. She spent most of the time talking to him in her mind: she wrote him imaginary letters, which she sent in the air, looking at the clouds, the birds, the stars, asking them to give her little one those words and give him a kiss. She imagined him sending news too, trying to visualize him well, happy and in good health.

"You look so happy! You are growing, getting stronger!" she told him.

"By enchantment... these words reach you, touch your eyes."

"Mommy loves you, and she's thinking about you right now..."

"Good night, my sweet, sleep well."

As the days went by, she was able to confide his pain to Iphigenia, without masking it, but she tried to avoid his father noticing anything, since he showed signs of being in full recovery. Ganymede, however, though physically weakened, was not – nor had he ever been – deaf or feeble. His apparently sleeping soul was still inside, all those years, and that light that was missing in her daughter's eyes did not go unnoticed.

"Is it common for Theo to be away like this for so many days?" Calliope asked her parents, one afternoon after eating, sitting together in the living room, talking.

It was a lazy afternoon, the women had worked in the kitchen more than usual, and the heat had made them even more tired. A certain numbness took over everyone, and the silence around them invited a rest, a quiet conversation.

Iphigenia, in a chair next to Ganymede's, was sewing the hem of a chiton.

"He always has a lot to do, in the city…" she answered.

"But there it is already more than seven days."

"It's true, he's never been away like that, more than a day or two…"

"Don't worry…" said Ganymede.

The two women had already gotten used to the fact that their father was improving, and they no longer jumped for joy, as in the early days, making a fuss every time he said something, demonstrating that his reasoning and ability to articulate sentences returned to normal. Calliope had instructed her mother and employees to have an attitude of complete naturalness about this.

"You're right, Ganymede… There are several people he has to talk to there.'

"The loquats have begun to sprout, mother," Callíope said, remembering seeing the trees laden with fruit that morning. – "Shall we make jams like before?"

"Yes! I've already warned the girls to prepare the pots, because we haven't had any fruit wasted! All are picked and given to the candy, we are left with pots that never run out!"

"I heard a carriage noise" Ganymede gets up, going to the window.

"It's Theo, after all," said Iphigenia, getting up too, looking outside.

Below, at the foot, the carriage was climbing, carrying Theo and Stratos, the servant who had accompanied him.

"But who's with him?" Ganymede asks, squinting to see better.

"Stratos, who went with him," Calliope said, sitting up, yawning.

"No… It's true… There is someone else, yes…" said Iphigenia.

"It looks… like a child…" Ganymede completes.

Calliope felt the hairs on her arms stand up as she got up, in a split second, to look out the window. And her heart missed a beat. Getting down from the carriage, beside Theo, still below, there was no doubt, it wasn't a dream, it wasn't a mirage. There he was, himself, her little Demetrius.

"Dimitriki!" his voice comes out in falsetto.

And she ran out the door, runing out of the house, her heart beating as if to get out of her chest, thoughts racing inside her head, in stark contrast to the time, for it seemed to her that everything she went slower, her movements and steps too slow, the space and seconds that separated her from little Demetrios not wanting to finish anymore.

"Dimitriki!"

Stumbling over the chiton, her hair coming loose, tears running down her face, tumbling down the path to the carriage, she sees the little one come running too, her eyes not believing what they saw, the world spinning around her.

"Dimitriki! Dimitriki!"

"Mommy!"

The sun, the house, the trees, life, everything seemed suddenly still, nothing really seemed to exist, just her son, little Dimitriki, whom she saw in front of her, as if fallen from the sky.

Barely making it, already losing his balance, Dimitriki running towards her with his arms outstretched, those meters seeming to never end, her son's face appearing sharply, his little eyes and his smile, his child's voice calling for her, even that at last only a step separated her from happiness, and at last she takes him in her arms, twirling him in the air, her baby, her treasure, her life.

"Mommy! Mommy!"

"Dimitriki!"

Filling him with kisses, she puts him down and bends down to look at him, holding his little face in her hands, barely able to see him through her tears, smiling, crying, her heart pounding so hard it hurt.

"Look, Mom! I got this puppy from Theo!" he shows a puppy that came staggering right behind.

Turning, she sees Theo a short distance away, and gets up, running towards him, still overwhelmed by the avalanche of emotion, and drops to her knees at his feet, taking his hand and kissing it over and over, eyes closed and cheeks wet from the tears that wouldn't stop flowing.

"Thank you... Thank you... Thank you..." Her voice couldn't get out.

"Calliope..."

He tried to lift her by the shoulders, but she didn't want to get up or let go of his hand, which keeps kissing, out of control with crying. Then he kneels down too, hugging her, and Dimitriki comes with the two of them, standing, wrapping them in his little arms, in a long, tight hug, the little dog twirling around them, running, jumping, wagging its tail.

And at that moment, with the tears taking away all the rest of the pain he had in his soul, Ganymede recovered completely his perfect health and, together with Iphigenia, watching the scene through the window, seeing his grandson for the first time, mute with emotion and inert of happiness, the two old people were born again.

Chapter XI
Aphrodite – goddess of beauty and love.

"Grandma! Grandfather!"

That was it all day.

On the day Theo brought Dimitriki back, letting go of each other's arms, Calliope's convulsive tears having ceased, she soon wrapped her arms around her son again to carry him to his grandparents while the boy talked nonstop about the trip, about the puppy, about Theo, whom he had adored, right from the start. When they entered the house, Dimitriki, running, threw himself into Ganymede's lap, who, overcoming the weakness of his seventy years, held him with the strength he felt quickly returning to his limbs. Theo's force-feeding had been worth much more than they'd realized.

And Dimitriki couldn't control the joy of having a grandfather and a grandmother, like the rich kids in town! The affinity between grandparents and grandson was immediate. From early in the morning, he was used to running to Ganymede, pulling him out of the house, jumping into his lap and holding on to his neck, wanting to go walk and run in the garden, the barn, see the animals , getting to know all the employees, listening to the old stories of the grandparents, handling everything and talking non-stop.

"Grandma! What is that?"

"It's the mill, where the grapes are kneaded to make wine."

"Can I see it?"

He kept asking questions, and he wanted to know everything. The family soon realized that they should buy a slave-teacher who would come and teach him how to read, count, add, and everything else. Sometimes he said things that made the whole family and employees laugh, and his success with his audience filled Dimitriki with excitement.

"Well, good night, children!"

"No. It's story time!"

At night, he liked to tell stories to his grandfather. Ganymede would then sit with him on his lap, and listen with interest to the things coming from Dimitriki's imagination, who mixed everything he had seen in his long life, creating characters, inventing places, without being able to put an end to the narratives. Someone had to intervene so that they could finally go to sleep.

"So he boarded the ship and left for good," Calliope was saying, in a book-ending tone, wanting to cut short the night.

"Not! How did he get on the ship?" scolded Dimitriki, "There was no ship!"

"He got on the mule, then! And gone forever."

"But what mule, mother?" Dimitriki laughs, "Where did you find the mule?"

"In the Assembly Council: there you find five hundred mules, all together!" said Ganymede, definitely recovered.

Iphigenia was also swollen with joy. She spent the entire day laughing, cooking, arranging Dimitriki's clothes, preparing his bath, wanting to know from Calliope all the details of his birth, looking and listening to her grandson like a tiny god.

"Mom!"

Calliope often caught Iphigenia in the kitchen in the mid-afternoon, giving Dirnitriki pieces of apple, pear, and almond cake.

"It's just a little piece, Calliope!"

"It's the third one I see!"

"Why, he likes it!"

"And what do you say, Dimitriki... ?"

"Thank you, grandma!" he answers, with his mouth full.

"You're welcome, my treasure!"

But little Demetrios' eyes sparkled even more when he was with Theo. He had a real crush on him. He wanted to imitate him in everything, from gestures to the way he spoke. Of a completely different nature from each other, Dimitriki admired Theo's quiet and gentle stillness. Next to him, he felt the security that every child instinctively senses. Theo would take him around the field, taking him by the hand, and Dimitriki would then let himself be led, trying to be quiet, but finally he was overcome by his own fallacy, and began to tell things, to talk about everything, to ask questions, Theo answered patiently, smiling to himself. In fact, no one was pleased with the boy's conversation more than Theo. In each other's company, silence or conversation was equally pleasurable.

"Theo, how am I going to repay you for everything, everything you did and do for us...?" Calliope asked him one day, watching her parents playing with Dimitriki, sitting on the living room floor, the little dog around them making a party.

In fact, seeing her happy, seeing her there, was everything to Theo.

"Callíope... There is nothing to repay... Because I owe you everything... All my life... To the Papa... To the mother... Lypso... Helios... You ..."

"How am I going to repay you for bringing me back my son?" she continues, seeing herself in his eyes, as she had always seen herself.

Theo had roamed all of Attica in search of Dimitriki.

First he went to the market, in the agora, where he had been able to find little. Then, at Phocion's house, talking to Phocion, to the other servants, and to the new foreman, he managed to find the trail of Tartarus and find out where he was, going to him. Phocion, too, had every interest in finding Dimitriki, and Tartaros as well, for he regretted having fired the foreman without further punishment: if he so wished, he could take more drastic legal action in relation to that vile insubordination. Tartars was well aware of Phocion's fondness for Calliope and the boy, and it would be easy to prove it to the authorities.

Had it not been for his haste and anxiety to find the child, perhaps Theo would have killed him, because it was not without much anger that he encountered Callíope's former foreman. And Tartaros wanted money to pass on the information.

"Listen to me,' Theo said, his voice coming through clenched teeth, leaning Tartarus by the neck against the wall with only one hand, glaring at him with his eyes. – I have a lot of money here, and what I want to know is worth more than all the money in the world, but you're going to tell me right away, without seeing the glint of a single coin, or you're going to tell the magistrates! Choice!

"Well, until..."

"Talk!!"

Anyone would realize that Theo was no joke, and that behind that gentleness there was a bull willing to fight to the death for what he had to defend. Tartarus ended up saying everything. Dimitriki, though not in Athens, had never left Attica.

Theo loosened the hook in Tartarus's neck, letting go and finally turning to walk away, the former foreman catching his breath.

Theo was thoughtful, prudent, quiet and kind. He had a noble and honorable soul. But he was also a human. Of flesh and blood. He also had blood running through his veins. He turned and, in one blow, firm and violent, he landed a blow, a single one, containing all his rage, in the middle of the face of Tartaros, who fell backward like a tree, sprawling to the ground. Theo waited to see if the other was alive, if he wanted more. But seeing him whimpering, unable to get up, he left without having anything else to talk to that unfortunate man.

In a tireless search, he ended up finding the house that Callíope's son had bought, and within five minutes the owners resold it for the high amount Theo had offered. And he would never forget the moment when, next to the boy for the first time, he saw his little eyes sparkle when he told him he was going to go back to his mommy.

"I'm the one who'll always have something to repay, Calliope... Do you remember... I was Dimitriki's age, when Papa Ganymede brought me..." The simple memory of that day moistened her eyes. – I'm the one to thank... I'll always owe everything to your family..."

"Theo, you are family too."

The very hot night had found everyone tired, that weariness that overwhelms people when the heat is excessive, and not a breeze comes to ease the labored breathing, the discomfort in the skin, the heavy limbs, the untimely sleep. Shortly after dinner, Iphigenia and Ganymede went to bed, overcomed by the heat, and even Dimitriki let himself go straight to bed, after a refreshing bath, trying to find an escape from that malaise in sleep. Calliope and Theo were still in the living room, they didn't feel like going to bed so early.

Calliope had completely regained her spirit, spirit and joy. Back at his parents' house, with his son with her, and everyone in good health, nothing weighed on his soul any longer. Talking to Theo, it was as if she had never left that house. For the second time in her life, she felt as if the passing of so many years had been just a dream. Even more beautiful and elegant than ever, dressed in a dark blue one-shoulder tunic trimmed in gold, she played her sitar, gently plucking out a note or two, instantly inventing a melody, while Theo looked through the window, he watched the stillness of the night, the stagnant air, a numbness taking over the life outside.

"Calliope, come see... Come see the sky... it's brighter than I've ever seen it!"

It was one of those very hot nights when the sky is so clear and clear and the moon so big overhead it looks like things were hand-painted, the edges absolutely sharp, the colors strong and deep, under the dark cloak from the sky.

Calliope leaves the zither and goes with him.

"Let's go outside?" he proposes.

Leaving the house, into the garden at the door, the moonlight illuminates their path, tinting the vases, the trees, the tower with silver, towards which they slowly walk, quietly commenting on the beauty of the colors, on the flowers in the pots, the sweet smell of plants filling the air. Under that enchanted moonlight, it seemed to them that the soft notes of Calliope's zither accompanied them, in the perfume of the night, in the delicacy of that moment.

Side by side in the tower, elbows leaning on the wall, looking across the land below, Theo tells about the things in the house, about the changes that had taken place during those years, while Calliope listened, attentive, silent, to the eyes fixed on some gleaming speck.

"Do you remember that garden down there? The one where we used to go play?" he asks.

"Where we were hiding from the mother and Lypso?"

"It's all new, we made a flower bed, with some trees, we placed a bench, with an arch on top, it's all flowers now, I made it thinking of you. You have to see it, Calliope, you'll love it, it was very good."

Calliope watched him, watching his face, a smile on her lips, her head a little tilted.

"You need to go see," he continues, embarrassed.

"Why do I need to go see...?" she says, smiling softly. – I don't need to go there and see... I see everything in your eyes, Theo..."

Speechless, an unheard cold feeling in his stomach, Theo looks at Calliope in front of him, there, so close. In the moonlight, the soft sound of the zither still in his ears, the earth still around him, as if in revelation, he sees himself in her eyes, clear and sharp as a mirror, as he had never seen himself there, or in any another place. And like a powerful and irresistible magnet, their eyes move closer, finally closing, just as their lips touch.

"Calliope..."

He doesn't know what to say. But Calliope is still smiling, with those eyes, and Theo no longer has anything to talk about, or to think, or anything to fear, or doubt. There he was, reflected in her eyes, welcome in her eyes. Wrapping his arms around her slender waist, feeling her arms on his shoulders, and those lips he had dreamed of for twenty years, now he finally tasted them, it was his turn to be born again.

Where had the world gone, that there were only the two of them in that tower? The tower where for years he dreamed of her, alone at the end of a busy day; the tower from which he saw the Spartan, moving menacingly in the distance; the tower where he embraced Calliope, all wet from the rain, on that fateful day, whose night he saw him right there, crying desperately for losing her to the law; the tower from which Ganymede had wanted to throw himself, his soul bewildered; the tower that now witnessed and harbored that kiss...

"Calliope... I... How can I... I'm just a miserable ex-slave, Calliope..."

– Psst! – she gently puts her index finger on his lips. 'Don't ever say that again, Theo... Because you're the most dignified, honorable, bravest, most upstanding man I've ever met. And there is no citizen, no politician, no strategist, no magistrate, no artist, no one, anywhere, that compares to you, that comes to your feet...”

“Papa... I would like to speak with you, if I can...”

“Is there a problem, my son?”

“Papa, I believe so.”

Theo couldn't find the words. Unaccustomed to talking, he found the task ahead difficult. Calliope, who had come along for the conversation, remains silent awaiting the words of the two men.

“Yes?” asks Ganymede.

“Papa...”

“You two want to get married!”

The couple look at each other and smile.

“Wow, father, but how perceptive you are!” Calliope said.

“Insightful? I am an observer, children! Observer! Or do you think I missed the last few days, huh? Theo, by the way, was never strange to me how you felt about my daughter.”

“Papa, forgive me,” Theo says tensely, not knowing what the decision would be.

Ganymede looks over and over, and over and over, respectfully awaiting his words.

“My children... I am very happy to know that you two love each other and would like to get married. But I'm sorry to tell you that, by my plans, you were going to have to get married, even if you didn't love each other!”

Calliope and Theo look at each other, laugh, and hold hands.

You will be my daddy! says Dimitriki, jumping on Theo's lap, beaming with joy at the news.

'And I?” Calliope said, pretending to be jealous of that hug.

Calliope and Theo wanted to tell Dirnitriki right away as soon as they had Ganymede's blessing. They knew he would like the news, but they didn't think he would be the happiest of all. Dimitriki had a real crush on Theo.

Iphigenia, like Ganymede, had already noticed a certain change in the air in those days. Certain lingering glances in a split second or two; an extra little smile after a word; a softer tone of voice than usual. A woman understands these things very well.

Nothing could fill the hearts of Ganymede and Iphigenia more with joy than the union of Calliope and Theo. Life seemed to be reborn in the two old people, who until days before thought they had nothing left in the world, except to wait for death!

Ganymede had taken up the problem of succession, which for all those years had been put aside. If only she could adopt Theo and make him her heir! From a very young age, the boy had won the old people's affection, and now, with all they'd been through together, Theo was truly a son to them. But it was not possible to adopt a non-citizen, even if he was a free man.

The situation required a lot of study, with the advice of a good understanding of the succession issue and the various legal aspects.

By becoming a slave, Calliope had lost her bond with her father. She no longer had a family. It was no longer linked to a man, a citizen - father or husband -, to whom or from whom, intermediately, it passed goods. She could no longer bear children that they inherited from their grandfather. She had regained her freedom, but she had not regained her status as an epiclera – the daughter of the citizen Ganymede. She was just an ex-slave, just like Theo. Calliope was not Ganymede's daughter, and Theo was not a citizen. And the children they had wouldn't be either.

What did the laws say? Could they adopt one or the other after all? Could he test in their favor?

If Calliope could go back to being her epiclera, and Ganymede married her to a citizen, he would inherit from her father-in-law. And he would certainly find on the Pnix several citizens enthusiastic about the idea of marrying his daughter. But Ganymede was not even considering that hypothesis. He loved Calliope and Theo equally. She had seen her daughter suffer a lot; he knew his son's feelings well. Now he thought about their happiness, and he would find a way to achieve it. If the laws barred the way, the laws would have to change! Ganymede felt again all the impetus of a citizen with rights running through his veins. And still, he had in his heart the hideous memory of the moment he had seen Callíope leave as a slave. He wanted to make amends in any way for one of his mistakes that had caused so much pain to so many. He wanted his daughter back, by law.

"Dad… Why don't you go to town and talk to Phocion about it?"

"But, daughter, he is your ex-boss."

"It horrified him to think that Callíope had had a boss."

"Dad, I told you so. I was treated by him like a daughter. I believe he is the man who can help you with the legal answers you are looking for…"

"On here! More to here! Is good! They can stop!"

Ganymede's employees helped with the carts that had arrived, pulled eagerly by several horses, taking them to the place where they had been determined by the master, to unload their heavy load.

"Heads up! Watch out! Can't break!"

Behind the barn, the carpenters who were working a few pieces of wood, making a large table and benches for the banquet, interrupt their hammering to go help lower the large pieces of marble that Ganymede had bought from the Pentelic, the deposit near Athens."

"Is it from that girl, Papa Ganymede?" Asked the sculptor, seeing Calliope descend from another carriage that arrived from the city.

"Get off the marble, Demetrios! Calliope shouts at her son, who has already climbed the huge rock and sits up there, her little legs dangling."

"Yes, hers and my son, too" and he goes to meet his daughter and his wife, to see the day's shopping.

The family went to town almost every day in preparation for the wedding.

Iphigenia had put aside the bad impression she'd always had of the turmoil in Athens and had started to go along with her because, excited, she wanted to help her daughter with shopping, tidying up, ordering, arranging flowers, etc. And they returned home laden with jars of creams, oils and essences; of beads and stones; of fabrics, tassels, braid, fringes and railings, and of all the decorations that abounded in the city, coming from all corners of the earth, sold in the small shops next to Portico Pécilo, whose famous paintings Iphigenia was finally able to appreciate. Calliope liked to try new things, such as sandals with heels, colored powders to change the color of her hair, and sticky masses, which the women were using to pluck the hair from their legs and armpits, in excruciating but painful suffering. lasting effect. All in the name of feminine beauty and vanity.

"Let's go again today!" Calliope said in the morning.

"Yes," replied Theo, already reaching out to hand them more coins.

And at every turn around town, the family would gather in the living room, or in the kitchen, or in Calliope and Dimitriki's bedroom, to see the things they had brought, guessing, admiring everything, extracting from those moments all the joy they contained, finally breathing relieved.

"We brought the fabric for my wedding tunic," Calliope said one afternoon in the tower.

"And is there a problem with it? - Theo asked, noticing a strange tone in the bride's voice.

"It is white. I didn't want to bring it, but papa insisted..."

"And what's the problem with it being white?"

"Don't you think it's wrong for me to get married in white? After all, white is the color of purity, Theo..."

He takes her face in both hands, looking into her eyes.

"If so, Calliope... then there is no white that is white enough for you..."

Ganymede had decided to present the cops with statues as votive offerings, in honor of Athena, for so many favors the family had received, and had hired that sculptor in town, along with Fócion, his new and greatest friend, who thought the idea was very good and took advantage of choosing the artist.

He was one of the assistants of the great sculptor Miron, the one who had made the sculpture of the athlete – the discobolo – with whom he had worked on several of his works and, recommended by the citizens, came to sculpt some statues for Ganymede, in his own house. Ganymede would offer the goddess Athena, in the next Panateneas, the statues of Calliope and Theo, placing them on the Acropolis, next to the Parthenon, where there were already so many marbles and works donated by citizens who, like Ganymede, in this way sought to thank to their goddess. And, excited by the idea, he had also ordered two statues of his children to stay in the house at the entrance. Phocion, fully involved and moved by the latest events in which, alongside Ganymede, he had played a key role, had a statue of Calliope made for him too.

"It's the girl who dressed as Palas Athena!" comments the sculptor who, as an observer, remembered this episode that took place there more than seven years ago.

"Herself," Ganymede replies. – And I've been thinking, what do you think, if her statue is just the costume of the goddess, like in the procession? It's in honor of Athena, after all…"

"I think it's an excellent idea! The helmet, the shield, the armor, the owl! Great! And the boy?"

"The bride and groom were enjoying it too. Theo, though very shy, had opened up his horizons since he'd seen his image in Calliope's eyes, and he'd gladly accepted all that news."

"What do you think, Theo?" Calliope asked, showing the groom the tunics she had chosen. "With which chiton should I pose?"

"I like… this one…" he says, choosing the dark blue tunic, edged with gold, from the moonlit night, in the tower, "Can he get that shade of blue to paint?"

The two had to pose for the sculptor, which made Dimitriki amused. Calliope had a little work, because the boy, around her, took advantage of his mothers temporary stoppage to do his tricks and mischief, and to fill the sculptor with questions.

"Come on, Dimitriki! Come with me to the fields" Theo called him, trying to give the artist and his mother a little peace.

But Dimitriki would not settle down.

"Won't there be a little stone left to make a sculpture of me?"

Theo ended up commissioning a small sculpture of the boy, to adorn the garden he had told Calliope about, the night in the tower when Aphrodite had joined their eyes, lips, and hearts.

Calliope of Acropole, in light blue hoplite outfit, had a sober and elegant bearing, but natural and pleasant. Calliope tried to adopt the same look and posture she had had during the procession, as indicated by the corêgo Danilos. And Theo was serious, serious-looking – he didn't have much patience for posing, but the sculptor, too, found it easier to sculpt him, as the shapes were straighter, the robe falling smooth and heavy to the ground.

The house's Calliope, in the one-shouldered tunic chosen by Theo, smiled and had her head tilted, her body in a certain movement, a little undulation, one leg straight and the other slightly bent at the knee, a tiny foot showing under her bar of the chiton, the slender arms delicately holding a jar. For her, Calliope had to squirm until the sculptor found the position more feminine, lighter, more graceful. The chiton, falling gently in folds, was the artist's most exquisite work. Her fiancé wore the short white tunic, in a more relaxed position, the weight of his body on one leg, demonstrating strength, confidence and sobriety at the same time.

Callíope of Fócion, in Athena's armor, but without her helmet or owl, was smiling placidly, looking to the side, as if satisfied and happy.

But all the Callíopes and all the Theos had in their eyes exactly that same expression, that look, that the sculptor, with the soul and perception that only artists have, managed to capture and transfer to marble, and that would enchant all who would see such sculptures.

Thus, taking them to the Acropolis as a votive offering, Ganymede, overflowing with joy and gratitude, gave the city as a gift that art, those beauties, which represented everything that went on in his heart, which contained so much of his family's history. and, above all, they relied so much on their polis, Athens.

At home, returning from the procession of the Panateneas, Phocion was also as happy as Ganymede. Her Calliope was there, adorning her front door. And he thought of the wedding, the next day, of that girl whom he had taken almost as his own daughter, and whose family now, more than great friends, welcomed him as one of them, filling his heart with new life. He would never forget the paths they had to walk for that marriage to take place. Phocion remembers the day, almost a year ago, when he met Ganymede, shortly after he had delivered Calliope back to Theo.

The family had arrived in Athens shortly after lunch, and they went directly to Phocion's house. Iphigenia hadn't wanted to go: she'd lessened her aversion to riots, but she'd never been one for exaggerating anything. The foreman went to tell Fócion that the family had arrived and would like to speak with him.

"Now! Papa Ganymede! What an honor to finally meet you! But... my eyes deceive me! Dimitriki!"

Phocion did not know the little one had been found. His joy at seeing him again with Calliope was almost equal to that of Ganymede himself."

She had been saying goodbye to a young man she had been talking to, the son of an important family, whom Calliope had seen in the house a few times, and whom she had gone to see one night, two years ago, when he had just turned eighteen. Hastily called, she had found him feeling very ill. It had turned out to be nothing more than an excess of wine: unaccustomed to the drink, the abuse of which was common among friends, he had stumbled back home after a symposium, with Athena revolving around him. Calliope had helped him while he vomited and then made him drink water with a little honey. Since then, he has completely lost his taste for alcohol, and he saw in Calliope, not without a little embarrassment, an accomplice of that night.

"How are you, Calliope? What about you, Dimitriki? – says the young man, playing with the boy.

"We are well, very well!" Calliope smiles. "How about you? How is your family?"

Calliope and Theo did not want to enter, preferring to leave Ganymede and Phocion to talk alone. So they followed Dimitriki through the streets to the Market, accompanied by the boy, whose path was that way too. For the first time, the conversation of someone from the city interests Theo, who is normally so averse to nonsense that the townspeople liked to talk.

"Well, I have to go," said the young man, after spotting a group of citizens in a corner of the agora, surrounding that bearded bald man Theo had spoken to, so many years before, during the Spartan episode. "May things go well for you! Goodbye, Dimitriki! Always obey your mother! And study hard, learn things, and think about them!"

"So they're getting married!" said Phocion, taking from the tray the two glasses of wine that the servant had brought, pouring one to Ganymede.

The two old men feel an immediate affinity in each other's company, and they drink together with relish. A little symposium after lunch! Why not?

"I can't say it's a surprise to me..." says Ganymede, who has long known Theo's feelings.

"Neither for me..."

"Same?"

"The day Theo came to pick up Callíope, and told me the whole story of his incessant search to find her and take her back to his house, it was visible what he felt... Honored, he asked me the value that I should, by Calliope..." Fócion gives a smile. "As if I could assess a value like that, in cash... When I told him that he owed me nothing, he insisted on paying... At that moment, I granted Calliope her freedom, releasing him from any payment... He looked annoyed to me... But nothing compares to that look I saw in both of them, when face to face... They were like two mirrors facing each other... His eyes shone in the same intense and deep way... In that one instant I realized everything. Sounds like a great guy."

"You have no idea how much..."

"I believe I disappointed him, by releasing Calliope. I think he wanted to be the man who would set her free."

"No... I know my son, he doesn't think like that... It's all humility... For him, what mattered was bringing her back, so much for those who had freed her... He has honor and soul like never before saw in anyone."

Ganymede begins to tell the part of the story that Phocion did not know.

His illness and disability; Theo's commitment and love for him and the lands; Calliope's return home; the miracle of his having found Dimitriki again.

"He turned Attica inside out; he didn't rest a minute in his search for my grandson. Both my wife and I were born again thanks to this young man, our son..."

"No doubt!"

But even if Theo deserved all the praise, what had brought Ganymede to Phocion was something more practical. They wanted to consult the great speaker about Calliope's situation. Telling the whole story since the loan from Pasion, the banker, Fócion silently listening to all the details, was showing his new friend under what circumstances everything had happened.

"If you had looked for a specialist before signing this mortgage" said Fócion at the end of the report. "This is what we should all do, whenever it involves real estate, or a family interest... Our simple signature on a piece of paper can jeopardize so many things..."

"I know that well now," said Ganymede, who ached with the memory of the day in the agora when the banker had granted him the loan. "If you could see with what enthusiasm Pásion passed me that amount."

"I know the tricks of these men. They are adept at involving the interested party, who already come to them in a weakened situation. Do you have the document with you?"

"'Yes, here it is," Ganymede said, pulling the rolled-up paper from the folds of his chiton, which Theo had kept all those years in a chest with other things in the house that he thought important to keep but didn't want to see.

Fócion examined the paper carefully, reading the terms and amount of the loan, the established interest, the dates, and finally, the last clause, written at the end, the guarantee.

"This clause," he said slowly, "couldn't have been required, at least not in this way... Several things tarnish the deeds that led Callíope to become a slave... First, tie the loan payment to the harvest and sale event wheat is an unacceptable practice, by our laws... When you went to pay him, before the date, he would have had to accept the payment and pay the debt."

Fócion was thoughtful, looking at the paper, mulling over phrases and concepts in his head, putting together facts, arguments and conclusions. He had always known, from her own accounts, that Calliope's situation not only had dark spots, but that it was, to say the least, irregular. But he had closed his eyes, he had been selfish, not wanting to meddle in the case, for he liked the girl like a daughter, and he didn't want to see her go. Which ended up happening anyway. He felt as much or more guilty than Ganymede for what had happened to Calliope. If Ganymede had lacked prudence and health, he had lacked soul. Now, given the chance to recover from his omission, from his mistake, he would definitely do it.

"I think our chances of succeeding with the magistrates are very good, Papa Ganymede.

"Do you really think?" Ganymede feels his heart fill with joy and hope.

But that wasn't all. He had one more legal issue to consult with Phocion. After exposing some more facts and details, he finally concludes the thought and awaits the response of his new friend, his consultant, his synégoros, representing him before the men of law.

"Are you aware that this is a very rare cause, with an unpredictable outcome?"

"Do you think it would be accepted?"

"Well, it could even be accepted, as you have the right to propose it and seek to see the legal decision. But the result, as far as this one is concerned, I can't tell you... It is indeed an interesting situation. Noble. But very difficult."

"Perhaps if I tell you more details of this story and the merits involved, you will understand my commitment. A little less than thirty years ago, when happier days stirred the Athenian horizon under the command of our great Pericles, I was passing by the agora once when I saw the slave trader finishing the day's sale, taking away a little boy of about six or so. seven years. My daughter Calliope was the same age, having been born in very special circumstances for me and my wife...."

And in the shade, in the courtyard of Fócion's house, Ganimedes tells the story of his family to his new friend who listened to

him silently, deeply, absorbing every word he heard, getting en-
thused and moved by the story as if it were a true epic told in
prose.

Outside, another afternoon was falling into the city, turning it
all golden, with the market ending the day, the stalls being disman-
tled, the small shops closing their doors, and people finally leaving
for their homes, when Ganymede finishes. speak and, after a short
silence, Fócion rests a hand on his shoulder:

"Papa Ganymede, my friend, I believe we do have a chance!
You can count on me for your cause! I'm going to start looking at
all the issues involved in this case right away; I imagine the whole
city will know about this trial! Let's try to find a way out of this
situation! Have you thought about writing all these facts? It would
make an award-winning play!"

Ganymede was going to ask the People's Assembly to grant
Athenian citizenship to Theodoros.

Chapter XII
Posseidon – god of the sea.

The weeks that followed were of intense work for Fócion. He soon realized that those two causes would be the biggest ones he would have sponsored in his life as a citizen, perhaps precisely because they not only dealt with themes so deep in their legal, religious and political roots, but also dealt directly with people so dear to him.

Because he had taken a liking to Calliope's family in the same way he had taken a liking to the girl herself. And it was with new blood that he got up every day and from an early age he started to make contacts, talk to people, gather data and documents, find out about the court agendas, the names of the magistrates in service that year, their characteristics, and even their personal lives. Every night he returned home and took inventory of names and dates, crossing out some, putting a mark on others. He wrote long speeches and reread them aloud, looking for the right tone, not exaggerating, but giving the necessary emphasis.

The mortgage issue would be judged by the court of helieia, with the grand jury of the people - the heliasts, chosen from among citizens over thirty – whose number of members the magistrate would determine as he understood the importance of the case.

Theo's application for citizenship would be considered by the Ekklesía, the People's Assembly, and it would take six thousand favorable votes from those present to obtain it. And such proposal should still be previously approved by the Assembly, to then enter the agenda.

Phocion found out the names of all five hundred assemblymen that year and, after detailed study, found that month whose fifty prítanes seemed to him most inclined to approval. It was a good month, with mild weather, without heavy rains or droughts, not even less lightning storms. No bad omen would lead the magistrate or the epistatist – presidents of the court and of the Assembly – to suspend or postpone their respective sessions. Phocion even consulted an oracle: he wanted to obtain from all sides, if not the assurance that everything would go well, at least the certainty that nothing would get in the way. He would, like Posseidon, stir the seas of citizens' ideas about justice and law.

The cause of the mortgage would first be submitted to the fifty prítanes of that month, who would then take it to the assembly, and this would certainly receive the request as a public cause - a graphè - since it originated from a crime of illegality, and still covered on the question of citizenship, indirectly. And then the case would be referred to the court of helieia, to be judged by the popular jury, certainly with a high number of heliasts. In this case Fócion would act as a public prosecutor, not being able to abandon the claim, and running the risk of being sentenced to a fine if he did not obtain a fifth of the favorable votes, and would still lose the right to file another graphè in the future - which would prevent the other case, that of citizenship.

But even so, studying all the points of the situation, he articulated how only he was able to do so in order to have the two cases judged on two consecutive days, which he managed to tactfully mark, that month which he judged the most favorable. On the first day, the cause of the mortgage, seeking to solve Callíope's situation. And the very next day, Assembly day, the request for Athenian citizenship for Theo. That family's lot was cast.

"Calm down, Ganymede," says Phocion, taking a seat beside him, after the sacrifices and prayers are over. – Everything is under control; when called, you will answer the questions I ask, as agreed. Don't be afraid to stutter: all people get nervous at this time, it's normal. The magistrate and the jury know very well what you are feeling. Better a natural stutter than forced self-confidence: this one they distrust. And you won't have to lie, so just trust my questions and give the answers.

Phocion had similarly guided all the people he had listed as witnesses, including Theo, who was waiting outside the moment when he would be called to testify.

On that day, the whole family came to town, even Iphigenia. But they could not enter the courtroom, so they stayed outside, waiting. Theo could not hide a certain nervousness. He wanted things to go according to his father's wishes, to see him well, so that he wouldn't suffer another disappointment. Calliope was still so delighted with her little boy's return that nothing else seemed to matter to her. Slave, free woman, "citizen," all of this was unimportant, as long as Dimitriki was right by her side. And Theo, too.

The day was very clear, but without that intense heat so common in the city. The two women sat in the shade near the door with Theo, their eyes glued to Dimitriki, who had already tried to find other children around, and they railed around the fountains, the statues, the flower beds.

"Watch out, Dimitriki!" Callíope draws his attention. "Don't step on the flowers!"

"Check it out!" Iphigenia smiles, watching her grandson make a circle of children and talk at length while the others listened quietly. "How he is taken! Wants to talk to everyone! Look! The others start laughing at what he says! What a temper! Who did he pull, this boy?

Calliope raises her eyebrows ironically.

"Demetrius! Don't pull the girl's hair!"

Pásion had been called to appear at the trial and, although he did not appear exactly as a defendant, since Ganymede did not ask for his conviction, he had also appealed to a friend who would defend him, such as his synégoros. Both synégoros had already taken to the magistrate, on another day, taking the oath, the documents they considered useful for the process: texts of laws, the loan agreement, the list of witnesses they intended to call, their written arguments.

Fócion had decided not to seek Pásion's conviction for the illegality and bad faith of the mortgage clause in the loan agreement. Such an attitude would lead the banker to defend himself as he could, and given his financial power and influence with certain citizens – he knew everyone in the city – the result of the action could be disastrous for Ganymede and Calliope. It was not revenge that moved Ganymede, but his desire to see his daughter restored to the bars of citizenship. So Phocion chose not exactly to spare Pasion, but to call him as a witness, corroborating the facts. In this way, Pásion would come before the magistrate and the jury, the heliasts - for that cause, three hundred, as decided by the magistrates - and there, exposed in all its vileness, would give the heliasts the chance and freedom of, appreciating the case of Calliope and Ganymede, indirectly judging the one who had already harmed so many.

Of all the testimonies, certainly those that most touched the heliasts and even all those present – which were many, Fócion had made a real campaign to fill the room – were those of Theo and Ganymede, reporting, through Fócion's questions, all the details of the loan, the attempt to prepay the debt, the excellent wheat crop coming out of those inhospitable and almost uncultivable lands, the confiscation, the afternoon when the banker's agent had come to collect the debt, the sad moment when Calliope had left; of Ganymede's disease, and of years of hands tied in the face of the law. The testimonies of the former agent of Pásion; of Tearion the baker; of some employees of Ganymede; from two of the sytophylakes – the wheat inspectors in the agora; of some doctors Theo had taken to examine Ganymede; and the banker himself, came to confirm what was being reported.

Not a great many laws regulated the lives of citizens in Athens. Fócion's defense was then based more on concepts, on principles, on the general rules established by the great speakers, and above all on the Constitution, guiding the values of justice, legality, legitimacy and citizenship.

After hearing the witnesses, Fócion recalled, in his final speech, whose duration was regulated by a water clock, all the arguments that supported his position: the mortgage clause was null, since it linked the payment of the loan to a future and uncertain fact, preventing early redemption of the mortgage; the applicant had sought to pay the debt before term, and had been unable to do so given the banker's refusal to receive the amount; the creditor then constituted in default, leaving the debtor unencumbered in the conservation of the thing owed, whether the money or the harvest; the confiscation of wheat gave rise to the renegotiation of the debt, if not its extinction, given that the debtor's fortuitous event was independent of his will; the banker, as a free man, but not a citizen, could not enter into the enjoyment of the property of the property given as guarantee; and still, and above all, the sale of the Calliope girl as a slave escaped all the norms established by the great Solon, whose laws promulgated more than one hundred and fifty years ago and inscribed in wooden prisms, revolved around their axis in the Pritaneu, to view of all citizens, by the sacred fire of the city, showing everyone that practices such as the sale of a citizen's son or daughter, with very few exceptions, no longer had a place in that society of good men, and that Ganymede, taken by a numbness and heartbreak that had weakened him for more than eight years, since the episode of the confiscation, he had been unable to do anything, seeing his only child leave, no longer the daughter of the honest and honest citizen he had always been. Therefore, given the facts and laws reported and proven, given the irreversible and irrecoverable lapse of time during which the family had deprived themselves of their rights, their health and, above all, the company of their only daughter, the citizen did not come Ganymede asks for pecuniary compensation, since it is irrelevant in the face of the greater evil; he came, rather, to seek the reestablishment of the rule of law.

"Only requesting from this court the irrefutable declaration of nullity of the aforementioned mortgage clause, with retroactive effect, also annulling the acts and deeds arising therefrom, restoring Mrs. Calliope, daughter of Ganimedes, widow of Cassandro, to her original condition and indelible as the daughter of a landlord and residing in Attica, as the family desires, as the law dictates, and as the gods and goddesses of the city of Athens command".

People who watched the debates were speechless with emotion.

Some jurors wiped tears from the corners of their eyes with their fingers.

The synégoros of Pásion saw that his friend was capable of getting out of there still imprisoned, perhaps even lynched. He thought it best not to counterattack, since nothing was asked of him except his testimony confirming the facts. He only alleged, regarding illegalities, that Pásion, as a former slave, did not have complete control of the citizens' laws, and was unaware that certain practices such as the aforementioned clause and the sale of a citizen's daughter were prohibited. A good defense going off on a tangent, although it was a lie, as he knew all the laws very well, even better than the vast majority of citizens. But there would be nothing to fear Pásion and his synégoros, finally, because the magistrate could not pronounce a sentence outside the order, which was only a declaration of nullity of a contract clause and its effects.

"Let the heliasts proceed to the vote" the magistrate determines, after a brief silence.

After deliberating among themselves quickly and without noise, the three hundred heliasts neatly came one by one to deposit their jetons in the umas . Each had two jetons - small metal discs, with a hole in the center, crossed by a beam: hollow in one of them, massive in the other, so that they were recognizable at the touch of a hand. The massive beam jeton served to acquit or grant the request; the hollow beam, to condemn or deny. Each heliast cast their vote in one ballot box, and the remaining jeton in another , for control.

The magistrate then, with his assistants, counted the votes.

"Having counted the votes of the heliasts after the discussion and debates in accordance with the laws of the polis, I proceed to deliberate. This court, through its members, by unanimous vote, saw fit to accept the request of citizen Ganymede in favor of his only daughter. Pursuant to the powers conferred on me by the laws of the polis, I declare null and void the mortgage clause contained in the loan agreement entered into between citizen Ganimedes and Mr. Pásion, banker, for all legal purposes. I further declare, therefore, in the same way, null and void the act by which the sale of Mrs. Calliope, daughter of citizen Ganimedes, widow of Cassandro, was effected, restoring her to her condition of epicleric daughter, subject to the rights of third parties in good faith who may have been harmed by the acquisition, since it was null and void".

At this moment, Phocion stands up and asks to speak, interrupting the magistrate's deliberation, who looks at him impatiently – no magistrate likes to be interrupted.

"Your Excellency," he begins. "With your permission. I am the third who acquired Ms. Calliope. In this act, in the presence of Your Excellency, of all the heliathists who deliberated on this cause, and of all the citizens present here, I waive the right of action against Pásion for the aforementioned illegal sale."

Phocion would not enter the vile question of fighting in court for the value of his dear Calliope. He wanted, as much as Ganymede, just to see things put back in their proper place.

"The Fócion citizen" resumes the magistrate, "buyer in good faith, in this act, waives the right of recourse against the person who harmed him through said sale."

There being nothing more to deliberate and decide; is the sentence.

I declare this process closed.

May Themis, the goddess of justice, lead and enlighten us,

And may Athena protect us".

Ganymede bows his head, eyes squinting, his heart wanting to explode.

"Thank you my friend! Thank you very much!" he said to Fócion, finally, his eyes watering, the words unable to come out of his mouth.

"I'm the one who's grateful, my brother" says Fócion, also moved. "For having given me the opportunity to recover Calliope!"

Ganymede looks at his new friend, not finding the words to express what he has to say. That sentence gave him back his daughter. And eight years to live. And the honor of a father and a citizen.

"How many have you counted so far?"

"More than a thousand, but I believe they can be almost double, just here on this side, as many arrived in groups, I couldn't count them all."

Phocion had placed some employees around the Pnix, counting the incoming citizens for the Assembly. He needed to fill the room with as many citizens as possible in order to get, at the time of voting, the six thousand votes necessary for victory. For a long time, no item on the agenda had managed to bring to the Assembly all the approximately twenty thousand citizens enrolled in the polis. Most of the time, at most five thousand attended. This was the first hurdle to be overcome by Phocion. But the resounding success in the helieia, the day before, had served as a call to everyone's attention for Theo's citizenship application, the very next day, just as he had predicted.

In fact, there was no mention of anything else in the city.

Phocion was anxious. But it was still early, Athens lazily advancing into the morning.

The day had dawned already full of a different air, especially for Ganymede's family, who, moreover, had barely managed to sleep that night, both out of joy at Calliope's victory and out of nervousness for the Assembly. A climate of decision gripped them all. Certainly not even the athletes, on the day of the final competition, felt the same anxiety. Theo, the pivot of the matter, until the day before, had kept a certain indifferent reserve about the application for citizenship, but that morning, when he woke up, he had opened his eyes still in the dark with an unknown shadow covering his soul. Why so much fuss about the subject? How would that change his life? How would your blood run differently in your veins if you became a citizen? He wondered these things, walking around the garden of the house before breakfast, watching the dawn light up the fields he knew so well, when the bride came to meet him.

"Aren't you coming to eat?" she asks him, smiling.

"I don't feel like it..."

Thoughtful, he walks beside her into the house.

Again, Theo, the two women, and Dimitriki stood outside, at the entrance to the Pnix, beside an archer who took care of the arrival of the citizens. When Ganymede took a place at the very front, next to Phocion, more than fifteen thousand men were already gathered there, and many were still arriving.

This time, Phocion would have no one to call to testify or answer questions. It would be him, alone, speaking from the rostrum, defending that cause, sponsoring that request. But the decision, this would be what the citizens deliberated together. Much would depend on how Phocion would speak, but also on what was in those people's souls. And not everything was going well in the city lately. Always vibrant, Athens seemed to have an unshakable strength in its people. But in politics, things weren't quite like that. Those who believed that the war against Sparta was heading towards Athenian success were wrong. The great Alcibiades had just been defeated in the Ionian Islands, and overwhelmed, tired, sad, he had opted for self-exile in Thrace. How would the animosity of those men be there, faced with a request for citizenship?

The very strong sun in a cloudless blue sky made everyone sure that the gods agreed with this assembly. They started well.

The priests offered the sacrifices of the slain animals, then sprinkled the earth with the lustrous water. One of them then said the prayer, invoking all the gods and goddesses of the city so that, in that sacred place, everything would happen according to the will of heaven. The secretary read the name of the tribe that held the pritany that month, the archon who named the year, as well as the epistatt, who presided over the session, to whom he gave the floor. The Epistat then listed the projects and requests on the agenda that day. In order to be heard and understood by everyone, he spoke slowly, very loudly, and this cadence made the act even more solemn than usual. This was an important moment for Phocion. He wanted Ganymede's request to be one of the first to be put up for discussion and vote.

Citizen Ganimedes, resident in Attica, owner of olive and wheat producing land. Athenian citizenship application for the thirty-five-year-old former slave named Theodoros, who has been serving on his former master's land for thirty years.

Photion fixes a point with his eyes and focuses all his attention on his ears. Deliberation is quick.

The request received by the Council. Before the vote, will any citizens take the floor?

Phocion then gets up and goes to the rostrum, where an officer takes his data, checks his status as a citizen over thirty, owner in Attica, widower, two sons in the army, unblemished reputation, up to date with his obligations to the gods . One of Athens' most respected citizens. The officer places the crown on his head, making him, in that instant, sacred and inviolable, and he ascends the rostrum, having an overview of the Assembly, nearly twenty thousand pairs of eyes and ears turned to him, silently awaiting his words. For a few seconds he scans the audience with his eyes and then, taking a deep breath, begins to speak, slowly:

"That enlightened by Zeus, guarded by Apollo, guided by Hestia and protected by Athena, we may know how to behave and deliberate according to the will of all the gods of this city, and so may prudence and wiser understanding prevail. Gentlemen, magistrates, priests, citizens of Athens. Great is the emotion that brings me to this rostrum today. Much for the same reason that moves all the speakers who come here to speak to you, which is the honor of addressing those who decide, with their vote, the destinies of the polis. But mainly because I can be here today talking to you about a man of unequaled value.

"Gentlemen, when talking about this man, more than talking to you about a single person, I will be talking about an entire nation, the Athenian homeland. Because the man to whom today is sought to confer Athenian citizenship contains in himself everything that our ancestors fought so hard to defend, preserve, keep alive, which is the Hellenic spirit. Gentlemen, who are we? Where do we Athenian citizens come from? What is "being an Athenian"? Certainly, some will say, it is to love this land, to give ourselves body and soul to it, to abandon everything in its name and in its honor, and in honor of its gods. But, the more profound ones will say, it is also, and even more, born of other Athenians, who in turn were born of the Athenians who settled here in remote times. For them, being an Athenian is more in the blood than in the soul. For them, serving the army of this city and fighting battles for it is enough to become a citizen. But, gentlemen, how many of us have had to face the real threat of losing everything – the lands, the sacred fire, the family, life – as happened to the boy we are talking about, Theodoros? Yes, many here will remember, it was he himself who, years ago, alone, having only his own body and soul to look for strength, faced the Spartan envoy, invader of the lands of Ganymede, in Attica, at the gates of Athens. Faced with an adversary all the more powerful the more hostile and better equipped, Theodoros had at his side something that his antagonist could never have known: the true love for the Athenian homeland, for the sacred ground of our ancestors and heroes. A love detached from formalities, instructions, orders from superiors. The love of your master, Ganymede, first. Afterwards, the love for his house, his home and his gods, since as a slave to this connected family, he was introduced into the rites and he had always respected them, as his own, from an early age. And finally, the love for the land, the land that he himself made to produce, made to sprout, made to generate the fruits that identify the Hellenic presence on the ground: the vine, the wheat and the olive tree. Faced with danger, he did not hesitate to fight for that homeland, and defend it energetically, although devoid of any military training, only with the Athenian soul feeding its will, ready to perish in the name of all that our ancestors, generation after generation, they taught us and showed us to be worthy of struggle, praise and respect. In that instant, like an insurmountable wall, stronger and more powerful than the stones of the walls that surround Athens, it blocked the enemy's march towards the city, thus guarding our gods, protecting our lives, and saving our honor and dignity of men. Gentlemen, perhaps more than any of us, Theodoros has demonstrated that he has in him the Hellenic spirit where the greatest virtue is courage. But he went even further. Perhaps much further than either of us would ever think to go. With the kindness, prudence and wisdom that only happens to the enlightened, he decided not to take the life of that invader, but to spare him, since he was already defeated, and the land, family and soul of his people were out of danger. ancestors, in order to show us, all of us, where the true Athenian spirit lives. That is not only the ability to pray, to surrender, to fight, and to die for the polis and its gods, but after all that, still knowing the human spirit and what is divine in it.

"Because we, here in the city, full of ideas and ready to learn everything that comes to our eyes, novelties and small things that stun our ears more than add to our intelligence, we set out to extol urban finesse and qualities. But he, the rustic, the one who lives in it and works the land and who, without further detours, produces what sustains us and keeps us upright, which is food, he yes, he is the depository of the ancient values of our ancestors. Finding himself at the junction between the savage and the civilized, he knows the paths of civility, the shortcuts that lead to order, the order that we citizens have long struggled to see victorious...

"Being a citizen. What is it to be a citizen? I ask you all. Certainly the Hellenes, from whom we all descend, coming from the distant lands of the north for more than ten centuries in search of the ideal place to live and prosper, when they lit the sacred fire on this soil that we inherited from them and inhabit today, had a very notion clear of what we now call "being a citizen", and for what purpose they stipulated the rules that we still obey today. Follow the rites. Believing and fearing the city's gods. Never vilify the sacred. Fighting for the polis in times of war. Serve her in times of peace. Love it and obey it, in its benefits and rigors. Gentlemen, all this we do without even thinking about the origins of such commandments. But he, this man whose courage and nobility of soul were put to the test and indisputably stood out, he carries within his chest, he carries in the core of his being this notion, this respect, this urge to fight and die for the Athenian homeland without be given an order to do so, but because the love of this land is in his bowels. From an early age, as a very young child, he was introduced to the home and rites of this Attica family. And even though he learned from these Athenians about the tradition and history of the glorious Hellenic people, he was never forced to revere our ancestors. All the more valuable, therefore, is the feeling that has moved him throughout his life to honor and respect this family, and more than that, to love it, as well as its history, its gods and heroes, without ever claiming anything for himself, taking on his shoulders, in a moment of serious crisis, the responsibility and risks during all the years that the pater was affected by health problems, which prevented him from any act of citizen, now fighting not against the enemy of another polis, but against the excesses of life itself, health, bad weather, injustices. Here, gentlemen, is what our ancestors would certainly call a true Athenian citizen.

"Gentlemen, granting citizenship to such a man is an honor and a pride, not for him, because for those who already carry such values within themselves, it is unnecessary to see them boasted. It is, yes, honor and pride for us, to have in our midst a man of such character and nobility, and in whose soul we should all try to mirror ourselves, and, full of pride, we can then say that we are Athenians, like him.

"May us all enlighten and protect our goddess, Athena."

The Assembly was silent, taken by Fócion's words. Everyone always liked to hear the ancestors remembered, the Hellenic values extolled. Every man thinks of the things that life has already provided or inflicted on him. And everyone admires both Theo's achievements and Phocion's way of exposing them.

"Does any other citizen wish to take the floor?" Asks the Epistat.

Nobody speaks up.

"Let's proceed to the vote. Those of the citizens here present who agree to the granting of Athenian citizenship to the former slave Theodoros, as pleaded and stated, may you raise your right hand, and hold it up for the count."

Phocion and Ganymede, breath held, attentive to the movements of the citizens, saw the audience made up of thousands of men forming a compact block of mostly white chitons and himátions, at a single moment being as if covered by a yellowish cloud, practically all of them arms raised in silent and solemn approval.

"My friend, my brother" Phocion says to Ganymede, overcome with emotion, "I believe that…"

Ganymede could not articulate a word. He just looked at all those outstretched arms, not really able to believe what he saw.

The employees, arranged throughout the precinct, were each counting the votes of that part of the assembly that was theirs - they hadn't had so much work for a long time - and, one by one, they were bringing to the epistatt their respective counts, which other employees at the table they were then adding up. When the sum already exceeded ten thousand votes, several citizens began to speak, asking for the sequence of the feat, and the epistatist then took the floor:

"That enter Theodoros, and approach this tribune."

An employee then goes to the door and, outside, approaches Theo, inviting him to join him. Theo looks at Calliope, who takes his hands and stares at him too, smiling.

"May Athena be by your side, my dear!" said Iphigenia, seeing him follow the official, the archer giving him passage.

And the two women hear, coming from beyond the Assembly, the citizens burst into applause and shouts of "Save!" and "Praise be!"

"Mom, he did it!" Callíope says, her eyes full of tears.

Theo enters the Pnix, that sacred place reserved only for Athenian citizens. Standing in the doorway, legs refusing to move, he feels his heart skip a beat. In that instant, seeing practically all the citizens of Athens gathered there deliberating about the city and its destiny, he felt the magnitude of that institution. He was beginning to understand the deep values and feelings that led Papa Ganymede to stubbornly insist on his acceptance among them. A lump forms in his throat as he takes in an overview of the entire room, and his eyes finally fill with tears as he sees Ganymede looking at him, smiling contentedly.

"Come near, my boy," says the epistatist.

At the table, Theo was asked to sign some papers and, listening to some deliberations by the Pritans, he is taken to the rostrum next to the priest, who takes the floor:

"Illuminated by Zeus, Restia, Apollo and Athena, in this year of Archon Evagoras, in deliberation of this Assembly of citizens of the city of Athens, with sixteen thousand, six hundred and twenty-five votes in favor, the city of Athens grants citizenship to Theodoros, ex-slave purified and accepted by the gods at the home of Ganymede, who is registered from this date as an Athenian citizen in the same tribe as Ganymede, passing now to the solemn oath."

Theo stands beside the priest, who once more sprinkles the lustrous water on the ground he was about to tread, and also on his shoulders and head, saying to him, as he placed the crown on his head:

"Slowly, and out loud, my boy."

Theo repeated the priest's words:

"Kaì ta hierà ta patria timeto amuno dè hupèr hierôn."

Ganymede closes his eyes to better hear that oath, and even so, with his eyes closed, listening to Theo's voice, he says in a low voice to Phocion:

"Thank you, my brother, thank you very much. Athena, goddess of my city, my goddess of peace, of wisdom, our protector, thank you. I will without delay have statues made in your honor, which I will donate to your city, to my Athens.

And finally Theo finishes the oath, confirming the deed and its legality, being thus, from that day, admitted to the number of Athenian citizens, accepted at the table of the polis.

" ... meteînai tôn nirôn."

In this way Theo, as a citizen, entered into the sharing of the sacred things of the city of Athens.

Again the men burst into applause, while Theo, having returned the crown to the priest, went to Ganymede and, kissing his hand, bowed his head in emotion.

"Thank you, Papa..."

Moved, barely able to speak, Ganymede hugs him.

"My son... my son!"

"Papa, don't get tired, come sit down."

At the table, the epistatist takes up the floor again after asking for silence:

"Next item on the agenda: sending troops to the Arginusa Islands, proposed by the strategists.

There went the city for another naval onslaught, wiping out the finances of the state, underestimating the power of leadership of the Spartans and, above all, without a strong leadership themselves, thus walking with large and firm steps towards the final downfall.

And in the months that followed, nearly every boy born in the polis was named Theodoros.

Remembering that solemn afternoon at the Assembly, a few months earlier, when he had successfully defended the granting of citizenship to Theo, Fócion remains for a few minutes looking out the window, enjoying the end of that summer night, after arriving from the distribution of the sacrificial meat, which followed the procession on the last day of the Panateneas, the eve of Calliope and Theo's wedding.

On the already empty Acropolis, under the moonlight of the Athenian summer, the statues of the bride and groom, firm on the ground, beautiful, noble, full of history, placed there by Ganymede on that special day in honor of the goddess, spent the first night in her abode where by all eternity, by the donor's wish, should remain untouched, together with the others that were already there, enchanting the gods and men who came to visit them, showing the world the gratitude of that Hellenic family to its protective goddess, Palas Athena.

Grouped at the door, in absolute silence, the guests watched the father and the bride and groom. By the family's sacred fire, throughout the ceremony in which the father offered prayers and vows, Ganymede, Calliope, and Theo were as one person. They seemed enveloped in an aura of magic, detached from the rest of the world, transported to a special dimension, which gave the moment all the solemnity attributed to it by the ancestors, by the gods, by the souls of men. United were in the purpose, sincerity, harmony and joy of that act. Thrilled, the three had the same difficulty in holding back tears. The voice betrayed Ganymede in its sentences.

"Oh gods and goddesses of this city of Athens and Attica," he had said. – In front of the home of my ancestors, with the permission and blessing of the gods of this family, I give my daughter Calliope to my son Theódoros so that, with him, in this house, which is the house of both, keep burning, offer libations and pray together to her husband's home, my son Theodoros, to bear his children, to honor and respect him, submitting to him, continuing together the prayers and rites of this family, which is the family of both. May Zeus, Hera, Hestia and Aphrodite protect my children who are now united in marriage, giving them health and an abundance of goods, and may the gods receive this couple that I bless".

The three of them look at each other, mute, their gestures paralyzed, their voices stuck in their throats, their eyes wet with emotion. They experienced the depth and sacred value of that ceremony. Only they knew in their hearts exactly the arduous and tortuous path they had walked in their lives, over so many years, to finally be there.

And having his hand kissed first by Theo, then by Calliope, Ganymede took the hands of his son and daughter in turn, kissed them and, holding them for a few seconds, looking into the eyes of his children, united them, feeling in this moment the greatest joy he had ever had in his entire life.

Outside, amidst the flowers, the music, the sun and the coming and going of the employees, the guests were already settling into their seats, at the large table under an awning, where the banquet would be served, followed by the symposium right there, with the presence of women, idea of Theo. Everyone was waiting for the bride and groom and family, and the most anticipated moment at weddings, when Iphigenia lifted Calliope's veil. Everyone knew that the couple already knew each other, that they had grown up together, and that there would be nothing new in that meeting. But Calliope and Theo, having removed the veil that separated them, to the sound of the musicians singing the hymeneus, finally saw in each other's eyes the same image.

Although Ganymede always ordered that the wine be mixed with the water in the crater in mild proportions, in order to avoid the excesses of the drink, some guests managed to become more cheerful than expected, with their jokes and jokes, typical of a wedding day, making ironic comments about the time to untie the belt, uttering sentences full of double meanings, looking at the newlyweds wanting to see them blush.

Only Phocion noticed when, at nightfall, the bride and groom withdrew and Theo, between the columns at the entrance, took Callíope in his arms, and entered the house, going at last to his room – their bedroom.

Tired, as night had already arrived, but experiencing an unheard of joy in living, Ganymede himself had already gone to bed. Iphigenia takes Dimitriki to bed to put him to sleep, a lamp in her hands lighting his way.

'Grandmother! Why don't Mom and Dad come sleep here with me in this room? It's pretty big here."

"They want a room for them, honey! And they want to leave this one to you! Goodnight darling.'

"Grandmother! Shall we see my statue tomorrow?"

'Let's go, my dear! Now, sleep, let's go" - she says, at the bedroom door.

"Grandmother!"

"Yes, my treasure?"

"What is 'untie the belt' "?

Dimitriki pissed her off.

And the dawn wakes up that family for the new times that have finally begun. In the bride and groom's bedroom, both naked amidst the tangle of sheets, still not believing that fate had reserved that happiness for him, Theo is secretly savoring the sight of Calliope beside him, sleeping the end of sleep: the contour of her face, the line her eyes closed, her mouth in a relaxed smile, her long black hair, loose, spread across the pillow. They had taken a long time to sleep...

"Good Morning!" she says, finally opening her eyes for him.

"Good Morning!"

The morning light, brightening the room, announces a new day, invites people to live, predicts a new life and new dreams to be achieved.

"I do not believe!" Calliope said, with a smile in her voice.

"In what?"

"I'm finally able to say "good morning" to you!!" With her fingers, she strokes his hair.

That inside her heart, since she was a teenager, she had a strong, affectionate and special love for Theo, that was nothing new for Calliope. During all the years full of setbacks she had gone through, she had never stopped thinking about him with all the affection, her eternal and best friend, her hero, her soulmate. But on that morning following the wedding night, after embracing and making love for a long time between the soft sheets reaching a height hitherto unknown to her, the sun had come to wake her and found her happy, fulfilled, with a new smile on lips and, for the first time in her life, completely in love.

Epilogue

The festival of Posseidon, at the temple of Cape Sounion, had always been one of the favorites of the Athenians, who especially liked that place of blessed beauty, that piece of land high above the waters, entering the Aegean Sea, rushing towards the Cycladic islands , at the end of which stood the temple of the god of the seas.

It was the solar year, when the cycle ended at the end of which the agreement between the solar and lunar years was reestablished, adding an intermediate month of thirty days – the Poseideón deuteros – between the months Poseideón and Gamelión, in the dead of winter. And then the festival was celebrated.

Despite the cold, the whole city rushes to the coast to see that beauty towering over the mountain in honor of the god of the seas, and to worship him. Theo has promised to take the whole family, so they leave the countryside very early, as he also has matters to resolve, as always, including talking to some homeowners in the city: he was thinking about a possible move of the family to Athens, leaving the land and the production of cheese and oil under the care of employees, who would start to supervise, going there every two or three days. Spartan hostilities had long been tiring peasant families, and he thought it was time to spare his own from those fears and uncertainties, especially now that Calliope was carrying another baby in her womb... Besides, Dimitriki, he had just finished of adopting, he was of school age and they didn't want to be away from him for so many hours, they would like to be around and see him every day at all times. Calliope also likes the idea of coming to live in Athens: she missed the city life she had learned to love. Only the father and mother are reluctant because, already aged, they feel tired and lack the courage for such a radical change. They've lived in the country all their lives, and the bustle of Athens doesn't attract them like the younger ones. But they are ready to do whatever Theo decides.

It's a very sunny afternoon, despite the time of year, and the carriage takes the family through the crowd on foot. Early that day, people had already started to leave the house, taking children, old people, dogs, etc., and carrying baskets of provisions for the day, as the walk was long, steep and tiring. Upon arrival at the top of Sounion everyone was breathless and almost unable to enjoy the wonderful view of almost three hundred and sixty degrees of sea and blue sky that surrounds the temple inside which stands the statue of Posseidon, pointing to the sea. Some were already with enough wine in their heads, making them funny, some brave, others still quite inconvenient, speaking obscenities to the women, including those who were accompanied, giving immense work to the guards scattered along the road, who had at all times to intervene in a fight, as there was no lack of punches, kicks, heads split by thrown pots, etc. Theo stopped here and there, to enjoy the view, to rest the horses, for Dimitriki to pee. They arrived in time to find a place from which they could see the procession enter the temple and from which they could leave more quickly, without being trampled by people who, at the end of these festivals, no longer had the patience to walk slowly, and actually stepped on everything and everyone who appeared to them. And as the entire population arrives and settles down, no space visible to anyone else, a compact mass of people gathered there for the same purpose, gradually calming down, and finally a sober and respectful silence takes over the sanctuary.

Huddled together in the crowd, Dimitriki between Theo and Calliope, holding a bundle of dried figs soaked in honey that her grandparents had bought her from a roadside stall, they enjoy this rare moment whose splendor had brought everyone there in that winter day: the sunny sunset on that infinite horizon, changing the colors of the sky, from a very clear and bright blue, to a pinkish, which turns into lilac to finally turn a deep, incandescent red, with the giant sun slowly sinking into the sea, the columns of the temple acquiring a hue at first very white, then golden by the sunset. Ifigênia and Ganymede have eyes full of tears, for the beauty, for the solemnity, and for the memory of their son Helios. Calliope, deep in thought, remembers at that moment everything that had happened to her, and to her family, and to her city, all those years ago. The birth of Dimitriki. The pain in the absence of your little boy. The death of loved ones. The excesses of politics and war. The doubts and weights in the hearts of so many people. The Athenian people's labyrinth of emotions. The joy of finally being with the family again. The new baby that was coming. And Theo. Theo...

"Look, Mom! Up there! The first star!! How big!!" said Dimitriki, pointing to the sky with his greased little finger.

Calliope looks up and sees in the reddish evening sky a huge solitary star, a different star, never seen before, very high, the first at night, shining strong, intense and sovereign in the firmament, as if totally dominating not only Sounion, but also the whole earth, illuminating sky and sea, cities and fields, roads and houses, palaces and temples, people and animals, thoughts and gestures. Amazed by the vision, her eyes magnetized in that glow, time seems to stop, and an unprecedented peace floods her heart, coming from that mighty star, with its Light taking away all the bitterness of those so difficult years, freeing your soul, bringing all the Answers, all Truth, and all Peace. A deep, true, total, absolute and eternal peace. Enchanted, reborn, renewed, rising to go, she does not lift her eyes from the sky, which is darkening little by little, other stars joining that one, blinding her light, finally making her get lost among so many, and , with a sigh, Calliope feels the certainty deep in her heart that that mysterious star will again shine in that same piece of heaven, and its magnanimous glow will bring to the hearts of all the people and cities of the world that same infinite peace that took hold her at that moment. With the star's glow imprinted on her eyes and soul, she turns her face to Theo, overcome with emotion, unable to say anything. But no words were needed. He smiles at her with the same peace, his eyes already reflecting the same glow. Theo had always seen everything in Calliope's eyes.

THE END

About the Author

Cindy Stockler was born and raised in the city of São Paulo, Brazil, and graduated in Law at the Sao Paulo University Law School. Influenced by her legal background as well as by her grandmother, a writer at her time, Cindy Stockler writes fiction novels describing in detail the places and habits of the people she depicts, frequently with a light approach to legal matters that ordinary people sometimes see themselves involved with. Always doing thorough researches, Cindy Stockler likes to give as accurate an account as she can to her stories, like the one she did as she wrote *Calliope, the Slave from Athens*, a story happening in the V century B.C., as well as her following novels, in totally different times and circumstances.

www.ingramcontent.com/pod-product-compliance
Lightning Source LLC
Chambersburg PA
CBHW021436020726
47499CB00006BA/2025